3

Ryan Cawdor never heard the swampies

One moment he was up and walking; the next he was rolling over on hands and knees, the G-12 pulled from his grip, someone's arm around his throat, another attacker hanging on his waist, kicking at his legs. A stench of gasoline and sweat assaulted his nostrils as he grappled with the oily bodies.

There were three of them: two men and a woman. Muties, like the ones they'd seen on the day they arrived in Louisiana. All were about five feet tall, stumpy, squat and muscular, in torn pants and shirts, their feet in flapping sandals of hacked rubber. All three breathed noisily through open mouths.

Suddenly the woman raised a small crossbow, aiming it jerkily at Ryan's belly.

The thought darted through his mind that this was a squalid and foolish way to die.

JAMES AXLER

DEATH LANDS

Neutron Solstice

A GOLD EAGLE BOOK FROM

W**O**RLDWIDE

TORONTO • NEW YORK • LONDON • PARIS
AMSTERDAM • STOCKHOLM • HAMBURG
ATHENS • MILAN • TOKYO • SYDNEY

First edition March 1987

ISBN 0-373-62503-0

Printed in Canada

Prologue

A GLISTENING PEARL OF sweat ran down between the woman's breasts, across the flat stomach, into the vee of curling dark hair. Another drop slid past her parted lips, over her chin, hung suspended for a moment, then fell through the smoky air and landed with delicate precision on the polished blade of the tiny silver dagger.

Her dark skin was smooth, her tumbling hair as black as the wing of a raven at midnight. She was naked, sitting cross-legged in the dirt, a yard from a smoldering fire of hewn cottonwood branches. It was difficult to guess her age. From her body you might have thought she was in her early twenties. Then you might have looked into her face.

The cheeks were pocked and scarred, with open sores weeping around her mouth. The lips were full, slightly parted as she panted in the heat. Most of her teeth were missing, and those that remained were yellow and chipped, jostling each other for space, like tumbled gravestones.

But it was her eyes that held you like an insect trapped in a web.

They were pale as watered milk, with a thin membrane drawn across each cornea, like a veil of finest lace. Beneath the pallid shroud the eyes moved, darting and jerking.

Her right hand gripped the knife, the hilt made from the middle finger of a man, the joints bound with silver filigree, an uncut ruby set at its pommel. The blade was about four inches long, razored on both edges, the tip needle-sharp. The flickering light in the reed-roofed hut revealed lettering engraved along the blade in twining, ornate script.

La Mort Lente.

The slow death.

In her left hand the blind woman clutched a small fluttering feathered creature. A red-winged blackbird, head turning from side to side, its tiny bright eyes rolling against the sheen of its plumage.

Inside the hut were more than a dozen men, most wearing cotton trousers, some with ragged shirts. Nearly all of them had tightly-curled cropped hair, with faces that betrayed an African ancestry. They knelt in the dirt, eyes locked on the woman's mutilated face, hands folded in their laps, as if in prayer.

One of them rose and scattered a handful of dry powder on the glowing ashes of the fire, sending a cloud of dense white smoke toward the hole in the roof that served as a chimney. White smoke tinged with scarlet filled the hut with a bittersweet scent.

The woman lifted her hands, bringing both the silver knife and the fluttering bird nearer the blind eyes. She breathed in deeply, her body trembling, the nipples becoming erect, fire-tipped, like cherries. She opened her mouth, whispering to the waiting men in a voice harsh and grating. The language was a sort of French, a debased and corrupt form of the tongue that had originated four hundred of years before with Creole settlers from Haiti.

"As I see, so shall this far-flying singer upon wings see."

The hut was silent and still, and only the frail scratchings of the bird's claws upon the skin of the woman's hand betrayed movement. Outside, the wind had fallen away as night set its grip tighter upon the land.

"For us and for the baron and for life beyond and life within, I do this thing."

"Do this thing," came the mumbled chorus from the watchers.

The hands came together, the point of the knife seeking the gleaming eyes of the blackbird. Slowly, with the care and skill of long practice, the woman pricked out both of the creature's eyes, blinding it. A thread of bright blood streaked the feathers of its chest as it opened its beak and gave out a piercing screech of pain and black terror. But the woman held tight.

"Sing not and speak not and see not. But let the pinions bear upward that we might see where hope shall beckon."

She lowered her head and breathed on the injured bird, soothing it, stroking the feathers at the nape of its neck with her fingers. Opening her right hand and letting the stiletto fall in the dirt, she cupped the left hand so that the bird nestled there, unmoving. Then she raised her arms toward the hole on the roof.

"Fly free!" she cried.

For a frozen moment, nothing happened. The loops of graying smoke curled lazily up toward the sky. The bird turned its head from side to side, as if desperately seeking a salvation from its darkness. Minute specks of blood dappled the woman's forearm.

"Fly free," she repeated.

The red-winged blackbird finally made a feeble half-hearted effort to fly, beating its wings in a flurry of motion. It rose halfway toward the chimney hole, then faltered. There was a gasp of horror from the men as it fell, then rose again, and finally fell a second and final time. It plunged into the fire, flailing as the air filled with the stench of burned feathers. No one tried to save it. That would not have been appropriate.

It was a balding, wizened man who broke the shocked silence. "Why? Why did it not show the road that must be taken?"

The woman turned her opaque, sightless eyes toward the speaker, and he took a hesitant step back, as though he'd been struck across the face.

"There is a season for all things. A season to live and a season to die. Even the proudest of men must one day fall into decay. Stay quiet while I look inward."

She began to rock slowly back and forth on her heels, her hands weaving an intricate pattern in the smoke-filled air. Quietly she started to hum a queer, keening tune that had no words. Then gradually the harsh Creole lyrics came through, telling of a land where there was only honor, humility, truth and courage. Yet a land where the shadows roamed, even in the brightness of dawn. Where a midsummer banquet was darkened by the whispering of distant thunder.

The song ended, and they all heard the rising wind outside the hut. The blind woman stopped rocking, stretching out her arms, jerking her head back so the sinews in her throat stood out like cords of wire. Her breath came fast, her body shook as if gripped by fever.

Suddenly she relaxed, gazed across the room, over the fire. Her mouth dropped, and for a moment her face held an expression of simpering idiocy. That, too, passed and she spoke.

"As stands the baron high, so shall he be brought low. Not from within but from without. He..." Her voice faded.

"What? What will ail him?" whispered the bald man.

The woman trembled, mouth sagging. Her eyes gaped wide in terror, the whiteness dreadful, as if someone pressed them from behind. Then she screamed.

And again. A rasping, high noise, like a stallion being put to the gelding.

"They come!"

The voice filled the hut, spilled out through the thin walls into the moist warmth of the surrounding land. It hung in the air like a raised fist.

She screamed again, locked into her trance. "They come!"

"Who? Who comes?"

She ignored the question, once more screaming the same two words. "They come, they come, they come!"

Outside, the swamp stretched limitlessly in all directions as far as man could know. Within its depths there was a slow stirring, as if it could sense something happening, something utterly new.

Chapter One

RYAN CAWDOR STIRRED and opened his eyes.

The last tendrils of the mist were clearing away. On the floor the pattern of raised metallic disks no longer glowed. The same pattern on the ceiling of the hexagonal chamber reflected his own face, distorted and blurred. The walls were of smoked armored glass, tinted a deep blue. It was much the same as other gateways that Ryan had been in. Maybe a little cleaner and in better condition than some of them.

He took a quick glance around him. Something else struck Ryan. This particular gateway was warm. Indeed, after his recent sojourn in the biting chill of the land that had once been called Alaska, it was uncomfortably hot.

Even though it had been days since he'd been wounded, the small cut on his left hand still stung. Then, he had been in the extreme northwest of the country, still in the grip of nuclear winter. From the heat he guessed that they were somewhere down south, and toward the east. By his calculation it was around the middle of February.

Around the chamber, all slumped over like untidy bundles of clothing, were Ryan's six comrades. Four of them had been with him since they had traveled on the armored War Wag One, with the Trader, roaming across the Deathlands of Central United States, buying cheap and selling dear. They'd been fighting for life in a country that was still ninety-five percent devastated from the great nuclear war of January, 2001, nearly a hundred years ago.

The first of them to be showing signs of recovery was J. B. Dix, the Armorer. Around forty years of age, lean and compact, J.B. knew more about weapons than anyone alive. His battered fedora sat at a rakish angle on his forehead; his wire-rimmed glasses had slid down his thin, sallow face.

He blinked awake, his right hand going in a conditioned reflex to the Mini-Uzi that rested across his lap. The big Steyr AUG 5.6 mm pistol was holstered on his right hip.

"Hot, Ryan," he said.

J.B. was a man of very few words. And all of them were relevant.

"Yeah," replied Ryan. He thought about standing up and decided he didn't quite feel ready for that, not just yet. The patch over the empty right eye socket had moved a little, and he edged it back into place. The butt of his pistol—a SIG-Sauer P-226 9 mm handgun with fifteen rounds in the mag—banged against the glass, and he reached to his hip to adjust it. On the opposite hip Ryan carried a panga with an eighteen-inch blade. His immediate and obvious armaments were completed by the Heckler & Koch G-12 automatic rifle and fifty caseless rounds of 4.7 mm.

Nobody in Deathlands ever worried about having too many weapons.

"Doc looks ill," commented J.B.

Ryan glanced across the gateway chamber at the oldest and most mysterious member of their party.

Doctor Theophilus Tanner. "Doc." Tall and skinny, aged around sixty, with peculiarly excellent teeth. Doc had a deep, resonant voice, and often spoke in a strangely old-fashioned way. He was sprawled on his side, breathing noisily through his gaping mouth. His battered stovepipe hat had rolled across the gateway chamber. The ebony sword stick with the silver lion's-head top was in his lap, and the bizarre Le Mat percussion pistol was holstered at his belt.

Doc had been rescued from the ugly township of Mocsin, his mind better than half gone. But he seemed to have a lot of arcane knowledge, touching on the technology of the past. The far past, even before the bombs and missiles ruined the land.

Next to him, Finnegan and Hennings propped each other up. The former, stout and short, carried a gray Heckler & Koch submachine gun with a drum mag of fifty rounds of 9 mm and a built-in silencer. Hennings was a tall black man with an identical HK54A gun by his right hand.

Old friends from the days with Ryan Cawdor and J. B. Dix on the war wag, they were tough-fighting men, fiercely independent, each with a dark and macabre sense of humor.

Both men wore identical clothes, more like uniforms: dark blue high-necked jumpers, with matching pants. Both in black midcalf combat boots, with steel toe caps.

Lori Quint lay next to Doc. Ryan had noticed over the past few days that the old man and the six-foot blond teenager had been becoming increasingly friendly. It wasn't that surprising. In Deathlands the first thing you needed was a reliable weapon. A friend came a close second.

Lori had been the second wife of mad, ragged Quint, the Keeper of the redoubt in Alaska that concealed the gateway. The long fur coat that she wore in the chilly north was by her side, but now she wore a short maroon suede skirt, hiked up around her long tanned limbs. The red satin blouse was torn and stained. She stirred as consciousness came creeping back, the tiny silver spurs on her thigh-boots of crimson leather tinkling with a thin clear sound. Her only gun was a small pearl-handled PPK .22 pistol.

Ryan, feeling the familiar dizziness and pressure behind the eyes from previous jumps, eventually decided to make an effort to stand. At his side, Krysty Wroth was coming around. He looked down at her, filling with a great wave of affection. That was the best word he could believe about it. "Love" was a word that was not much used by Ryan Cawdor.

"By the Earth Mother, Ryan, it's hot in this place."

"I figure we're somewhere far to the southeast."

"Still in Deathlands?"

"Mebbe beyond."

With no apparent effort, the girl uncoiled herself to stand by him. Ryan was a good two inches clear of six feet, but she was less than a palm's span below him. He marveled at her amazing powers of recovery. Though the others were all moving, moaning and sighing, Krysty's green eyes were bright as ever, and she was leaning against the glass wall, arranging her staggeringly bright red hair with long fingers. The girl wore khaki coveralls, tucked into a beautiful pair of cowboy boots, also from the Alaskan redoubt. They were hand-stitched in blue calf, overlaid with silver falcons, wings spread wide. The toes of the boots were knife-sharp, chiseled from silver. Her gun was also silvered, a 9 mm Heckler & Koch P7A-13.

In the next few minutes they all managed to stand, though Lori felt sick, kneeling with vomit drooling from her mouth. Doc knelt at her side with a cracking of knee joints, putting a comforting arm around the girl.

"Where we come? Hot. Never known hot. How we come to this? Walls different color."

"Tell her, Doc," said J.B. "Like to hear how you explain it to the dummy."

Doc Tanner scowled at the Armorer. "I would be obliged, Mr. Dix, if you would refrain from calling Miss Quint a dummy. She is not a mute. Nor a mutie. That foul imbecile Quint never educated her and kept her in a state of terror. She is as bright as you or I." He paused for a moment. "Certainly as bright as you."

"Fireblast!" swore Ryan. "It's bastard hot. Guess I'll leave my coat here." Dropping the long garment with its white fir trim to the floor, he hesitated, then retrieved a white silk scarf with weighted ends from a pocket.

"Why hot? My head hurts." Lori stood and leaned against Doc. Finnegan seemed as though he was going to make some joke about the oddly matched couple, then caught Ryan's good eye and closed his mouth.

"The pain will abate, child," Doc said. "We are now in some other, hotter part of what was the United States. Unless we have been carried to one of the gateways that was established in... But let us not consider that for a while."

Ryan listened, puzzled. Doc occasionally dropped strange hints about the gateways and what they could do. As if he possessed more knowledge than he possibly could.

"No, we enter this chamber, built long years ago, before the great nuclear conflict that destroyed this earth as we knew it, and the mechanism operates. Instant matter transmitter. From here to there in *that* much time." He clicked his bony fingers together to emphasize the shortness.

Lori's face was utterly blank, but she nodded as if she understood.

"These transmitters were known as gateways. They were hidden in many locations throughout the land. I imagine most were destroyed. But they were well made, using what was called the state-of-the-art technology. Many survived, hidden within a variety of redoubts.''

"Like home?'' she asked.

Doc nodded, his long white hair drifting across the high cheekbones. "Precisely, Miss Quint. Like that vision of Dante's last circle of the inferno that you knew as your home. This is a gateway. A part of Project Cerberus. Research from scientists that was to run to the very end of endless night.''

"When was we home?''

This time Doc shook his head. "Alas, I have no really accurate chronometer, Miss Quint. But my memory, addled though it often is, recalls a transmission time of less than .0001 of a nanosecond. Of course, it seems longer because of the recovery time from the molecular scrambling and disassembly.''

In the few jumps he'd made, Ryan had wondered how long it took. On one he'd checked the chron on his left wrist, but it didn't seem to have moved at all from the beginning to the end of the journey. Doc's explanation hadn't made it any easier to understand. All he knew was that you got into one of the surviving gateways and closed the door. An infinity of scattered time later, you were in another gateway, perhaps three thousand miles away.

"So we was there and here at same time?'' asked Lori, in her slow, almost tranquilized voice.

Doc smiled paternally at her, but the hand that squeezed the top of her thigh, where skirt nearly met boots, was far from paternal.

The old man turned his smile on Ryan Cawdor. But it was quickly replaced with a taut expression of horror. The eyes bulged wide at Ryan. Doc's grip on sanity gradually seemed to be returning, but it was still frail.

"The men of science, Ryan. Upon my soul, ladies and gentlemen, but they are such inhumane scum. They seek better and better ways of slaughter. Oh, the sights I saw when I was...oh, the horrors!" He closed his eyes, swaying like an aspen in a summer wind. "A young man, a taxi driver from Minneapolis, a petty thief...nothing vicious in him. Seen him used as a guinea pig for one of their nerve toxins. Seen him trying to bite his hand off, gnawing to the bloody bone. Children, from Asia, experiments for the agency that...rubbing their own excrement in great ulcerated sores that they had torn in their own flesh. Oh..."

He began to weep. Lori put her arms around him, hugging his frail body as he sobbed uncontrollably.

For a moment, everyone avoided eye contact. It was Ryan who broke the silence.

"Best we move."

"Yeah," said J. B. Dix.

THE DOOR TO THE GATEWAY opened smoothly. The anteroom was filled with chattering banks of computers and ranged equipment that hummed and whirred. Red and green and amber lights flickered. This was the cleanest and apparently best-preserved gateway control room that Ryan had seen.

Above the small panel of numbered and lettered buttons by the side of the chamber door, there was a notice that Ryan had seen before. Up in the Darks, where it had all begun for them.

"Entry Absolutely Forbidden to All but B12 Cleared Personnel. Mat-trans."

This time there was no small room between the controls and the actual gateway. There was a massive door of vanadium-steel at the far side of the room.

"Blasters ready," ordered Ryan, taking out the SIG-Sauer pistol, steadying it, his finger firm on the trigger.

Everyone drew rifles or pistols and ranged around Cawdor as he reached for the door. In the humid heat it felt cool to the touch. To the right was a green lever, pointing to the floor, with the word Closed printed on it. Ryan grasped it and tugged it upward, toward the Open position.

When the door was only a couple of inches ajar, Ryan eased the lever back to the neutral position, pressing his good eye to the slit and squinting both ways along the corridor that ran outside.

"Anything?" asked J. B. Dix.

"No. Pass the rad counter."

The Armorer handed him a small device, like a pocket chron, that measured the radioactivity. It cheeped and muttered quietly, showing no more than a minor surface level. There were places scattered throughout the country where it would have howled out the danger. These hot spots were often near cities or towns where there had been either missile complexes or communication centers.

"Safe?"

"Yeah."

Hennings was at his elbow as the door hissed open the rest of the way.

"Fucking hot, Ryan. Help sweat some of Finn's fat."

"Careful the sun don't fucking burn you blacker, Henn," replied the stout little man.

"Cut it, you two," snapped Ryan. "Come on. Keep tight and careful."

Nobody needed telling where to go.

Ryan led the way, as always. Then came Krysty, light on her feet, two paces behind. Hennings was third in line. Doc, with an arm around Lori, was in the middle of the group. Finn was last but one, with J.B. bringing up the rear, about ten paces behind everyone, constantly turning to check that nobody was trying to come up behind to cold-cock them.

The corridors were a pale cream stone, seamless, curving slightly to the right. About four paces wide, and about twelve feet high. Lighting was contained in recessed strips. There were no doors on either side.

"This a redoubt, Doc?" Ryan asked.

"Perchance not, Mr. Cawdor. Not all of the gateways were built within the large storage redoubts."

The corridor wound on. Ryan's guess was that it was going to come a full 360 degrees. Every now and then they passed beneath what were obviously defensive barriers, locked away in the ceiling. And every thirty or forty paces they walked under the cold gaze of small vid cameras, set in the angle between wall and curved roof.

"Nobody?" called J. B. Dix from the rear.

"Not a smell or sight of 'em," Ryan replied.

"There's nobody," said Krysty Wroth, voice utterly decisive.

"Sure?"

"Sure, lover," she said.

In the century after the nuclear apocalypse many parts of what had been the United States were disastrously contaminated by all forms of nuclear poison. Chem clouds, bitter winter, acid rain and lethal doses of radiation had all combined to produce a multitude of genetic mutations. Muties came in all shapes, sizes and forms.

In many cases their names gave clues as to what they were like and how they acted.

Stickies had strangely developed hands and feet that enabled them to grip almost any surface. They were hard to kill.

Sensers were able to see into the future, mainly in a very limited and often inaccurate way.

Doomies could only feel when some disaster was going to happen. They could rarely be specific, but their premonitions were generally correct.

Crazies were . . . well, crazies were plain crazy.

Krysty was a kind of mutie. Ryan had found it difficult to handle when he first became aware of it. After they'd first made love. She had mixed talents. Her long hair was slightly sentient and seemed to move of its own volition. She could often sense trouble, in the way that a doomseer could. Also, she had unusually keen sight and hearing.

But her greatest attribute was generally hidden. Her late mother, Sonja, had always drilled into the girl the key phrase: Strive for Life. She had come from a settlement called Harmony, which had a reputation as a sanctuary, as peaceful hamlets were called. Krysty had been taught there by her mother, and by two good men, her uncle Tyas McNann and his friend Peter Maritza. They had taught her to respect the Earth Mother, Gaia, as she was called, after the Greek goddess of the earth.

Though it exhausted her, Krysty was capable of disciplining her mind and body to such an extent that she could unleash a terrifying physical strength.

It wasn't just humans that bred muties.

In his thirty or so years, Ryan had encountered just about every kind of genetic perversion that a diseased mind could imagine. Fish and fowl. Insects from the locked rooms of a dying nightmare. Animals and snakes and birds. All distorted into obscene parodies of their original forms.

Ryan believed that this odd circular redoubt was devoid of life. Krysty just confirmed his suspicions. The air tasted clean and untouched. Once you'd smelled death, you never forgot it. Not ever.

It was only about three minutes later that they reached what looked like the main doors. The corridor opened to a room about ten paces square. The walls showed faint shadow-shapes, squares and rectangles, where pictures or notices had been hung. But the entire complex was clear. Whoever had been there when Armageddon came had done a good cleaning. Nothing remained, not even dust. It was all hermetically sealed, waiting for human beings to return.

"There's no control panel," said Finn. "Not like the others."

The walls around the doors were smooth and clean, lacking any kind of opening mechanism. Ryan looked to Doc for help.

"I confess I'm baffled. The individual design of some of the gateways was outside the scope of the Cerberus people."

"Blast it. Got some grens." As usual, J. B. Dix was direct in his thinking.

"I suggest caution, Mr. Dix," replied Doc. "Some of these main entry ports are highly sophisticated. If we were to fail to blow it open, then we might find we had permanently closed the building's only exit."

"So? What do we do?" asked Ryan. "Feels warmer here than anywhere."

"Got to bring fresh air in every now and then. Been going for a hundred years, give or take. So some outside air and humidity leaks in. I am of the opinion that the controls for this might be in some hidden master unit."

"In the big fucking fire!" swore Hennings. "That mean we can't get out?"

"Wait," said Lori, pushing past them all and walking slowly, fearfully toward the dully gleaming great doors.

"What's she going to do?" hissed J.B. "Lean her tits on it?"

"Shut up, Dix," warned Krysty. "Looks like the kid knows something we don't."

About six feet from the portal, Lori hesitated, then took two more long strides forward, her little spurs tinkling.

At first nothing seemed to happen.

Then like a metallic giant unclenching his fists, the doors began to slide ponderously back, letting in a waft of humid air that made all seven of them gasp. The doorway was nearly forty feet wide, and when the doors finally stopped moving, a stretch of corridor, around two hundred paces in length, was revealed. At its end was a steel wall with an ordinary-sized door set in it.

"Come," said Lori, stepping briskly forward, followed by the others with varying degrees of reluctance.

On the right-hand wall someone had neatly stenciled the word *Goodbye*.

"How d'you know just to walk up to it like that?" shouted Ryan, his words ringing out above the echoes of boot-heels.

Turning her head over her shoulder, Lori answered, "Back door out home. Quint show me. Earth slip and cover it. Look same. Eyes see us and open door. Eyes of dead men."

"Mebbe boobied, girl," called Hennings, running past her, stopping at the door and pushing cautiously at the handle. "Locked!" he bellowed.

"No," said the girl, moving him aside and taking the handle in her right hand. She pulled it slowly toward herself.

It was unlocked.

Henn followed the tall blond girl out into the daylight. Ryan came next, with the others at his heels. He stood on the threshold of the building, staring out. The light was oddly diffused, with shifting green shadows moving in the doorway. He drew a deep breath, filling his lungs, tasting the air, savoring it like a connoisseur.

Ryan Cawdor had visited many parts of the continent. He had walked the cracked avenues of New York City, through the groves of whispering vegetation with poisonous flowers and berries on every corner. Gazed across the oily brew of chemicals to the charred stump of what had once been a mighty statue. Something the locals mostly called Libberlady.

He'd been in the cold and ice of the north and down in the glowing rad-crazy wastes of the southern deserts, where chem clouds flamed from east to west. If J.B. was right, and they were in the southeast, then it was new territory for him.

"Some ozone," he muttered. "Can taste gas. Mebbe in the ground or water. Fireblast, but it's hot and wet here."

Already he was sweating, a trickle of perspiration running down the small of his back. From habit he glanced behind him, seeing to his surprise that virtually all of the gateway was below ground. Creepers twined all about the shallow concrete single-story building, covering it with an impenetrable mat of gray-green foliage. His first guess was that this superb natural camouflage was the main reason the gateway hadn't been entered and despoiled.

"Here we come," said Finnegan, staring out at the unbelievable landscape around them.

Krysty shuddered. Within the deeps of the limitless swamp that stretched all around them, she sensed a slow stirring.

It was not a good feeling.

Chapter Two

THE BLIND WOMAN SAT trembling on a large wooden chair, leaning against the high quilted back, arms folded across her breasts. She wore a thin cotton dress, with a dark brown stain on the right hip. Her right hand fiddled with the slim silver knife, sheathed on a cord around her neck. Every few seconds her pink tongue flicked nervously over her dry lips.

All around her, in the lobby of what had once been the Best Western Snowy Egret Inn of West Lowellton, near Lafayette, Louisiana, men bustled about their business. Not one of them looked directly at her. If Mother Midnight had been summoned by their lord, then it was best to avoid any entanglement. The scar-faced woman was notorious as one of the most cunning of the witches. The magicians of the day were known as houngons, and were frightening enough. But Mother Midnight was one of the dark wizards, called bocors.

Cross her, and she might wish you dead. Might touch you on the cheek with a long fingernail and whisper the single word, *Thinner*. That had happened only a month ago to tall, strapping Stevie King. Slowly but surely, he began to waste away. Within twenty days he died, shriveled to less than eighty pounds.

And now something had gone wrong. All through the bayous the whisper had gone out of a disaster at a ritual. So the baron wished to see her.

Her sensitive nostrils caught the sharp scent of marijuana, and she turned toward the sound of steps, hearing them stop near the chair.

"He will see you now, Mama Minuit."

There was not the usual respect in the young man's voice, and the woman tasted fear on her own tongue. The baron ruled over a vast area of the swamps, all around Lafayette. Apart from the renegades, every soul for fifty miles around paid dues to Baron Tourment. Even the Cajuns, deep within the Everglades, would not cross him.

She stood and reached out a feathering hand for guidance. The Best Western had been the headquarters for the baron ever since she could recall. But he moved from room to room daily, fearing assassination. The hand that gripped her fingers was soft as a girl's, and she could smell scent.

"This way. There is a step, then another."

She wasn't going to ask why she'd been summoned, in case she got the answer she dreaded.

She wasn't going to ask.

"Why does . . . ?" she began.

"He will tell you."

"Oui," she said simply.

The carpet was soft beneath her sandaled feet, muffling their steps. Her sense of direction was excellent, but even she lost track of the twists and turns of the endless corridors. Twice they passed clunking machines that made ice for the baron and his army. Once they stopped, and she heard the thin whining of an elevator. They went up one floor, then along more corridors. They entered another elevator. As her bare shoulder brushed against the sliding metal door, she felt the faint whipcrack of a static shock. Down a level.

She realized that the young man holding her hand was teasing her. Playing some cruel jest by taking her a winding way, making the darkness around her into a bewildering maze.

"How far?"

Ignoring her, he quickened his pace, dragging her behind him.

"How far, friend?"

"Soon." There was a measured pause. "And do not think I am your friend, Mother."

Then, clear and distinct, her ears caught the sharp click of a gun being cocked. She winced in the expectation of the shock of a bullet. But nothing happened. The man at her side giggled, feeling the sudden tenseness of her hand.

"That is not his way. Not a swift death."

"I know it," she replied, her voice shriller than she'd intended.

The last public execution had been around the beginning of the year. An old man who'd stolen a chicken for his family and had been caught by the sec men.

They'd stripped him, his pale, sagging belly almost concealing the shrunken genitals. Poured gasoline over him and ignited it. The flame was almost invisible in the bright sunlight. He'd capered and jigged, his hands beating at the fire. The leader of the baron's sec men, Mephisto, had handed the old man a can of water, which he'd immediately poured over his own head.

The water had been boiling hot.

Smoke and steam had mingled in a deadly halo about the old man's skull. Layers of skin had come peeling off like discarded decorations at Mardy. Careful not to sully his immaculate white suit, Mephisto had splashed his vic-

tim with more gas, flicking a match to light it. The cold
liquid had streamed over the man's body, over his groin
and his legs. The flames, with the more beautiful blue tint
to them, had danced all over. The pubic hair had scorched;
blisters burst out by the hundreds.

Mother Midnight had seen none of this, relying on one
of her followers for a description. But she'd smelled burning hair. Roasted flesh. Heard the mewing and gagging of
the old man. The hiss as Mephisto poured more boiling
water over the fire.

Flames and water.

Flames and water.

Flames.

"Come on," snapped the young man, jerking the witch
from her reverie.

She was pulled into a room and was left alone. She
coughed, trying to establish the size and shape, but the
sound was muffled, as if large drapes hung everywhere.

"The ritual of the bird, Mama?"

He used the Creole French that she always used in her
ceremonies, rather than the anglicized patois of his followers. His voice was deep and resonant with a pleasant
amiable tone to it.

"It was bad, Baron. Real bad."

"Everyone leave us."

There was a scurrying of feet and a jostling in the doorway as if too many people were trying to get out at once.
The woman heard the door close, then silence broken only
by a susurrating creaking sound. Leather and wood and
metal moving against each other, under tension.

Mama Minuit had never seen Baron Tourment. She had
spoken many times with him. Even made love with him.
Her body knew his dimensions. All of them.

She knew that he was immensely tall. Three inches over seven feet. Though his fingers were like steel, his body was weak, the knees and hips unable to fully support him. To compensate, he wore a clumsy exoskeleton of steel struts and bindings around his lower torso and legs. His hair was short and curly. She also recalled that his penis was about twice ordinary size, thick and long, like the forearm of a young child. He had thrust remorselessly between her wide-spread thighs, tearing her, so that blood gushed over her legs and belly.

She had never conceived. Nor had any woman he had ever serviced. But she knew that the baron still lived in hope of a son and heir.

"I heard of the red-wing slain. Falling into the flames to perish."

On an impulse she dropped to her knees, conscious of him looming over her. She could smell his body. Musk and soap, mingling.

"I have never seen the like."

"You put out the eyes?"

"Yes."

"And released it clean? It was not harmed? The wings were unbroken?"

"Yes, lord."

His breathing was slow and steady. The only other sound the woman heard was the surf of her own blood seething through her ears.

"It fell to the fire and was consumed?"

"I have never..."

"You have said that."

"Forgive me, lord."

"For what? There was a ripple in our world, and you asked for the strangers' ritual to be performed. It has been done before. And it will be done again. This time, it went... I am disappointed, *madame*. I am very disappointed."

"It proves what I had said. There had been signs before. When there has been a great tide or the earth has shaken. The insects, the snakes and the birds. All behave in..."

His hand touched her face, and she stopped speaking. The middle finger of his right hand touched her jaw, beneath the left ear. His spatulate thumb probed under the right ear.

"Tell me once, woman. Why?"

The palm of his hand was across her lips, pushing them against her broken teeth. There was the warmth of sweet blood in her mouth.

"There are strangers come. But they are not as we are. Not Cajuns. Not your men or women. Not the wolf's-head renegades from the other side of the town. They have come from nowhere."

"And the signs are bad?"

"As bad as can be. Never..."

The finger and thumb began to tighten, making the cartilage pop under the skin. The woman moaned, but the grip was inexorable.

"That is all? There is nothing more you can say to aid me with these strangers?"

She desperately racked her mind for something that might satisfy Baron Tourment, might spare her from his cold anger.

"No?" he said, voice as soft as the touch of a butterfly's wing. "Then you have failed me."

The hand closed on her jaw, squeezing, the nails digging into her flesh. The skin burst under the pressure, and the woman tried to scream for mercy. But already her windpipe was clamped shut. First the left side of her jaw was dislocated, then the right joint cracked apart. She tried to bite the black hand, but it was too tight against her lip.

Blood was filling her mouth, and she struggled to swallow it. The hand pincered in, harder and tighter, until she couldn't breathe.

Her veiled eyes protruded from their sockets, blood trickling from the corners. More blood came seeping from her broken mouth, from her nose and from both ears. It was as though her entire skull was a great sponge, filled with crimson blood, and Baron Tourment was squeezing it slowly dry.

The giant black braced himself on his splinted legs, lifting Mother Midnight until her bare feet hung clear of the carpet, kicking and jerking. He wrinkled his broad nose at the stench as she lost control of both bladder and bowels and fouled herself. But his grip didn't relax for a moment.

The last sound she heard, deep within her own head, was a soft cracking, like a man setting his heel to a fresh apple.

"Adieu, Mama," whispered the man, opening finger and thumb with a gesture of revulsion, allowing the corpse to drop to the floor at his feet. He wiped the blood from his hand on his dark cotton shirt.

There was a polite knock on the door of the luxury suite.

"Come."

"It's over, Lord?"

"Yes, Mephisto. It's over. Remove that and dispose of it to the pets." The grating Creole French was gone and the man spoke perfect English.

"And then? She saw something?"

"I think so. Something could be real bad. Pass the word for extra care."

"Who can they be?"

The massive black creaked across the room and collapsed inelegantly on a long sofa, stretching the exoskeleton and sighing.

"Not that white butcher kid and his friends?"

"Lauren and his gang?"

"No, Mephisto. The bocor woman here smelled something new. From outside the swamps."

Mephisto grinned wolfishly. "It is a vengeful spirit come to punish you for your evil, Baron Tourment."

It was dangerous to make that kind of joke, but the sec boss had judged the moment well.

"You think maybe that? Do I do wrong? No. A man like me shouldn't worry about something like that. It may even be blasphemous."

He threw back his leonine head and laughed uproariously at his own joke. Mephisto joined in, stopping when the baron pointed a long, bloodied finger at him.

"But take care. Who knows what manner of creature moves amongst us?"

Chapter Three

"THIS PLACE IS fucking something else," complained Hennings, swatting irritably at a huge mosquito that had battened on his shoulder.

"These bastard fly-bugs are the biggest I ever saw," added Finnegan.

"Muties," commented J.B., laconic as ever.

The Armorer used his pocket sextant to take a sighting of the glowering orb of the sun through the dense foliage of the forest surrounding them. It confirmed his original suspicion that they were in the Deep South, around two hundred miles west of the old port of New Orleans.

"Cajun country," said Doc Tanner, pausing to wipe sweat from his brow with a massive kerchief with a swallow's-eye design.

"What's a Cajun?" asked Ryan, easing the shoulder strap of his weapon.

"Around five hundred years ago, back in the 1600s, the French settled on a part of the east coast that would later be known as Nova Scotia. The soil being fertile and the climate temperate, the settlers called their paradise Acadia. More than a hundred years later, the British drove them out of the region and the Acadians fled south to these parts. Acadians got corrupted to Cajuns. Simple, isn't it?"

Nobody said anything, and Ryan wondered, as he had a hundred times in the past few weeks, just how the old

man came to have such a bottomless supply of knowledge.

AFTER LEAVING the small redoubt they had tugged the
door shut behind them. At J.B.'s suggestion, they had put
a tracer on it so they could find their way back through the
labyrinth. But the tiny trans didn't work.

"Damp," said J.B. disgustedly. "Don't have another.
Have to watch our path real careful."

Ryan led the way, following the faint remains of a narrow two-lane blacktop through the trees and shrubs. Never
in his life had he seen anything like this place. Not even in
his dreams.

Though it was nearly noon, the sky was filled with a
dull, hazy greenish light. On both sides of the road there
was the sullen glint of water, rainbow-tinted where oil lay
on its surface. Cypress and pecan saplings twined about
each other, with groves of beautiful oaks and graceful
elms. And over all of the forest were the smothering veils
of Spanish moss, dangling from every branch like spider
webs. As the sun broke against it, the moss seemed to shift
and alter, diffusing the light in shards of white and gold.
Where the shadows gathered, the moss changed color like
a chameleon, from green to gray.

Two hundred paces from the building, they came across
what had been the security gate. There had been triple-
layer barbed wire with porcelain conductors, evidently
meant to carry a lethal dose of electricity. But over the de-
cades the planet had struck back at the man-made intrusions. Fallen trees had smashed the fences; long creepers
had brought down the guard towers where machine guns
rusted in the gloom.

It took several minutes for Ryan to lead his party over and under and around the tumbled trees, using his panga to hack away at the clinging ivy. Several times he heard something scuttling away from them but did not see what it was.

They came to a fork in the road, and Hennings stepped across to examine the remains of a notice board rested crookedly against the stump of a dead azalea. But as he attempted to pick it up, the wood crumbled in his fingers, rotted by beetles and the humidity.

Passing more fallen barriers and fences, Ryan realized how tight the security must have been when the redoubt was built, way back at the end of the twentieth century. Now it was all wiped away by the bombing and by the weather that followed.

"Much nuking down here, J.B.?" he asked.

"Never been hereabouts. Recall some trader in a gaudy house near Windy City saying they used some kind o' new missiles. Kills life and leaves things standing."

Both men started, looked upward through a break in the covering branches, seeing a great white bird with beautiful plumage soaring far above them. Neither of them recognized the creature as a snowy egret.

"What we going to do 'bout food, Ryan?" asked Finn, stopping to shoo away a cloud of tiny orange flies that gathered around his flushed face.

"This road's got to lead somewhere. We all got food tabs. Place like this might have dirties living close by. Take their food."

The idea of getting food from the backward muties who were supposed to live deep within some of the more isolated swamp areas wasn't that attractive to anyone.

"There," said Lori, pointing ahead, where the trail narrowed by the remains of a high fence. It was now a tangled heap of rusting steel.

"Looks like there could be a real highway yonder," Hennings said.

He was wrong.

It was a back way into a kind of park. There was a wooden causeway, floating on the watery mud that flooded the area. Some of the logs had rotted and broken, and others shook dangerously as Ryan stepped carefully on them. Leading the way, he warned the others to be cautious and keep ten paces apart.

The trees became sparser, comprised mainly of intertwined mangroves set in the water, some leaning and toppling. The water opened into a kind of bay, offering a visibility of up to a couple of hundred paces. The sun was a watery gold, sailing in a sky dotted with purple and black clouds. Intermittently Ryan noticed that the surface of the swamps was broken every now and then by a rippling splash, as if something had moved or jumped. But it was always the actual enlarging rings of water that caught his eye; he was never quick enough to see what was doing it. Once, as he was standing on the edge of the piling, staring down into the thick brown water, he was sure something large passed underneath, setting up a sullen rippling on the surface.

"What's that?" asked Krysty, pointing at a thick square post with the number 25 deeply etched into its sloping top. At its base was a black plastic box.

"Looks like a small trans. J.B. what d'you reckon?"

"Could be. Antipersonnel, mebbe. Pick up intruders by the gateway. Fire gas? Looks like it's well iced by now."

Doc stopped to peer at it, running his gnarled fingers over the carved numbers.

"Upon my soul, but this rings a far-off and tiny bell in some back room. I believe . . . no, it eludes me, I fear."

The next two posts along the causeway had rotted away to mere stumps. At a curve in the trail, many of the logs had collapsed into the murky swamp below, and they had to leap the gap. Doc surprised everyone by leaping across like a startled gazelle, but Lori found it harder, eventually removing her high boots and throwing them across first, and finally jumped with little difficulty.

Finn slipped on landing and opened a small cut on his hand. He bent over to wash it in the swamp. "Water's warm," he said, raising his hand to his lips and licking it. "Warm and salty."

"Not that far from the sea. Only a few miles from Gulf o' Mexico. Few years back they had vicious acid rainstorms here. Strip a man to his bones in a few minutes if'n you got caught in one. Seems calmer."

"Them clouds is gathering," said Hennings, pointing with the muzzle of his gray HK54A submachine gun.

The sky was blackening, the violet becoming a deep royal purple. The sun ducked and dived behind the clouds, sending shadows racing across the water.

"Best move faster," urged Ryan.

Passing more wooden posts, he automatically noticed the numbers. They stopped at a post numbered 18.

"You are approaching the end of the Audubon self-guiding nature trail. Remember, the planks may be slippery, so use the handrails and ropes where provided. Children should hold the hand of an adult."

The disembodied voice was so sudden and shocking that Ryan slipped and came within an ace of tumbling head over heels into the turgid slime.

"Fucking fireblast!" said Ryan, recovering his balance and his composure.

The voice went on, creaking a little like an old farm gate in need of oiling, occasionally fading and then rising again.

"In the basin directly in front of you are thousands of tiny green turtles. If you see or hear something slithering in the water, then it just might be old brother alligator. But they have been carefully selected to prevent them growing too big, so don't be frightened."

There was a click as the tape loop reached its end.

"Activated by a low-intense beam," said J. B. Dix. "Works like a basic gren trap."

"A hundred years old and still working," said Krsty Wroth, moving close to Ryan.

As the seven continued to walk along the wooden causeway, they passed several of the stumps, but only a couple were working.

Number 7: "Wandering along the Audubon self-guiding nature trail, most visitors will have, even in this vast solitude of mud and water, a sense of kinship and friendliness with the environment."

"Like a hole in the fucking head," spat Finnegan, slapping angrily at one of the insects that had settled on his neck for its afternoon fix of fresh blood.

"Remember, no picking or taking, please! The delicate ecostructure can easily be damaged by the careless hand of man. Some creatures here are real messy housekeepers, so watch where you step."

This time the tape didn't stop. It just began to repeat itself, gradually slowing down, drawling and blurring its speech until it died with a crackling, hissing mess of static.

They walked on in silence.

"LOOKS LIKE DRY LAND," said Hennings, pointing ahead with the muzzle of his blaster.

The cathedral of towering trees that surrounded them was thinning out a little, occasionally letting the sun dart through, creating pools of brightness all over the tangled roots of the mangroves. They spotted several large birds swooping among the upper branches. Ryan had never seen creatures like some of these. Brown-feathered birds, with great leathery bills that hung like sagging shopping bags.

"How deep d'you figure this swamp, Doc?" asked J.B., leaning out over the side and shading his eyes with his hand, peering into the clouded depths.

"I wouldn't be surprised to find them, technically, bottomless. The water will grow thicker as you go deeper. Muddier. Until muddy water becomes watery mud. Then thicker mud, slimy and clinging. Perhaps a hundred feet or more before you reach anything that could be regarded as solid."

"Another speaking tree," said Lori, indicating the last of the posts, with the numeral 1 carved deep into it. As they drew level, the ancient mechanism creaked to life.

"To wonder is to begin to understand . . . understand. Welcome to the Audubon self-guiding nature trail. The leaflet you are holding will help you to . . . to . . . to . . . to appreciate the wonders of this part of the Atchafalaya Swamp, the largest natural swamp in the entire country. To wonder is . . . entire country . . ."

"Kind of strange listening to a voice from the past like this, even if it is going all wrong." Krysty shook her head.

As if involving actual effort, the tape began to grind around once more, with many jumps and starts and repeats.

"If you...finish with it, replace it for use of those...after. Help to preserve this vital part of our living heritage so that they...by the great-great-great-grandchildren of us all, a hundred years in the unguessable future."

"Unguessable," echoed Ryan. "Son of a bitch sure got that right."

As the tape jerked along, Finnegan sighed and sat down on the edge of the causeway, less than twenty paces from the murky edge of dry land. He leaned over the side, trailing his hand in the warm salty water, straining to hear the faint voice on the tape.

Above them, the sun had disappeared once more behind the gathering clouds. Twice in the past few minutes they had heard the whiplash of lightning as it slashed to the earth.

Half-listening to the voice from the past, Ryan Cawdor walked a dozen paces beyond it, then stopped where the last logs of the walkway were rotting and settling into the crusted mud of the shore. Tiny orange crabs scuttled and darted among the jumbled debris. Near the pier a metal can bobbed on a sullen swell, still bearing the recognizable words Miller Lite. Ryan had seen dozens like it before. They had been containers for beer, or sugary drinks that had foamed and fizzed when opened. He'd seen pictures in old magazines in redoubts.

"The Audubon trail is controlled by the National Parks movement. Remember…man…harmony…environment. Man in harmony with his environment."

Abruptly, Finn screamed and threw himself back on the moss-stained planks, rolling to try to get away from the enormous alligator that had come bursting from the stinking ooze. Jaws gaping open wide enough to swallow a buffalo, with rows of sharp, triangular teeth, the predator raked the air as it sought its prey.

Chapter Four

THE HECKLER & KOCH G-12 automatic rifle has a laser sight that makes it extremely accurate over any distance by day; and equally so by night with its infrared laser nightscope.

J. B. Dix had once explained to Ryan why the three-round burst, such as the G-12 features, had been introduced, back before the long winter hit the world.

"On full automatic, most rifles, like the M-16, tend to start rising after four or five rounds have been fired. Difficult to control. So you fire a succession of three-round bursts. Interrupts the cycle before the muzzle comes up at you."

Everyone was startled by the eruption of the monster reptile from the swamp. Some reacted more quickly than others.

Doc struggled to drag out his nineteenth-century pistol, but Lori jerked out her popgun. Krysty and the Armorer were equally fast in readying their blasters, with Hennings a split moment faster to try to save his friend's life.

Ryan, with his H&K G-12, was first and quickest of all. As he spun around, finger already dropping to the pistol-grip trigger, the alligator was less than ten yards away from him, and Finnegan was desperately scrabbling away from the yawning chasm of its jaws. Muddy water streamed off the horny ridges along its spine and its tiny hooded eyes stared unblinkingly at its potential victim.

Ryan snapped off five successive three-round bursts, bracing himself against the recoil, firing from the hip against the advice of all the approved manuals. He'd owned the oddly-shaped blaster for only a few days, and still found it odd not to be surrounded by spent cases, pinging all about his feet. But the nitrocellulose caseless cartridges were all used up in discharging the 4.7 mm bullets.

The first triple burst, sounding to an inexperienced ear like a single tearing explosion, ripped into the edge of the sodden wood, a hand's breadth from the monster's snout. Wooden splinters exploded, showing white beneath the surface. The next four bursts all caught the mutie alligator, raking it from the end of its jaw, along the side of its questing head, into the light-colored belly with its softer armor.

Blood spouted over Finnegan, soaking his face and chest. Shards of jagged bone were torn from the creature's savage teeth, pattering into the water. One of its eyes disappeared, the whole cavern of the socket disintegrating under the high-velocity fire from Ryan's weapon.

The reptile was kicked back into the water, off the edge of the causeway, its claws tearing away at the wood. Propelled at an extreme velocity, the rounds punched into the target with fearsome force.

There was no need for anybody else to fire. More than a dozen bullets had ripped the alligator apart, sending it flailing and thrashing, throwing up a great pink spray that darkened to crimson, covering its death throes. Hennings helped Finnegan to his feet, and they stood on the edge of the torn planks staring as the monster passed from life. The others, including Ryan, with his finger still on the trigger, also watched carefully.

"Bastard that big could still come at us," he said.

"Be fine way to go. After all he's fucking eaten," grinned Hennings, one hand still on Finn's shoulder. "Being that fucker's dinner."

"Why did you sit down there?" asked J.B.

Finnegan shook his head, wiping the mutie's blood from his face and neck. "I asked a man that. Tail-gunner off War Wag Three. Dean Stanton, his name. Little runty guy with a lot o' balls. Once seen him throw himself clear off a high bridge into a couple of feet of water. Near Missoula. We dragged him out and I asked him why he done it."

"And?"

"And he said it just sort of seemed a good idea at the time."

Finnegan began to laugh, hanging onto Hennings for support. The laughter was contagious, and they all began to laugh, even J.B., easing away the tension of the fat man's near escape.

"Crazy bastard," called Ryan, patting the stamped sheet-metal housing of the automatic rifle. It was damned near the closest he ever came to showing any affection.

"Thanks, Ryan," said Finn.

"Sure," he replied.

The alligator was nearly still, no more than a twitching corpse. Around it the water was stained a deep brown-red, and small fish began to appear by the hundreds near the carcass.

As Ryan and the others looked on, fascinated, the dead alligator, better than fifty feet in length, began to jerk and roll, its white belly up, the fish tearing at it.

Within less than five minutes the corpse had been stripped to raw bones and shreds of tattered sinews.

Hennings whistled. "Phew! Those are mean bastard fishes. I heard of 'em. Called pianners."

"Piranhas," corrected Krysty. "And you're right, Henn. They are mean bastards."

It was a relief to finally set foot on dry land at the end of the walkway.

There was a small stone building, with a roof of woven reeds, standing among a grove of oaks. Its windows were unbroken, and although the stucco on the walls had peeled, most of it remained undisturbed by the elements.

It was an odd sight in a world where the great bombings of 2001 had reduced virtually every building to rubble. Ryan could almost count on the fingers of one hand the number of times he'd seen prenuke architecture intact like this.

"Figure the low land protected this place?" he asked J.B.

"Has to be."

"No."

"What's that, Doc?"

Doc Tanner rubbed at a green stain on the side of his stovepipe hat. "Not the lie of the land, my dear Mr. Cawdor. Have you not heard of a little toy called the neutron bomb?"

"Neutron bomb?" asked Ryan. "What the fireblast was that?"

"I heard of it," said the Armorer slowly. "Took out men and left the houses. That it?"

Doc nodded. "A simplistic summary of the effects, but accurate enough for our purposes."

The door of the little building was open; the weather had apparently cleared out whatever it might have held.

With the aid of Ryan's long machete, they hacked through a screen of tumbled vegetation about forty feet thick, which screened off the walkway and ultimately kept the location of the redoubt and its gateway a secure secret.

On the far side was a crumbling road, winding southward. Standing on the cracked pavement, they heard no sign of life, just the occasional crying of a distant bird and the endless clicking and chirping of insects.

"There's more water," said Krysty, pointing ahead. "Cross the road."

It was a slow-flowing muddy-brown river, wide as the eye could see, moving toward the east; it washed out the remains of the highway. Finnegan, still visibly shocked by the near miss from the mutie alligator, dipped his hand cautiously in the water to wipe off some of the blood. He touched a finger to his mouth.

"Fresh. Not salty like the other."

"How come this has risen, but the swamps back there look like they're 'bout the same height they was before the war?" asked Krysty, puzzled.

At first no one answered; then Lori spoke.

"All rivers bigger. No people drink them."

"That's the fucking most stupid thing I ever heard," laughed Hennings. "Rivers rise because there—"

Doc Tanner interrupted him with a raised finger, crooked like a claw, the nail yellow as old ivory. "Mock not, my somber-hued brother. Think that we are close to the delta of the old Mississippi River. I would surmise that even now, a century later, barely one-fiftieth of the people live and work in its basin. No factories to drain it. No rest rooms, flushing away millions of gallons. No drinking, as Lori said. No commercial uses at all. No wonder the levels of the streams and rivers have risen."

"You figure we're stranded here?"

The old man looked sideways at Ryan. "It is conceivable. Perchance we should go back and try the gateway."

"What the bastard big freeze does *perchance* mean?" hissed Finnegan, but nobody answered.

"East or west?" asked J.B.

Ryan looked both ways. The vegetation was stiflingly thick to the east; to the west it looked a little clearer. Along the edge of the river there almost seemed to be some sort of cleared pathway.

"West," he replied.

It *was* a path.

Not very wide, flirting with the water, but it was most definitely a trail. After a few paces, Ryan dropped to his knees among the bushes, peering at the marks in the soft ground.

"Animal?" asked Hennings.

"No. There's something looks like deer. Cloven hoof, sharp. But there's human feet. Deep tread, working boots. Recent. Let's be careful."

The warning wasn't really necessary. Even young Lori had been with them long enough to realize that life was lived astride a singing blade.

While she had been with them in Alaska, one of the party had mentioned problems to Ryan. She recalled his answer.

"Problems? Solving problems isn't our business. We deal in death."

She sensed what that meant.

As before, Ryan led the way, gun cocked and ready, his finger on the trigger. Everyone followed in their places, their own blasters ready for instant action.

Once Ryan thought he caught the sound of human voices ahead. But Krysty's mutie hearing didn't register anything, so he figured he was mistaken.

It was an error that within an hour would culminate in the death of one of the party.

THEY FOUND THE VEHICLE less than a quarter mile along the trodden path. It was beached, like a long-dead swollen whale, pulled in among the trees, its rear wheels still in the water. At first glance it looked like a boat on wheels. Its six wheels held it about eight feet above the mud; it had small metal ladders on each side, and the biggest, fattest tires that any of them had ever seen—their diameter was at least six feet. Ryan poked at the tires, finding them amazingly soft and underinflated.

"Swamp buggy," pronounced Doc Tanner confidently. "Deep tread on the tires. Go through or over just everything you can imagine. Land or water. As well as anything that lies between."

J.B. clambered up a ladder and peered inside. "Seats for eight. Couple o' cans of gas. Steers with a rudder kick-bar. Box of old scattergun shells. Fish hooks. Something looks damned like a ramrod. Figure it can't be. Only blasters from two hundred years back use a ramrod. Muzzle loaders."

"See anyone?" called Ryan.

"No."

"I can drive it," said Finnegan. "Let's get the fuck out of here 'fore they come back."

After a moment Ryan nodded his agreement. There was a simple rule you learned in the Deathlands. If you held it, then it was yours. If someone else held it, then it belonged to them.

The swamp buggy was about to belong to Ryan and his comrades.

THE TRADER HAD ESTABLISHED routines for most occasions. Even for stealing someone else's transport.

"One gets in, slow and easy. Watch for traps. Small landwag, one man can watch. Big one takes two or three.

Don't start it until the last possible moment. Say again. Don't start it until the last moment. Once you make a noise, then they're on you, and you got borrowed time. Once it's running, get the chill out of there."

Finnegan sat in the driver's seat of the buggy. Krysty, Doc and Lori took the other seats, each watching a different section of the land and river around them. Hennings, Ryan and the Armorer moved into the surrounding forest, their eyes and ears ready for the return of the men who owned the vehicle.

Once he felt he could master the controls, Finn gave a low whistle. The three men fell back, ringing the swampwag with their backs to it, eyes raking the shifting wall of green all around them.

"Which way?" asked Finn.

"Cross the river. That's where the old road went. Must lead to a ville of some kind."

"Ready?"

"Ready, Finn," replied Ryan.

The starter was a three-inch nail, bent and smoothed from use. Finn grasped it, pushing on the gas pedal a couple of times. His left hand nursing the throttle, he twisted the starter.

There was a spluttering muffled cough, like a sleeping bear waking in a deep cavern. Finn tried it again. A puff of thick blue smoke spurted from the exhaust, but the engine still wouldn't fire.

"Again!"

"Bastard won't . . ."

"Come on, Finn. You're going to bring every citizen for miles."

On the third go the engine very nearly caught, turning over a dozen times, then dying away. Krysty half stood in her seat, pointing to her right; to the west.

"I hear someone, Ryan. Men running."

At the fourth attempt the engine of the swampwag fired, filling the small clearing with a deep throaty roar. Smoke rushed from the exhaust in a choking pall. Standing on the ladder, rifle at the ready, Ryan gestured for the others to climb aboard.

"Go. Fast as you can, Finn. Go 'cross the river. Make for cover."

"Only blasters they got look like they come from a hundred years 'fore the nukes," said J.B.

The massive wheels began to rotate, throwing a spray of mud and brackish water in the air.

"All the tires give power," shouted Finnegan, kicking at the rudder bar to steer the buggy into the water.

Ryan watched behind them, where Krysty had warned of men coming fast. But there was no sign of them. He suddenly realized that the bottom of the ladder was going to be immersed as the buggy slid fully into the river and he hastily climbed aboard. Clambering up, his eye caught a movement near the bottom of the short ladder: the scaly spade-shaped head of a huge water moccasin emerged above the water, and the two deep-set eyes gazed blankly into his.

The utter depth of feeling made the short hairs bristle at the nape of his neck.

"Left, you gaudy bastard bitch!" cursed Finnegan, wrestling with the unfamiliar controls.

"Open her up!" yelled the Armorer, one hand hanging on to his beloved fedora hat.

"She's open wider than a low-jack whore's legs already," replied Finn, sweat streaming from his chubby face.

They were about halfway into the serene brown water when men appeared on the bank.

"Five of . . . no, six. Seven," amended Hennings, leveling his gray Heckler & Koch submachine gun, steadying the drum magazine on the side of the swampwag.

"Hold fire," warned Ryan. "We already stole their buggy. Let 'em deal the first hand. See what they're holding."

Krysty shaded her eyes with her hand, peering toward the men silhouetted against the elusive sun as it broke through the clouds.

"Nothing much. Nothing automatic. The one on the left with the scarf around his head has a . . . some kind of long blaster. He's thumbing back on a sort of hammer."

Hennings stood up. "I'll waste them all, Ryan?"

The buggy was very close to the belt of sycamores that lined the far side of the river. Another ten seconds or so, and they'd be under their cover.

"Hold it. There might be hundreds of the double-poor bastards round here on both sides o' the water."

"I'll just warn them some," said the black, bracing himself and squeezing the trigger.

The blaster was set on continuous, and a stream of bullets flowed out, with a sound like tearing silk; it kicked up a line of spray a few paces from the watching men.

Finnegan glanced over his shoulder, whooping his approval at his old friend's success. "Teach them suckers not to fuck with us!" he crowed, his enthusiasm making the swampwag veer alarmingly to one side, nearly sending Hennings toppling into the water.

"One of them's got a blaster aimed!" shouted Krysty warningly.

Hennings waved his hand derisively toward the group of natives, clenching his fist in a power salute.

Ryan watched the men pick themselves up after Hennings's burst of fire and scatter. All but one. He stood still, a long rifle at his shoulder, rock-steady.

There was something menacing about the man's deadly calm. There was the look about him of someone who knew precisely what he was doing, not frightened by the shattering effects of the fire from the buggy. Ryan could almost feel himself inside the man's skull.

He considered the windage, the elevation, the drift, the distance.

Then he squeezed and squeezed again.

Ryan turned toward Hennings, tasting the immediacy of the danger like cold steel on his tongue.

"Get down, Henn!" he shouted.

The tall black glanced sideways at him, the smile of triumph still on his lips. From the corner of his eye Ryan spotted the puff of gray powder smoke as it billowed from the muzzle of the long gun.

A moment later he caught the crack of the explosion. Almost simultaneously he heard the unforgettable flat wet slap of lead striking flesh. Hennings gave an "oh" that held more surprise than fear or pain.

"No," said Finnegan, half standing, losing control of the swampwag for a moment, sending it skittering sideways, down the river.

"Keep on it," yelled J.B., nearest to Hennings, holding the black man as he folded into his arms, blood gushing from the back of his head.

Ryan sprayed the men on the bank with his blaster, getting a vicious satisfaction from seeing three or four of them go down, kicking and jerking. But the man with the musket had reached the safety of the fringe of low scrub.

The buggy jolted and tipped as it reached the far side of the river and moved up the sloping bank. The six wheels worked independently, grinding over the tangled roots of the bayous. Mud and water splashed up off the huge tires.

Low branches scraped across the top of the swampwag, leaves crowding in on the crouching men and women. The moment they were totally under cover, Finnegan kicked the engine to a stop, letting it idle and die in a grinding of fears; vaulting off his seat he got back to where J.B. still cradled Hennings.

"How is...?"

Both Finnegan and Hennings had ridden with the Trader on his expeditions for some years. They'd both seen a lot of deaths. Both of them knew the truth.

The leaden ball had struck the black man just above the right eye, leaving a neat dark hole from which a little blood seeped, bright scarlet against the skin. The exit hole was huge: a chunk of skull the size of a man's fist had been punched out in jagged fragments, blood and brains slopping all over the bottom of the buggy.

Krysty, Lori and Doc stood helplessly by, looking down at the felled man. Lori was crying silently, her shoulders shaking, tears sliding down her smooth cheeks, pattering into the spreading pool of blood.

Hennings's eyes were open, blinking in shock. Though the brain damage was clearly terminal, a shred of life still remained. His eyes sought Finnegan, fighting to focus on the red face of his oldest friend.

"I'm here, Henn," said Finnegan, leaning over the dying man.

"Going dark, Finn."

"Yeah. Mebbe a storm on the way."

"What...?"

"What blaster?" guessed Finnegan. "Some fucking musket from the cave days."

"Good shooting." Hennings's tongue flicked out across his dry lips.

"Not fucking bad, friend."

Not far to the west, there was a dazzling burst of sheet lightning, followed by a deafening peal of rolling thunder.

Henn struggled to speak. "Do this mean what I think it do?"

Finnegan nodded. "It do."

Hennings's eyes remained open, but life slipped away, leaving them blank and empty.

As the first heavy drops of rain began to fall about them, Finnegan lowered his head and wept.

Chapter Five

FOR NEARLY TWO HOURS the rains came pounding down so hard that it was impossible to move. There was a stained brown tarpaulin inside the swampwag that they managed to pull up over themselves, keeping the worst of the storm off. But even then the rain was so devastating that it seeped through the canvas in a fine spray, soaking them all. Water collected in the bottom of the buggy, diluting the blood from Hennings's corpse, turning the crimson to pink.

It was the worst storm that Ryan Cawdor had ever experienced.

It wasn't the banshee gales—he'd heard those farther north in the Deathlands. But the lightning and thunder were almost continuous, pounding at the ears until the senses began to totter. The rain swept in, seeming at times as if it were a solid shroud of tumbling water. At one point J.B. stuck his head from under the tarpaulin, taking care to remove his glasses first, trying to see if there was any sign of the storm abating. He pulled back a few seconds later, blinking and gasping.

"Can't breathe. Drown out there, in open air. That's the trouble. No damned air. Just water."

By the time it eased to a persistent drizzle, the noise of the thunder drifting inland, it was close to dusk. The purple-black clouds remained, hiding the setting sun.

During the two hours, Finnegan hardly spoke. Not that conversation was easy above the noise of the thunder and the drumming of the monsoon on the stretched canvas sheet. He sat, his head in hands, beside Hennings's corpse. He ignored all attempts to console him. Only Ryan's words about having iced several of the natives seemed to cheer him at all.

For some time Ryan had worried that their attackers might be creeping around, readying an ambush. But the experience of the Armorer convinced him that as long as the rains lasted they were safe.

But now it was quieting.

"J.B.? What d'you reckon?"

"Go."

"Where?"

"Same way we said 'fore Henn bought the farm."

"South. Way the blacktop was going. Move until it gets dark?"

"Yeah. Stay in the swampwag. Best chance we got. It's noisy as a butchered sticky, but it can go over any kind of land and water. We got the blasters to hold anyone off. Go south and then find a good defensive position for the night. That's the way I see it."

Ryan agreed.

Hennings's sudden death had depressed him, made him question what he was doing as the leader of the group. When the Trader had walked off into the night and never returned, he handed over the command of the party to Ryan. And what had Ryan done with it? Taken a handful of comrades on a crazy expedition through a mat-trans gateway.

Then, in only a few days, three of the original eight were lost. Tall, sullen-faced Okie, one of the top blasters, a girl who kept her own counsel. Hunaker, with her cropped green hair and her incessant taste for anyone of either sex at any time.

And now Hennings.

"We're going to move," he said, throwing back the tarpaulin, standing and stretching. He tasted the flatness of iron on his tongue, carried on the drizzling rain. There was also a hint of the sharpness of gasoline in the air.

"What 'bout Henn?" asked Finnegan.

If Finn hadn't been there, Ryan probably would have dumped the body over the side of the swampwag into the swollen muddy river.

"We bury him, Finn," he replied.

THE VOICE WAS SWEET and pure, ringing like a crystal goblet, unsullied by the rain and the dark and a friend's violent death.

> Amazing grace, how sweet the sound
> That saved a wretch like me . . .

The digging was accomplished with a short-hafted trenching tool they found in the back of the buggy. After going a couple of feet down, Ryan and J.B. were for stopping, but Finn took the shovel, wordlessly continuing in a frenzy of action; mud and clods flew to either side as he bent to the task; he paused only when the grave was a full five feet deep, the sides slick with the rain.

"Now" was the first word he said.

With a touching dignity, the fat man lifted his friend's body and laid it out straight on the short, cropped grass. He took some rags from the buggy and wiped Hennings clean, then closed the eyes firmly. Folding the arms across the chest, Finn placed the HK54A submachine gun in the cold graying hands.

"Gimme help with a piece of that tarpaulin, Ryan," said Finn.

Together they cut a piece off, struggling to keep it as straight as possible. While Finn steadied the corpse, Ryan wrapped the stiff cloth around it like a shroud.

"Keep him for a whiles," muttered Finn. "Way from the...fuckers."

As Finnegan gently put the body into the grave, Lori began to sing.

"I once was lost, but now am found..."

All of them stood around. J.B. had looked at Ryan meaningfully when Finn took the dead man's blaster and wrapped it with him, ready for the grave. Standing orders from the Trader had always been that a dead man's possessions, especially weapons, should be shared among the survivors. Ryan shook his head at the Armorer. Times had changed. They all had blasters. There was no point in burdening themselves with another.

Besides, he figured that Finnegan would have tried to chill anyone who aimed to stop him.

"...was blind, but now I see..."

Doc mouthed the words along with the girl. But none of the others had ever heard the tune before.

The rain came in gray sheets, dripping from the ghostly veils of Spanish moss. Small pools of water glistened in the folds of the canvas shroud, reflecting the somber sky. The wind had fallen to a gentle breeze. With full darkness still an hour or more away, Ryan was becoming concerned that they might be vulnerable to a sneak ambush from the locals.

"Want to say a few words, Finn?" he asked.

"I don't fucking know any words. Someone else best do it." He looked around the circle.

Ryan did it, knowing it was his job. It wasn't for anyone else, once Finn had refused. That was the way of it. First the closest comrade, then the leader.

That was the way.

"This is Hennings, on his last ride. Hennings...I don't even know his other name—Finn?"

"Arnold," muttered the fat man.

"Arnold? You certain?"

"Yeah."

Ryan wiped a bead of rain from his nose. More water had run behind the patch on his left eye, and he lifted it, allowing the cold liquid to trickle down the unshaven cheek.

"Henn was a good blaster. Never run from you. Always stand at your shoulder in a firefight. There aren't many men you can say you trusted with your life. Henn was one of them. Now he's gone and we'll all miss him. Times we'll talk of him, around a good fire." He stopped, looking at the others. "That's all I got. Anyone else?"

Finn nodded. "Yeah. Just ride easy, Henn. I'll see you over the next hill."

The slopping chunks of wet earth fell on the tarpaulin with a flat, final sound. Each of them took a turn, with Finnegan snatching the shovel and filling in the rest of the dirt and flattening it as best he could.

"We got a marker?" he asked. "Can't just walk away from Henn and fucking leave him here like a dog."

"It's best, Finn."

"How come, Ryan?"

"Put a marker, and they'll find it. Dig him up. Do...do fireblast knows what to him. That's not right. Few days, and the grass'll cover him snug and safe."

Finnegan nodded his agreement.

And so they left Hennings, sleeping alone and undisturbed among the trees.

ALTHOUGH THE SWAMPWAG was equipped with headlights, Ryan figured it would be suicide to drive after dark. It would be like carrying a great sign asking folk to blast you. As soon as it got too dark to drive safely, Ryan ordered Finn to pull off the road among a grove of live oaks.

J.B. found some strips of dried fish in the buggy, and they divvied them out. Ryan appointed guards, in pairs for extra safety. A fire was too hazardous, but the night promised to be mild and humid.

Krysty sat next to Lori. ''That was a right pretty song. I think mebbe I heard old ones sing it, back in Harmony. Where did you learn it?''

The girl looked down, blushing in embarrassment. ''Back redoubt, Krysty. Quint sing when he ice someone. Every time. I hear lots time. Called 'A Mazing Grace,' I think. Seemed right sing for poor Henn.''

''Guess it was,'' said Krysty.

ALONE IN HIS BED about thirty miles from where Ryan had set the camp, Baron Tourment lay in an uneasy sleep. The grotesque exoskeleton lay propped at the side of the king-size bed, once available at a special A tariff for visitors to the motel. The heavy curtains were drawn across the picture window, shutting out the last shreds of the storm's lightning.

The giant black, who often had nightmares, generally slept alone nowadays. After twice strangling bed companions in his sleep, he had agreed to forgo more deaths.

He was restless, tossing and turning, tangling the sheets about him. Once during the night he dreamed, his right hand touching and fondling himself, bringing himself to an erection of terrifying proportions. Beneath the pillows was a silver-plated pearl-handled Magnum pistol that he'd found in the loft of a big house on what had once been the exclusive side of West Lowellton. His hands reached for the heavy pistol, caressing it, stroking the cool metal.

And all the while he was asleep.

Just before dawn he began to thrash and mumble, but the words were inaudible—apart from the repeated muttering of "Strangers, strangers."

RYAN AND KRYSTY took the last watch of the long night. They took turns circling the swampwag at a distance of between fifty and a hundred paces. The false dawn came whispering in, with a pink glow in the east and the promise of a fine morning. Then darkness returned, followed at last by the sallow light of true dawn.

"Wake the others, lover?" she asked.

"Soon. Let 'em sleep long as they can. A jump really scrambles up your head. And losing Henn like that..."

The sentence trailed away into the stillness. The air was cool, with a faint mist hanging over the trees behind them. They heard the delicate clicking and chirping of insects, rousing for the new day, and the songs of birds to the east.

The Atchafalaya Swamp was coming to life.

Krysty laid a hand on Ryan's arm, just below the elbow. "Why do we do this, love?"

"This?"

"Keep running. Fighting. Now... dying?"

"I figure you can live easy or hard. Easy, and you never stand up for a thing. Hard, and..."

"And what, Ryan?" Her grip tightened on his arm, making him wince at her latent power.

"Once you start with fighting and killing, Krysty, then it's killing and killing and more killing."

"Why? When do you stop?"

"When the reason for the fighting and the killing is done and ended."

"When will that be?"

"Maybe tomorrow. It's always going to be tomorrow. Until one day you find it's come. That's all there is."

About a mile ahead of them, a thin column of gray smoke was curling up into the morning sky. Ryan and Krysty noticed it simultaneously.

Ryan set his boot on the ladder into the swampwag. "Time to wake 'em," he said.

Chapter Six

AFTER SOME DISCUSSION they agreed that the safest bet was to leave the buggy behind, hidden under cover, ready in case they needed a fast-footed run from danger.

J.B. suggested that they split into groups, circle around and then meet back at the swampwag, but Ryan insisted they stay together.

"No. With Henn gone we're low on blaster power. You, me an' Finn. Doesn't mean Doc and the girls don't pull their weight, but we're the professionals. Best we stick close."

The promise of a good day was vanishing fast. The sky was chameleonic, shifting from a pale blue streaked with pink to a deep purple with black clouds slashed across it.

Ryan, as usual, took the point position, keeping as far as he could to the side of the blacktop, in among the shadows, blaster at the ready, finger close on the trigger. Krysty came second, twenty paces back, on the opposite side of the road. Then Doc and Lori, who were becoming increasingly difficult to separate, with Finn a farther twenty yards behind them. J.B. brought up the rear, keeping a good hundred paces off, on the same side of the road as Ryan.

The temperature was already rising, humidity making the going tough. Ryan estimated that it was already close to the hundred mark. He was glad that he'd left his beloved fur-trimmed coat behind in the gateway.

A large mosquito, wings shimmeringly iridescent in the hazy light, settled on Ryan's left wrist, readying itself to feed. "Bastard!" Slapping at it, he crushed it in a smear of blood.

There weren't many signs that the blacktop was actually used very much. Oases of vegetation sprouted from cracks in its surface. A sharp curve to the left was followed by one to the right. At each turning Ryan held up a hand, slowing the others until he checked out what was around the bend.

Moving back, he called the rest to him, using the prearranged signal of touching the top of his head with his left hand. One by one they came up, J.B. at the rear.

"Road goes straight, but we're close to a ville of some kind. And there's a guard box over on the left, near a side trail."

As they neared it, moving closer together, Ryan was first to see that the small building wasn't a guard box at all.

"It's a phone booth," said Doc wonderingly. "I vow that it has been..." He seemed awestruck. "...many a long year since I have seen such an artifact."

The box, with some of its glass still intact, leaned to one side. The letters 'AT&T' were still visible on it. The group stopped to gawk at it.

Above them the sky had darkened as it had the previous afternoon, with a jagged spear of silver lightning occasionally crackling down. To one side there was a large pool, reflecting the sullen clouds. Beyond the water several buildings were silhouetted in the distance, seemingly fairly undamaged.

If a whole large city had really escaped the nuking of 2001, it would be an astounding thing to see. Certainly Ryan Cawdor had never seen anything like it before.

Finnegan stepped closer, stopping about a dozen paces from the booth.

"Some fucker's in there. I can hear it moving."

"Get back, Finn," ordered Ryan. "Don't take any chance with..."

The words died in his throat when he saw, as they all did, the creature that Finnegan had disturbed.

"A fucking rat," said Lori. It was the first time any of them had heard her swear.

In the Deathlands there were all kinds of mutie creatures. But none of them had ever seen a rat like this one. It was much larger than usual, hanging on the plastic receiver cord, gnawing at it, while its fiery red eyes stared at the invading humans. Its coat was white as driven snow.

"Albino," said Krysty. "I had a pet mouse back home called Blanche. She was like that. Pink eyes and white coat. No pigment."

Almost contemptuously the rat scurried down the cable, pausing in the open door to pick its way delicately over splinters of broken glass, then running across the road and stopping on the edge of the bushes. Finnegan drew his Beretta 9 mm pistol, steadying his right hand with his left.

"No," snapped Ryan. "Don't be a stupe, Finn."

"Why not? We can waste any local double-poor swamp muties."

"Just like Henn did? Come on, Finn."

During the brief conversation the rat made a leisurely escape.

THERE WERE FURTHER COLUMNS of smoke, and soon they could actually taste the flavor of roasting meat. Finnegan was all for pushing on at best speed, going in with blasters spitting, taking what they wanted and icing anyone who stood in their way.

He was overruled by the others.

"Slow and easy, Finn. Usual way. Let's go and do it."

SPREADING ACROSS HALF the roadway was a tumbling mass of brilliant azaleas, a rainbow of brightness, dazzling in the dullness of the morning. Away beyond were the buildings of the town, but the smoke from cooking fires was closer. It emanated from a dip in the land in which lay a maze of shallow swamps.

"Flowers pretty," said Lori, staring open-mouthed at the display.

"Road sign, yonder," said Krysty, pointing to a small rectangle of dark green, well over a mile beyond the flowers.

"It name the ville?"

She stood on tiptoe, straining, her face wrinkled with concentration. "La something. Yeah. Layayette. Lafayette, and it says West... Can't... West Lowellton. Nearest place looks like it's called West Lowellton. Maybe Lafayette's farther."

Doc looked across at her. "I believe that Lafayette was a city, Miss Wroth. Perchance West Lowellton is a suburb of it."

A dozen muties appeared from behind the azaleas. Suddenly and silently. One second the road was clear; the next second the creatures were there.

"Fireblast!" breathed Ryan, dropping into a blaster's crouch, gun braced against his hip, checking to make sure the others had fanned out.

About forty paces ahead, the swampies stood in a frozen group, staring at the invaders as if they were men from deep space.

Ryan checked them out, trying to guess precisely what their mutation was, wondering if it might be safest to simply chill the whole lot of them in a raking burst of lead. But there might be three hundred of them around the next bend.

The first thing that struck Ryan was their stocky build. Not one was taller than about five-two, and not one, including the single woman, weighed less than about two-twenty. Most of them had negroid features, with flattened noses and thick lips. Their hair was short and curly, and came in all shades from black to white, through red and yellow. Ryan noticed that their eyes protruded slightly, surrounded by nests of scars, like old tattoos.

None of them had fingernails.

As they glared at Ryan and his companions, their mouths sagged open as though their noses were blocked. There was not a blaster among them, though several had peculiar small crossbows strapped to their forearms. Each one, including the woman, wore long pangalike knives at the hip.

They were dressed in cotton shirts and patched short trousers, with flapping sandals on their feet, hacked from chunks of old tires.

For several heartbeats nobody moved on either side.

Then Finn opened fire.

Immediately all the others started shooting. After all, who was going to stand there shrugging his shoulders and complaining he hadn't been involved in a tactical planning discussion?

Two muties raised their feeble little crossbows as if to retaliate, but the wave of fire sent them crashing down in a tangled heap of thrashing arms and legs.

Ryan saw his triple bursts wipe three of them away. First the woman, two 4.7 mm rounds smashing into her neck, nearly severing the head from the torso.

"High," muttered Ryan, automatically adjusting his aim. Finn's actions hadn't entirely taken him by surprise. The chubby blaster had never been known for his patience. And after Henn's murder...

The swampy beside the stricken woman was on a crutch, half his left leg missing. Ryan shot him through the stomach, spilling his tripes in the dirt.

Ryan's third victim had already been knocked off balance by one of his falling comrades, and Ryan's bullets hit him through the upper chest, on the left side. A clear heart shot, fatal within thirty seconds or so.

Perhaps fifty rounds were fired by Ryan's party, laying them all down. Peculiarly, none of the muties screamed or cried. Just a faint mewing from the dying.

In the loud silence, Ryan turned to face Finnegan, who was clearing the Heckler & Koch, reaching for spare ammunition.

"Open fire like that again, Finn, and I'll ice you myself."

It was said very calmly, with no obvious anger. But the blaster flinched and looked down at his boots. "Sorry, Ryan. You know how..."

"Yeah, I know how. But not again. Now let's get the fuck outta here before—"

There was a stifled scream from Lori. Everyone else was sufficiently experienced to know that all of the muties were down and done. Finished. But the tall blonde had been staring at the twitching corpses with a morbid fascination. Now she stood, pointing with her dainty blaster, her eyes wide with terror.

Three of the corpses had risen and were walking unsteadily toward them.

"By the three Kennedys," exclaimed Doc, taking a shaky step backward, away from the horrific apparitions.

Ryan knew that stickies were notoriously difficult to kill, but this was something else. The three . . . another one was struggling to rise . . . *four* muties had all taken terminal wounds. One had half his intestines hanging out, looping around his feet so he stumbled and nearly fell; bending to pick them up, he draped them over his arm, looking like an old picture Ryan had seen of an elegant Roman senator in his toga.

A second had an arm hanging by a thread of gristle with tattered rags of muscle bloodily weeping from the stump. Ryan had shot that one. A third had been shot in the face, the bullet dislodging an eyeball so it dangled prettily on the scarred cheek. The fourth had two massive bullet wounds in its chest and upper abdomen.

"They can't," said J.B. in disbelief. "They're dead."

"Then why aren't they fucking lying down?" asked Finnegan.

One of the swampies had managed to fire its crossbow, the bolt flying short and burying itself in the earth near Krysty's feet. She stooped and plucked it from the ground, looking at the sticky patch of brown oil smeared around its point.

"It's poisoned," she warned.

The four staggering muties were only fifteen paces away, lurching like drunken customers leaving a gaudy house at midnight. Ryan noticed that their wounds, appalling though they were, didn't seem to be bleeding as much as they should be.

"Again," he said, opening up at point-blank range with the G-12 automatic rifle, the burst of the caseless ammunition sending all four figures dancing and toppling. He raked the four bodies repeatedly, using thirty rounds to make sure they wouldn't rise a second time. Blood spurted, and chunks of flesh splattered into the air, with gouts of crimson, carrying splinters of bone.

After the racket of the guns, the silence was intense. The bodies lay still, torn apart by the ferocity of the shooting.

"If there's more of them, they'll be on top of us any time now," warned Ryan.

"How could they?" asked Doc Tanner, moving and staring down at the mutilated corpses. "Such wounds, and they rose and walked." He squatted down, oblivious of the blood soaking around his cracked boots.

"Where?" asked the Armorer.

"Away," replied Ryan. "Must be more where that smoke was. I don't want to face more if they're that bastard-tough to put the stopper on."

"Sure. Back to the swampwag? Or into the brush?"

Standing up, his hands slobbered with dripping blood from probing at the carcasses of the muties, Doc interrupted, "Amazing. My dear Mr. Cawdor, it is truly amazing."

"What?"

"These poor creatures, genetically mutated as a result of the neutron bombing, have developed a dual circulatory system. Two hearts, two sets of lungs, two sets of arteries. That is why they are difficult to slay."

"Zombies," breathed Krysty. "By Gaia! They are truly the living dead."

"Nukeshit!" Ryan looked at her in surprise. "You don't believe that stuff. They're muties. Just muties. All muties are different, Krysty, but they're still muties. Right?"

The moment his words were out, he wished he could suck them back and swallow them. The girl glared at him for a long-held moment.

"I know about muties, Ryan. So do you."

"Hey, I'm . . . I'm sorry, only . . ."

She nodded her understanding. "I know why. Doesn't make it right."

"I hear them," said Finnegan, hastily reloading his blaster.

They all heard it. A distant ululating cry, rising and falling like the howls of hunting wolves. It sounded like an awful lot of swampies were heading their way.

"Let's move," said Ryan, turning away from the water and running unhesitatingly into the heavy undergrowth alongside the track.

A DESPERATE CHASE it was, and lasted all morning, and well into late afternoon. At one point there was another torrential downpour but they didn't dare stop for shelter, in case the muties just kept coming after them.

Ryan, Krysty, J.B. and Finn were able to keep going with no great strain. Battle-honed and fit, they could have run for a day. Lori, despite the handicap of her high-heeled boots, did well enough. But for Doc Tanner it was a torturous pursuit.

At first they more than held their own, ducking and weaving along paths that danced and twisted like a break-back rattler. Ryan led the way, his steel panga drawn, slashing the branches that blocked their progress. Every few minutes he'd hold up his right hand for a brief rest, while all of them fought to control their breathing so they could listen for the sound of the muties.

The banshee wail seemed closer for the first couple of stops, then it faded away until it was no louder than the humming of bees. But by the fifth check, Doc was in a perilous state, dropping to hands and knees, his chest heaving, sweat dripping from beneath the high hat.

"I beg you, gentlemen and ladies, to go on and leave me behind. I have my trusty cannon," he said, half drawing the ancient, ponderous Le Mat percussion pistol. "I assure you that I shall give a good accounting of myself, and I shall take some of the monsters with me."

"Save a round for yourself, Doc," urged Finnegan, readying himself to move on deeper among the trees.

"No. Finn. You keep on this path with the women. I insist that—" Doc tried, but Ryan turned on him with a ferocious anger.

"Shut that fucking mouth, Doc, or I'll bust it. This isn't some old-fashioned fucking game of heroics. If you were gut-shot, I'd be first to leave you. But you aren't. J.B. and me'll stop and slow 'em some."

"Usual on the paths?" asked Finn.

"Yeah. Straight when there's no doubt. Any choice, take alternate right and left. Dagger slash on the nearest bush or tree."

Finn nodded and began to move, while Ryan and the Armorer readied an ambush for the swampies who were following. Lori helped Doc up on his feet, but still he hesitated.

"Come on, Doc," called Finnegan. "Have no fear."

The old man came close to a smile; it trembled uncertainly on the edge of the white lips. "You say to have no fear, my plump companion." An ironic laugh. "My own words to myself, a hundred times a day."

"Come on, Doc," urged Krysty. "Uncle Tyas McNann used to quote something 'bout being of good cheer and playing the man."

This time the smile was broad and genuine. "I know the saying, lady. But the man who said it died moments later."

"Get the fuck out of here," said J.B., leaning against a tall sycamore, his gun a comfortable extension of his right hand.

The four of them melted into the undergrowth; the only sounds were the sucking of the increasingly muddy earth at their boots. Ryan and J.B. waited, as they had waited in a dozen different places and times, for the enemy to come to them.

IT WORKED.

They didn't need a signal. Ryan was the leader, so when he squeezed the trigger, the Armorer was a split second behind him. In such thick cover it was difficult to count the enemy. And with the muties' talent for recovering from mortal wounds, Ryan wasn't about to go and check them out. But at least eight went down, hit hard, and the others fled into the bayous, splashing and crying out to each other in odd, bubbling cries.

It was necessary to try the same trick again around four in the afternoon.

Doc has passed out, his breathing shallow, heart racing like a pump engine. Normally, if they'd been out from War Wag One, there'd have been a medic among them with drugs. But out there in what had once been called Louisiana, they had nothing.

"Take five rest," said Ryan. "Me and J.B. will go do it to 'em again."

The swampies had learned their lesson and were approaching more cautiously. But four or five of them went down under the combined fire of the Armorer's Mini-Uzi and Ryan's caseless G-12.

"Take five," ordered Ryan, once they had all caught up with each other.

"I regret," panted Doc, "that I truly can no longer even walk, let alone . . ."

"We'll hold up here," Ryan interrupted. "Either those zombie bastards leave us be, or we stand and fight 'em. No other way."

The ground had been getting wetter and wetter, until at every step their boots sank inches deep into slimy muck. The sky had cleared and now had only a scattering of light orange clouds, floating high and untroubled, intermittently visible through breaks in the green curtain that was draped overhead.

While they waited, Krysty stood a little apart from the others, her head to one side, listening hard. The long red hair rolled over her shoulders, bright in the half light.

Ryan came and stood by her, putting a hand on her wrist. She smiled at him.

"I'm sorry 'bout the cracks on muties," he said.

"It's fine, lover. I know how it is."

He kissed her gently on the cheek, tasting the faintest hint of gasoline from the dirt and mud. "You hear them, love?"

"No. They backed off at the last firefight. But I can hear . . ." She shook her head.

"What?"

"I heard a dog barking. Then it sounded like a pig snuffling. Not far ahead, but the wind's against me for good hearing. I thought I heard a woman's voice. Singing. Mebbe another swampie village ahead of us."

They'd been running more or less blindly, picking anything that looked remotely like a trail, even narrow animal tracks. Now they were in a small clearing with some exceptionally tall elms around them, covered with the white Spanish moss, so that they resembled a mute assortment of frozen brides draped in stained wedding lace.

Ryan hesitated. If they turned back for the swampwag, they might encounter the muties. They couldn't go right or left either. The deep waters of the salt swamps had been closing on them on both sides. That left only straight ahead, where Krysty Wroth had heard sounds of active life.

The sound of a gas engine came to them from behind; deep and throaty it was, exactly like the noise of the buggy's engine.

"Swampies?" said Finn.

It didn't seem likely that any community as brutish as the dirties who'd attacked them could drive a swampwag. But whoever it was, there was a better than even chance that they weren't going to be friendly. Anywhere in Deathlands the odds were never better than even.

"On," pointed Ryan.

THE SWAMP CLOSED IN even more, leaving only a path less than six feet wide that wound among the high-rooted mangroves. Several times the mud and water mingled, and they waded through slime that reached above their knees. Remembering the giant alligator, everyone was edgy, concentrating on the slick surface of the mud as they progressed.

Several of them, not just Krysty, heard the dog bark again. And, drawing closer, they also heard the sounds of a small rural ville. Ryan advanced cautiously forward, and the others followed in single file, moving from quivering tussock to mud thick as molasses, stopping at the sudden apparition that seemed to spring from the very swamp itself.

A skinny white man, in a red shirt and white cotton breeches. He had long white hair and a neat beard. He held out both arms to show that he was weaponless.

"You are fatigued, *mes enfants*. Welcome to the humble ville of Moudongue. Here you may rest, and here you will be safe."

He turned on his heels and after a brief pause, Ryan Cawdor and his party followed the old man. There really wasn't anything else to do.

Chapter Seven

"IF THEY WAS GOING TO fucking butcher us, then they'd have fucking done it by now!"

"Finn makes sense, Ryan," said J.B. "Why bring us here?"

Ryan Cawdor shook his head. "Damned if I know. I just know that something here doesn't set right."

"I feel that, too," added Krysty. "There's a scent . . . a taste . . . I don't know."

"It seems to me, if I may venture my humble opinion, that we are better off here than out in that wilderness of mud and water, being pursued by the living dead."

"Lori says Doc speaks good."

Ryan shrugged. "Sure, no wonder. They promised to feed us in a few minutes, didn't they? Just make sure everyone keeps on their guard. And make sure that we eat different things. In case they've put sleepers in it."

He walked to the side of the hut, feeling the narrow planks bend under his weight; he looked out through the slatted blind, past the mesh of the mosquito netting and across the square of the small ville, down toward the swollen river.

There were about thirty small wooden houses in the ville of Moudongue, set in a rough rectangle along the river. Two or three swampwags were tied to the posts of a wharf.

The old man, who'd told them his name was Ti Jean, entered, followed by three young, slatternly women in dirty dresses of plain cotton. They carried dishes made of turned wood, with some battered metal forks and spoons.

"You are hungry. We feed you," he pronounced. "Later, you join us for dancing. We sing old songs. 'Jolé Blon. Hippy Ti Yo. Mamou Blues.' Dance to the...how do you say...accordion. A good time. It's Mardy, and we all love every man."

"Will you stay and eat with us?" asked Ryan, hoping to find out something about the area.

"No. I regret not. But eat and drink. The beer is good. The wine—" he shrugged expressively "—not so good. The crawfish and red snapper are fresh as tomorrow's sunrise. Gumbo and collard greens. Rice in plenty. Eat well, *mes amis*. Later we talk."

The dishes steamed enticingly. Following Ryan's orders, they tried to eat different things, but it wasn't easy. Everything looked and tasted delicious. Finnegan, in particular, managed to tuck into sizable portions of almost every sumptuous course.

Ryan sampled the crab meat chowder and some trout cooked with spiced rice. The beer was flat and thin to his palate. But he was surprised to find such good eating in such a wretchedly poor hamlet. He said as much to the Armorer.

"It's Mardy. Fat Tuesday. These aren't like them swampies. These are them Cajuns that Doc spoke of."

As they were wiping up the last smears of juice with fresh-baked cornbread, Ti Jean reappeared, smiling like an indulgent father to see how well they'd eaten.

He had obviously been drinking; the sour smell of home-brewed beer hung on his breath. The French accent was more noticeable than before, but he was still in a high good humor.

"Well eaten, *mes copains*," he slurred. "Now you may join us for our feasting of Mardy. Older even than the sky-bombs that changed the world. You said there had been trouble with the muties of deep-swamp. They will not come here."

While some of the women tidied the hut, clearing away dishes and beakers, Ti Jean told them a little about where they'd landed up.

"Lafayette's not far off. West Lowellton is closest suburb. There is fighting there."

"Fighting?" asked Ryan. "Between whom?"

"The baron and the renegades."

"What baron? Local lord of the ville?"

"No, Mr. Cawdor. More. Much more. Baron Tourment controls this whole...what is the word? Region? *Oui*, this region is his. We are his. Even the muties. We call them *les morts-vivants*."

"The living dead," said Doc Tanner quietly.

"We can control them. Use them as slaves. But they are dangerous. Not to be trusted. They live in hovels deep within the bayous. The lost ones. We guard against them. Now and then they take babies."

"To ransom? For money? They ask you for jack for the babies?" asked Finnegan.

"Non, non," Ti Jean replied, laughing. "They take the little ones to eat."

RYAN WAS INTERESTED in knowing more about the renegades. From his experience, any man who stood against a local baron was likely to be a better man than those who lived on their knees in virtual serfdom.

Ryan felt that Ti Jean was not being entirely open. To look at, he was the most hearty, trustworthy old-timer in many a country mile.

But Ryan intuitively felt that it would be better not to turn your back on Ti Jean.

His unhappiness was compounded by not being able to understand what the villagers of Moudongue were saying to each other.

Doc whispered that he could speak a little French, but the people hereabouts spoke a bastardized patois that he suspected was Creole French.

On the surface, all was well.

There was a long room at the far end of the hamlet where everyone had assembled, and were drinking, dancing and bellowing out incomprehensible lyrics at the top of their lungs. Ryan made sure that everyone in his group carried their blasters, but he was reassured to find that the men of the small ville had no guns, though everyone wore a long thin-bladed knife at the hip. The building shook to its rafters from the heavy stamping that passed for dancing in the bayous, to the accompaniment of a fiddle and an accordion; the latter was played by an immense fat man, his shirt sodden with sweat, toothless mouth open, revealing a tongue that was bizarrely forked.

"The Two-step de Bayou Teche" was followed by a driving song with a heavy beat, called "Un Autre Soir d'Ennui." Gradually the members of Ryan's group split apart as they entered into the spirit of the dance. Doc swung Lori away, his legs kicking sideways, knees cracking audibly, whooping his pleasure, the girl smiling like a pretty doll in his arms.

Finn was eyeing a skinny girl who looked to be around thirteen. She sashayed up to him and whispered something into his ear.

"Can I dance, Ryan?" he asked.

"Stick to dancing, Finn. Don't leave this room, or I'll slit your fat windpipe."

"Sure thing." The fat man grinned and went wheeling away after the sprite in her torn dress.

J.B. leaned against the bar, rubbing a pattern in the spilled beer with his forefinger. A huge woman, fully six and a half feet tall and weighing around 350 pounds, came over and tapped him on the shoulder.

"Dansez, mon petit?" she asked.

"What did...?" began the Armorer, but not even waiting for an answer, she jerked him forward, pressing his face into her rolling breasts, nearly knocking his hat off and sweeping him onto the crowded dance floor.

"Want to dance, lover?" asked Krysty.

"Better offer than J.B. got," he replied.

"Want it more formal?"

"Yeah," he said with a grin. The beer was loosening him up, and the food had been as good as any he'd eaten in...in a long time and a lot of miles.

"Sure." She composed herself, brushing back an errant strand of the fiery hair from her cheek. "Miss Krysty Wroth of the sanctuary of Harmony requests the pleasure of the next dance with Mr. Ryan Cawdor of...of where?"

The answer came in a crackling high-pitched giggle, from someone behind her.

"From the ville of Front Royal in the great state of Virginia, run by Baron Cawdor."

The blood drained from Ryan's face at the sudden voice.

Once, years back, a whore in a gaudy house somewhere near Denver had kicked him in the groin in an attempt to rob him. He'd broken her arm to teach her a lesson, but the shocking pain remained a powerful memory. It had felt like the breath had been sucked clean out of his body.

The feeling now was similar.

"What'd you say?" asked Krysty, turning on her heels.

"He's the youngest runt o' Baron Cawdor. Richest and most powerful man east of Ol' Miss."

The speaker looked to be around three hundred years old, but was probably somewhere between sixty and ninety, with a filthy fringe of hair around a peeling scalp. He was not much over five feet tall, with a drooping shoulder that made him look like a hunchback. He was dressed in a variety of rags, held together with mud and spittle.

His eyes were bright as stars.

Ryan gaped at the hideous apparition. There was something vaguely familiar about the old, old man, but he couldn't set his mind to it.

"You don't know me, Ryan Cawdor, do yer?"

The noise of the music and bellowed singing was so loud that nobody apart from Krysty and Ryan had heard the dotard's chattering, or shown the least interest. Instead they concentrated on having a good time.

Finn whirled past, hugging the young girl. On the far side of the hut J.B. was still almost suffocating in the embrace of the giantess. It might have been a trick of the flickering oil lamps, but Ryan could have sworn at that moment that the Armorer's feet were a good eighteen inches clear of the planking.

But all of that blurred compared to this totally unexpected confrontation. The Trader had known a little about Ryan's background. About the lost eye. About the emotional scars.

But even the Trader had only known the small glimpses of the past that Ryan allowed him.

Now this...

For a moment of scorching rage, Ryan was tempted to reach out and snap the scrawny neck of the diminutive old man to still his babble forever. But that would bring everyone in Moudongue down on them.

Oddly, it never occurred to him that the stranger might be chattering lies, might just have a snippet of useless information that meant anything or nothing. Somehow Ryan knew that this was the revelation that he'd feared for many long years.

"I think I know you. What's your name?"

The face contorted into an expression of vulpine cunning. The old man wiped a gnarled hand over the stubbled cheeks.

"Like to know, wouldn't yer, Squire Cawdor?"

Ryan eased aside the shirt, showing the butt of the SIG-Sauer pistol. "Name?" he hissed.

"Ryan? What does—" began Krysty, recoiling as he turned to look at her, the one eye glowing with a manic light.

"Let it lay, woman," he snarled.

"I don't rightly recall what my true name is," muttered the old man, licking his lips and speaking so softly that Ryan had to lean close to catch the words. He winced at the stale alcohol on the breath.

"What do they call you?"

"Pecker."

"Pecker?"

"Yeah."

A vacuous smile slithered across the wrinkled cheeks. The old man touched his stomach with his right hand, smoothing the torn shirt. He moved his hand lower, fondling himself, demonstrating how he'd earned his nickname.

"You know Ryan?" asked Krysty.

"Sure. Knowed him. Years back. He knowed me then. Don't know old Pecker now, do yer?"

The man put his head to one side like a bird sizing up a juicy morsel of food. Then Ryan remembered him—remembered his real name.

"Bochco. Harry Bochco. You were my...the dog-handler at the ville."

"Harry Bochco." The man tried the name out for size, running it around his mouth, repeating it and finally shaking his head in bewilderment. "Sometimes past I don't recall. You say it, then it was so. But I recall you."

"Then tell it," said Ryan wearily.

Against the noisy maelstrom of the Cajun dance, unheard by anyone else, the old man told it.

Chapter Eight

"FRONT ROYAL WAS THE biggest, strongest, richest ville in all Virginia. The nukes hit it hard, but the land's good. Fertile. Plant a bullet, and it grows a blaster. Baron Cawdor held it, in the Shens, from his father and his father 'fore him."

The music and the dancing swirled about them, but Ryan and Krysty were locked into the old man's story; the girl heard it for the first time; Ryan tasted the bitterness of old wounds, feeling the empty eye socket beginning to throb with ancient pains.

"Home like a fortress, deep in the hills. Oh, sweet Lord, those blue-muffled hills and the rolling forests. I swear it were near heaven. Ryan here, Lord Cawdor, was the youngest. Bravest. Proudest. Best with blade or blaster. Finest..."

"Get on, man," snapped Ryan.

"But only as he grew some. There were three in the litter. Morgan was oldest, and like Ryan here. Cherished him when we were little. Runt of the lot when young, Ryan was. The middle brother..."

"Harvey," whispered Ryan, barely conscious that he'd spoken.

"Aye, Harvey. Curse his fucking name. Twisted like a windblown rowan tree. I recall that when he were but ten years old, he took this kitten and a white-hot dagger and pushed..."

"Fireblast!" Ryan closed his good eye, fighting for self-control. "Keep to the center of the story, or I'll fucking... Go on!"

"You were only fourteen when Harvey struck. Your older brother, Morgan, was out with a landwag train, meeting up a trader from the Apps. Stickies mined the wag. None lived to tell."

The rowdy songs had momentarily ceased, and a young girl, her skin afflicted by disease, stood at the center of the long hut and sang a slow, sad ballad, alternating lines in French and English. Around her, the dancers had slowed, with everyone holding their partners tighter.

My yesterdays are always here,
Tomorrow is another now.
And none may say when life will end
And no man may say how.

Krysty had moved closer to Ryan, sensing the dreadful tension and memories roused in him by the old man's story.

"*They* said it was stickies," stressed Pecker. "I was there with me dogs—you said it was dogs, Lord Cawdor?"

"Don't call me that, Bochco. The name is Ryan Cawdor now."

"Where was I?"

"The dogs. After the stickies mined the landwag and butchered Morgan."

The old man giggled suddenly. "Them dogs was... Yeah, I was there with the dogs. The baron sort of figured that there was something didn't set right 'bout it. There was boot tracks in the hillside 'bove where the mine had been triggered.''

"Boot marks?"

Pecker started to sing to himself in a warbling, fragile voice. One or two of the Cajuns looked around, but nobody took much notice.

Well, I traveled four and forty miles
Mebbe was only three
But boots upon a stickie,
I never more did see.

"It was Harvey. I knew it then. Couldn't prove it, but I knew it.

"Then he poisoned your father's mind. The baron believed you'd a hand in Morgan's passing. Harvey kept whispering in his ear, like tainted honey. The baron near lost his mind with grief. Then, when time was right, Harvey sprung his trap on you.''

Though he fought against it, Ryan's right hand rose jerkily in the air of its own volition, brushing his chin, seeking the patch that hid the ruined left eye. A part of his mind was vaguely aware that the Cajun girl was singing another slow ballad; the only other sound in the room was the shuffling of feet as the dancers caroused about her.

It was a song of lost love and the pain that remains.

I miss him in the weeping of the rains,
And I miss him at the turnings of the tide.

Pecker was leaning against the table that served as a bar, reaching for a mug of beer, fumbling it so that it toppled over, the frothing liquid spilling on the scuffed planks.

"So Harvey and half a dozen of his sec men came for you. Kid of fourteen."

"Fifteen, Bochco. The day after my fifteenth birthday. Ten at night. Corridor outside my room."

THE FORTRESS AT FRONT ROYAL was one of the largest buildings anywhere in the East. It had been the mansion of a horse breeder, back before the long chill of '01. Ryan's father had built on it, repairing the work of his father and grandfather. Adding refinements. Fences and a moat. Blasters at every angle. You didn't get to be a baron by making everyone love you.

They had plenty of gasoline. Electric generators. A fleet of wags. A hundred sec men.

Harvey had tried to drug his younger brother, but a loyal servant named Kenny Morse had warned the lad not to eat or drink that evening. So when Harvey came with four of the sec men, they found Ryan awake and ready.

With his blaster cocked and ready in his right hand. A Colt .45 pistol that he'd stripped and oiled and cleaned himself. Because of his father's suspicion of him, Ryan hadn't been allowed a blaster, and he'd been restricted to certain parts of the fortress. But that hadn't stopped Morse from stealing the gun for him and instructing him in its use.

The blaster held seven rounds.

The first two rounds killed the first two sec men. Ryan had waited, just inside the doorway of his darkened room. Morse's last favor had been to remove a couple of the light bulbs, so that the attackers would be perfect silhouettes for the lad. As soon as he heard them coming, Ryan jumped out, firing.

Two shots to the upper chest and throat. Certain kills, sending the men in their maroon uniforms and polished knee-boots crashing back into the others.

The third guard took two bullets. One through the right arm as he dodged sideways, the next penetrating his skull as he tried to duck away to safety.

Harvey fired back at him with tracer bullets that hissed and flared in the darkness, bursting off the wall at Ryan's shoulder.

The last of the sec men had thrown himself flat on the floor, behind the jerking body of one of his fellows, firing short bursts from some sort of machine-pistol, but Ryan kept moving, dodging in and out of his room. His first shot at the man missed by inches, howling into the blackness at the top of a narrow flight of stairs.

The second bullet from the Colt drilled through the guard's open mouth: shattered his teeth, slicing his tongue to ribbons of bleeding flesh, angling upward through the palate to bury itself into the man's brain.

"You fired six, brother," yelled Harvey. "One to go."

"I reloaded," Ryan lied. Morse had only been able to steal a single magazine.

At that moment, the fifteen-year-old boy knew his life was measured only in short minutes. His room offered no escape: the window opened on a sheer drop of fifty feet to the stone flags of a courtyard. If he could make it past his brother to the stairs, then he might have a slight chance.

With Ryan Cawdor, even at just fifteen, to think was to act.

He dived headfirst through the doorway, rolling over and coming up, his finger on the trigger, squeezing off his last shot, not even waiting to see that he'd missed the crouching figure of his brother. He drew the horn-hafted dagger from his belt and sprinted through the dim light, hurdling the dying guards.

"Bastard!" screamed Harvey, trying to shoot him, cursing as the pistol jammed.

"Butcher!" cried Ryan as he closed in on his older brother.

Harvey was taller and stronger than the boy, but he lacked the ruthless determination. As they grappled, he managed to draw his own knife, and Ryan felt a cold fire across his ribs from the steel. But he also drew blood, cutting Harvey Cawdor on the upper arm, making him cry out in pain and shock.

Within seconds he could have killed him. And the rest of his life would have been utterly different. But there had been a sec man on a regular patrol in the corridor a floor beneath, and he'd come running at the sound of gunfire, arriving in time to drag Ryan away from his screaming brother.

The boy was quick enough, wriggling like a gaffed eel, to stab the guard to the heart, feeling the life flow from the man as his grip relaxed. But the interruption had given Harvey the moment he needed.

Ryan lived all his days with that memory. At times he felt he still had both eyes, so vivid was the image of the knife in his brother's hand, moving toward his face.

Striking.

He saw it. Actually *saw* the tip of the blade as it grated into his left eye socket. There was liquid trickling down his face that mingled aqueous humor of the eye with a little blood. Surprisingly little blood.

Shocked beyond belief, not realizing the devastating damage the knife had done, Ryan had staggered back, dropping his own dagger, his hands grabbing at his injured eye. Harvey had slashed out once more, aiming for the right eye, missing it by the width of a finger. The steel opened up a great jagged tear from the edge of the eye to the puckered corner of his mouth. This time blood cascaded over his chin and neck, soaking into his shirt.

In agony and desperation, Ryan punched out at the leering Harvey, feeling the man's nose break like a rotten apple. Then he turned and ran for the stairs, scarcely able to see, moaning from the pain. He never truly knew how he escaped from the fortress at Front Royal that hideous night. Perhaps a servant aided him. There was a door open. Driven snow from the Virginia winter chill on his face. Darkness, stumbling among the tall pines. A hand on his arm.

Had there been a helping hand on his arm?

Away, as far as possible. Running, running. Hiding and fighting. The years ground past until he had met the Trader and begun a new phase of his life, hoping that he had shut all of the past behind him forever.

He knew now that he had not.

BOCHCO BABBLED ON.

"After, there was a fearful inquisition. Poor Kenny Morse was put to death by Harvey Cawdor. So were others of the servants judged to have helped you."

"I did not know that," said Ryan quietly.

"The cobblestones of the great yard ran with blood. Harvey was in a fearsome temper."

"My father?" asked Ryan hesitantly.

"He was told by your brother that not only were you responsible for Morgan's death, but that you'd bribed the sec men to murder him. The baron named you wolf's-head with a lot of jack on your head."

"I heard that."

"Guess you didn't hear 'bōut the new Lady Cawdor."

"What?"

Again the crazed giggle from the old-timer called Pecker. "Yeah. Your father wed the whore, but it was Harvey that did the pleasuring. Only eighteen she was. Plump as a corn-fed chick. Hair like straw. I figured the old man was getting bats loose in the belfry by then, what with all that happened."

"My father died, I heard, Bochco. Was that the hand of my brother?"

"No, no, no, no. That was his wife. Lady Rachel Cawdor. The word about Front Royal was that she bound him with cords o' silk. Game of love, she called it. Then she smothered him with a pillow. He was frail by then. It was at Harvey's word."

Ryan licked his dry lips. There was a small room, locked at the end of a corridor in the west wing of his memory. Despite everything he'd done, someone had come along and forced the bolts.

And in a perverse, cathartic way, he was relieved that it was over and the door flung open and the secrets dispersed.

"Go on, Bochco," he whispered.

"He was dead and under the earth, feeding the worms and maggots, all in a day and a night. There was a babe born an' all."

"Boy or girl?"

"Boy, Lord Cawdor... I'm sorry, sorry, so sorry. *Mr.* Cawdor. Christened Jabez Pendragon Cawdor."

"My father's or...?"

The look on the old man's face was the answer. Harvey had sired the child, on his father's wife. His mistress.

"Hard to say which was most wicked, her or him. Mebbe they's twin shoots of the same dark flowering weed."

"And now?" asked Krysty. "Does Ryan's brother rule Front Royal? With the woman and his child? Is Harvey the baron?"

"Yes, yes, yes," babbled the old man, his eyes rolling madly. "The crow shits where the eagle should roost. Will you return, Mr. Cawdor, my lord, and claim what should be yours?"

"Harvey has it. Let him keep it. And let him have the fucking pleasure in it that he deserves," spat Ryan, turning away from Bochco, blinking as he found Doc Tanner and Lori at his elbow. "I didn't know you were..." he began.

"I beg pardon for dropping at the eaves, Ryan," said Doc. "The dancing was far too tiring. Lori and I are going to bed." Seeing Ryan's raised eyebrow, he added, "Yes. We are going to bed together. I may find dancing a little much now, at my age. But that does not mean I am totally impotent."

"Sorry, Doc," muttered Ryan.

"Apology accepted. Krysty." He gave a half bow.

"Good night, Doc. Good night, Lori. Sleep well."

"Thanks. And you," replied the blond girl.

"Doc," called Ryan, suddenly aware that the dance seemed to be breaking up around them with couples drifting away.

"Yes?"

"Did you hear any of that? About my brother and...and this," he said, fingering the patch over the barren left eye.

Doc smiled, looking startlingly, touchingly youthful. "Of course. But I had known it all along. Good night, my friend."

"Good night, Doc," Ryan said.

Chapter Nine

INSIDE THE HEAVY DOOR WAS a thick drape of black vel-vet. Mephisto eased it to one side, creeping through, al-lowing it to fall silently into place behind him. He paused, allowing his eyes to adjust to the dim light. A thick yellow candle, made from corpse fat, guttered in one corner of the motel room, filling the air with the pungent odor of am-bergris and squill.

The sec boss knew from long experience that it was best to be careful when approaching Baron Tourment in the night. His predecessor had died from a snapped neck for just such a foolishness.

"Lord," he called, from the safety of the doorway, keeping the heavy octagonal table between himself and his slumbering master.

"I heard you creeping on tiptoe along the corridor, Me-phisto." The sonorous voice sounded gently amused. "Though the knocking of that ice-chiller came close to drowning the sound."

"Shall I turn it off?"

"No, no, any machine that still functions from before the fireblast deserves every chance. What is it? You have news? I can tell. I heard the noise of the swampwag a half hour back."

Mephisto took a few more careful steps. His eyes had adjusted, and he could make out the calipers leaning against the side of the long bed. Tourment's bare feet protruded beyond the bottom of the blankets. The air-conditioning in the room whirred and hissed, keeping the awful damp heat at bay.

"He brought a bird from a ville."

"Where?"

"Moudongue."

"Aaah." He sounded like a great cat purring its satisfaction. "Our hunched friend Pecker, as they call him. Master Bochco as he is truly named. How many?"

"There were seven and now six."

"The black on the bayous?"

Mephisto nodded, knowing that Baron Tourment could see him well enough. "I have arranged a payment of food. But they killed a dozen of the *morts-vivants* and ran."

"To Moudongue, Mephisto?"

"Four men and two women, is the message."

"And they are still there?"

"Oui."

"The question is, where do they come from? Who are they? What do they want? Are they to be allies for the snow-head bastard and his wolf pack? Questions, questions, Mephisto, and no answers."

For a moment Tourment managed to stand without the aid of his exoskeleton, flailing his great arms in a fit of anger. But the effort was too much, and he crumpled backward onto the bed.

"Questions," he repeated softly. "Will they join the renegades?" Then he began to laugh. "But if they are strangers in Moudongue, at Mardy . . . I guess that mebbe there's nothing for us to worry on."

"Should I send men to the ville? Better to be safe than sorry, lord?"

"When they are sorry, then we shall be safe, *mon cher* Mephisto."

"Could they...they be blasters from the Deathlands? Hired guns?"

"Generosity. That was my error. I left them a little more than usual last year, and how do they repay me? By buying guns? Surely they would not dare, Mephisto, would they?"

"The people love you, Lord. Only the snow-head and his running curs... The rest are in mortal fear of you."

Tourment smiled indulgently. "If the saints in their wisdom had not wished them to be bled, then they would not have been created as hogs."

Mephisto laughed heartily, wondering as he always did whether the note of fear rang through his desperate merriment.

"You did well to wake me, Mephisto. If the strangers have arrived...the ones seen by the blind witch...then we should walk light. Take a dozen men and two swampwags and go hunting."

"How should we take them, Lord?"

Again he smiled lazily. "Alive, if you can. Specially the women. Oh, yes, Mephisto. I would have the women brought to me alive."

The sec boss backed out of the bedroom, nodding his eager agreement. When he closed the door, he leaned against it for a moment and took several long, slow breaths, finally recovering his composure.

Only then did he go to call for his men to go hunt in the ville in the swamp.

Chapter Ten

RYAN MADE LOVE TO KRYSTY as quietly as he could. Wrapped in a blanket, J. B. Dix was sleeping in the far corner of their hut, away from the door and window. His hat was by his side, and his Steyr AUG 5.6 mm pistol was tight in his fist. Doc and Lori lay side by side against a wall, the old man snoring gently through his open mouth.

Finn wasn't there.

Toward the end of the night's revelry, the mother of the girl that Finn had been dancing with had come along and whisked her away, chattering accusingly in Creole French at the plump blaster. But all hadn't been lost for Finnegan. The giantess who'd snatched J.B. had tired of his lack of enthusiasm and had sidled up to Finn. Nobody knew what she'd whispered, but it was the first time that either the Armorer or Ryan could recall seeing Finnegan actually blush.

As the dance had ended and Ti Jean had come to see them all through the small ville back to their own quarters, Finn and the woman had disappeared. The Cajun had laughed at it. "Marie has found a man worthy of her," he said.

KRYSTY HAD REACHED for him in the sultry humid darkness of the hut. Her long fingers spidered over his muscular chest and across the flat wall of his stomach, then down lower, finding him springing to a hard erection. He turned his head, raising himself on one elbow to kiss her. It was a long, lingering kiss, their tongues thrusting against each other.

"Yes, love. Oh, yes," she sighed as his hand touched her thighs. Her long legs opened to him, so that he could reach the moist warmth of her body. The tender bud of flesh hardened as her passion rose. She kissed him all over his face and neck, nipping with her sharp teeth, drawing a bead of crimson salty blood from his lips. He bent his head to nuzzle her breasts, the nipples swelling at the touch of his tongue.

Unable to control his fiery lust, Ryan had rolled on top of her, his hips rising and falling, letting her reach and guide him into her.

He climaxed moments before the girl, her nails raking at his bare shoulders, clutching him deep within her. She'd sighed, pressing her lips against his chest to quiet herself, fighting not to waken the others in the hut.

"I love you. By Gaia, but I love you with all of my heart, Ryan Cawdor."

"And I love you, Krysty." But the words still wouldn't come easily to his lips, which for so long had been used to a cold tightness when he rode with the Trader. Love and tenderness hadn't played much part in Ryan's life for far too long.

"You don't have to say it, lover," she'd whispered. "I can feel you feel it. That's enough for me." She kissed him as they rolled apart. "One day it'll be easy and natural. Trust me, lover."

"I do, Krysty." And he really did.

Around three he woke, pressed against her back, cuddling like two spoons, snug in a box. The contact was enough to rouse him again, but the second time she mounted him, sitting above him, grinning triumphantly down into his face. Her hair seemed to billow about her face and shoulders, even though there was no wind in the hut.

With all the dozens and dozens of women that Ryan Cawdor had taken to bed, none had been like Krysty. She had the most amazing control over all her muscles, so that he felt sucked and gripped into a cave of sexual heat that squeezed at him, milking him for her pleasure.

After the second time they both rose, naked, and walked to the window of the hut, peering out through the slats across the trampled earth of the square toward the sullen, rippling surface of the river.

They stood together, savoring the faint breeze that came sidling in through the blind. She shivered, and he put his arm about her waist, pulling her close to him.

"Cold?"

"No. It's not that. I think I hear engines."

"Swampwags."

"I don't know. They're far off, almost beyond my hearing. I don't know if I really hear them or whether I'm imagining."

"Are you a woman dreaming you're an eagle, or an eagle dreaming that you're a woman?" he asked her.

"Don't be so fucking runic, lover," she said. "Next you're going to be asking me to describe the sound of one hand clapping."

"No, I'm... Look, there in the shadows, to the far right."

If they hadn't been standing so close to the window, they never would have seen the movement. It was a man, bent low, scurrying across the gap between two of the wooden huts. He was followed by another, and then a third. As the last one darted across, Ryan caught the flicker of silver moonlight glancing off steel.

"He's got a blade," whispered Krysty.

"I knew that Ti Jean was a swift and evil bastard," said Ryan.

"It might not..." She stopped. "No. That's stupid. Course it means trouble."

"And the engines you hear."

"Yeah."

"Couple of hours to dawn. What can...? This Mardy festival, I heard of things like this. Some backwood villes where they pick a boy and let him do what he wants. Eat and drink what he wants. Fuck anyone he wants. For a special day each year. Then they slit his throat for the promise of a good crop. I wonder if..."

Krysty left his side, padding to her clothes. "Best get moving." She dressed with an elegant haste, tugging on her boots.

He joined her, pulling up his trousers, then fastened the buckle on his belt and checked his guns. Moving silently to the door and inching it open, he peered around the edge of the warped frame. He saw nobody out there. Yet his sixth fighting sense told him that the whole of Moudongue was bristling around them.

"I'll wake the others?"

"Yes. I'll wake Doc."

J.B. came instantly to full awareness, the gun probing out into the darkness, his eyes open. "What? Trouble?"

"Men on the move. Holding knives. Krysty thinks she hears swampwags, far off."

Lori came awake, trembling a little like a frightened fawn, eyes glistening. "What?"

"Trouble," said Krysty, matter-of-factly.

Ryan knew from previous experience that Doctor Theophilus Tanner wasn't the quietest of men when it came to being roused from sleep. He knelt beside him, cautiously extending his right hand and clamping it across the old man's jaws, holding the mouth shut. Simultaneously he hissed into Doc's ear, "It's Ryan. Keep still and quiet." Doc jerked and struggled, his hands scrabbling to free himself, but Ryan was far stronger, holding him down on the floor. "Fireblast, Doc! Wake up, will you? Keep quiet—there's danger."

Only when Doc was finally still did he release him. The old man sat up, rubbing his face. "Upon my soul, Mr. Cawdor, but you have a grip like a poacher's trap. What ails you now?"

Krysty answered him. "We've seen men moving around the huts with cold steel in their hands, Doc. And I heard engines, miles off."

"What about Finn?" asked J.B., standing at the window, flattened against the wall, squinting out. "He's with that giant whore."

"Where?"

Lori answered. "Saw big woman and Finn. Go to house with picture of bird on door."

"A white cockerel with a red band about its neck," exclaimed Doc. "Three down from the long hut where we all danced."

In a couple of minutes everyone was fully dressed and armed and ready. Ryan once more looked out of the shuttered window where J.B. had been keeping watch.

"Anything?"

"No. Thought mebbe I heard a noise, along to the side, by the river."

Ryan eased out of the hut, keeping in the dark lake of shadow and peering into the surrounding forest where the

Armorer had said he'd heard something. It was difficult to tell, but there could have been the faintest light of a fire. A dim red glow, but he couldn't have sworn to it.

J.B. joined him. "What d'you figure?"

"Get out. I reckon we should make for that township we saw. West Lowellton. This Baron Tourment runs Lafayette. Keep out of that ville. I figure we'll lose if'n we try and fight these Cajuns in the mud. Better we get into some ruins and make them play on our patch."

"We go and get Finn?"

Ryan nodded, slowly. "Yeah. You take Doc and Lori and go get him. I want to see what those bastards are doing by the river. I'll take Krysty. Meet you out where the trail narrows. Get to the far side of that and cover the path."

J.B. nodded and turned to go back inside the hut, then paused. "Chill the big woman?"

"'Course," replied Ryan.

ALL THE NOISES of the Atchafalaya Swamp were oddly muted.

Ryan led the way, with Krysty a silent shadow at his heels. There wasn't a light showing in the whole ville, but ahead of them they now saw that a large fire was lit deep into the curtain of the mangroves. The wind was drifting eastward, toward the ville, so they could smell the scent of the burning wood.

"I hear a drum. Muffled, slack kind of noise," said Krysty. "Beating slow and even. It's 'bout in time with a heart."

Ryan heard it, too, or more exactly, felt it, as though it was striking within his body.

Something suddenly scurried away from beneath the toes of his boots, making him jump. It vanished with a soft plopping sound into the river.

Now they were so close that they heard the crackling of the fire. They also heard an occasional mumbled chanting, rising and falling in the damp air.

Ryan stopped so abruptly that Krysty nearly bumped into him.

"What is it?" she whispered.

"Don't like this."

"What?"

"This whole fucking place. The heat. The damp. The fucking mud. That creepy ville with its songs and dances and all the time... always there's something fucking rotten going on. Since we met we've been in the cold, high country. That's better, somehow. This swamp is fucking evil, girl."

"I feel that, too. Mebbe stronger than you, lover. How's 'bout us turning right around and heading back for the gateway and getting out?"

"No, Krysty. Trader always figured a man had to go out and hit a lick for what he believed was right. If'n everyone turned their backs when things got mean, then I guess the world would just get real fucking mean. Let's go see what the Cajuns are doing out here."

Now they were within fifty paces of the blazing bonfire, close enough to make out figures moving in a shuffling ring around it. They were men and women, from what they could see through the dangling fringe of Spanish moss on the trees. The riverbank was only a few yards to their left.

"Look," breathed Krysty barely audibly, pointing ahead and slightly to the right.

Someone was standing rock-still, leaning against the trunk of a topless sycamore. It was one of the Cajuns who'd asked Krysty to dance: a large, squat man, wearing an old plaid shirt torn across both shoulders. He had a long beard, streaked with silver like a tree seared by lightning. There was enough orange light from the fire to show that he was cradling a blaster. It was a long, old-fashioned musket, like the one . . .

"The one that killed Henn," Ryan said.

Revenge was one of the sweetest-tasting dishes in all creation to Ryan. But he had been alive long enough to know that it was also a dangerous pleasure. If this was the man who had slaughtered Hennings, then it would be good to ice him. But only if it could be done safely.

The drums would drown out the noise of a cautious approach, Ryan realized as he studied the man, who was obviously supposed to be on guard. The stock of the musket, bound with baling wire, rested on the soft earth. There was a machete, similar to Ryan's own steel panga, sheathed on the man's left hip; a smaller knife was strapped to his right knee. Beyond him, the fire was burning brightly, the breeze carrying the scent of bitter spices to them.

At his side, Krysty looked up at Ryan's face, seeing the orange light flickering across the hard, almost brutal planes of the high cheeks, throwing his good right eye into shadow. The faint gleam of the strong teeth was revealed between parted lips. It was a face of total, cruel concentration. The girl knew that he was considering how best he could murder this Cajun: it showed in every angle of the taut face. Yet it was a face that only an hour or so before she had seen melt into gentle consideration in their lovemaking.

The Cajun's name was Henri de la Tour. As he leaned against the bole of the tree, he contemplated the hours to come. Once the rituals were finished, they would collect the outsiders and take them for the new ceremonies. But if the baron was interested in them, then they must not be unduly harmed.

Yet the girl with hair as red as glowing coals in a fire . . .

His head was sunk on his breast, and he lifted it, jerking a hand up in irritation at the feathery touch of an insect near his ear. The movement exposed the side of his neck above the collar of the shirt, uncovered by the long beard.

"Merde," he hissed. Even to someone who'd spent all of his life in the swamps, the insects could be torture. There had been a woman in Moudongue, named Jenny, whose skin had carried a subtle odor that was irresistible to the hordes of biting insects around the bayous. Poor Jenny. She'd tried getting help from the local voodoo priests. Even gone to Mother Midnight and begged aid against the swarming skein of fluttering flies that always hung around her long hair and face. In the end, Henri recollected, Jenny had been driven insane. Clearly mad, she had run screaming into the splashing shallows of the nearest slime hole, tearing great bloody gouges in her face. No one who had watched the frenzy of her thrashing in the gray-brown ooze tried to help her. It hadn't taken long for the sinister caymans, attracted by the disturbance, to slither from the banks.

Again there was an insect brushing at his hair, making him twitch with irritation.

He moved his head to precisely the right position.

De la Tour cursed fluently, slapping his hand to the point just below the right ear where the bastard *moustique* had stung him. Sharp and painful, where the big carotid artery carried the blood from the aorta to the brain.

In the darkness of the forest, the Cajun heard rain pattering on the leaf-mold around his worn boots. That was strange as it wasn't raining. Somehow it was hard to concentrate on why that should be so peculiar.

It was definitely raining. Henri could feel rain soaking through the collar of his shirt on one side, running over his skin. Warm.

"Chaud?" he muttered, puzzled by the heat of the rain.

He felt his lips move, heard the faint whisper of his own voice. But all of it was happening a long, long way off. Happening to someone else.

With a labored slowness he reached up to touch the place where the insect had stung him, feeling for the lump of the bite. It wasn't a lump at all. It was a tiny mouth, set in his throat. Pouting lips that intermittently spat blood into the night air.

The Cajun's left hand opened, and the musket dropped away to be caught by Ryan Cawdor before it could reach the ground.

Then the Cajun understood.

Through the murky slowness of his fading mind, he knew what was happening. He wanted to shout a warning to the others, busy at their ritual, but a hand, strong as a steel clamp, shut over his mouth, helping him as he felt his legs start to falter.

Ryan steadied the dying man, laying down the blaster with one hand, lowering the blood-splattered body to the earth. He actually sensed the moment that life departed.

The last cogent thought of Henri de la Tour was that he had, shamefully, lost control of his bowels.

"Pays the debt, Henn," said Ryan quietly, wiping his hands on the stubby grass that grew around the base of the trees.

IN SOME DOUBLE-POOR COMMUNITIES, out in the deserts, Ryan had seen ceremonies, sacrifices, hoping to bring some sort of fertility or rain or freedom from plague. They'd all been poor, shoddy events.

This was different.

The air tasted of fear. Followed by Krysty Wroth, the one-eyed man picked his way with exaggerated caution, closing in on the fringe of stunted bushes that hid them from the fire and the people around it.

There were eighteen: fourteen men and four women. All were naked to the waist, and sweat glistened on their bare flesh. What fueled the fire was rough-hewn logs, piled loosely in front of a broken block of concrete around eight feet long and four feet thick.

Spread-eagled on the makeshift altar was a huge boar, its skin pink in the light. A hemp cord was bound tightly around its long muzzle, muffling its shrill cries. It lay on its side, its legs and neck stilled with wire. Leaning against the stone rectangle was a long-hafted logger's axe, its edge glittering orange.

"They going to kill it?"

Ryan nodded. "Yeah. Got to be. I heard of some crazies out west kill like this. Trader said he once seen them slitting the throat of a girl child."

"What did he do?"

"Asked 'em first. They said it wasn't a girl. They said it was a goat. A goat without horns. I never forgot that."

"But what did . . . ?" she began.

"Iced them all."

"How about them?" she asked, pointing through the trees at the group of dancing Cajuns as they circled and shuffled through the trampled mud to the slow beating of the drum.

Ryan patted the butt of the gray Heckler & Koch G-12. "Could freeze the lot of them." He paused. "Mebbe. And mebbe that's not enough."

"There's others back at the ville."

"Sure. Could be other villes close by. No, best get our heels clean of here. Join the rest where we said now we know what's going down."

"You figure we could've been next, Ryan?"

He shook his head. "Mebbe, Krysty. Let's go."

They turned their backs on the fire and the bizarre ceremony in the deeps of Atchafalaya and carefully began to walk toward Moudongue.

They'd gone about a hundred paces when they heard the drumming reach a swift crescendo, then stop. The stillness was eerie. A man, his voice high and cracked, sang out some words in a foreign language. It sounded like *"Je suis rouge,"* whatever that meant.

The words were echoed by the rest of . . . Ryan almost thought of them as a congregation, like some of the church-belt crazies in Deathlands. There was a moment of awful teetering silence, as if the world around licked its lips in lascivious anticipation.

The faintest whistle of a steel blade sliced the air.

There was a solid, wet thunk.

Both of them heard the stifled squeal of mortal shock from the tethered pig. But they kept their faces turned and continued toward the ville and their friends.

AFTER THE EXCHANGE of whistled signals, Ryan and Krysty rejoined the others. Doc and Lori were sitting quietly together along the faint trail that they hoped led toward West Lowellton. Finnegan and J.B. stood watching the immensely tall Cajun woman. She leaned against a live oak, with little trace of animation on her heavy, brutish features. She was wearing only a coarse brown blanket across her brawny shoulders.

"They're butchering a pig back there at the fire," said Ryan.

"A pig?"

"Yeah. Better'n a goat with no horns." Only the Armorer would have understood the allusion; Ryan wrinkled his mouth in distaste.

"We going?"

"Yeah, J.B., I guess so. Why d'you bring the woman with you?"

"He wanted to fucking ice her while we was still fucking fucking," spat Finnegan angrily.

"You said…" J.B. started to protest, looking across the small clearing at Ryan.

"So why's she here?"

"She knows all 'bout this fucking Baron Tourment," said Finn.

The woman showed little interest in their discussion, busying herself with digging something from her cavernous nostrils, examining it closely, then popping it into her mouth and chewing with stolid relish.

"Mebbe she can show us a way out of here," suggested J.B.

The paths were tortuous in the darkness; Ryan realized that once the Cajuns discovered them gone, they'd be able to move faster and farther. Perhaps the woman *could* help.

"Tell her to show us the fastest way to West Lowellton," Ryan ordered Finnegan.

"We going to keep her?"

"Far as it takes."

WHILE THEY MOVED, quietly and in single file, through the dank wilderness, Finnegan walked alongside the towering woman, trying to converse with her. Now and again he turned to relay something to Ryan.

"Says it's about two hours. Says there's some pack of killers there. Led by a snow wolf. Don't know what that means. Fucking English isn't so good."

Somewhere deep to the left there was a rippling sound, as if some huge creature had moved gently from land to water. Everyone heard it, and everyone made certain a finger was on a trigger. Doc moved closer to Lori and put his arm across her shoulder.

"She says the buildings are still there from before. She calls it the 'great sleeping.' Says that West Lowellton is 'bout the only place this cocksucking Baron Tourment doesn't run."

"Ask her 'bout him," said Ryan, falling back a little way, gesturing for Krysty to take point so he could listen to what the Cajun had to say.

"Says he runs the dead and alive. Those got the death without ending, she says. Baron got a fortress not far off. Runs the villes all around. She says he's ten foot tall with a..." He laughed. "With a prick so long he ties it to his knee."

"What sort of power's he got? Sec men?"

Finnegan muttered the question. "Says he don't need that. Got the power. Makes it sound like some kind of wizardry, Ryan. Says he's the walking death himself. Says he can't be killed."

J.B. caught that, bringing up the rear of their small column, and he snorted. "Put him in front of my Steyr blaster and see if he's still walking and talking after six rounds go into him."

The towering woman heard him and giggled. It was a strange, thin, feeble sound, like that made by an ailing child, amazingly out of proportion to her build. Finnegan said something, and she leaned down to listen, one hand resting lightly on his arm. The other hand, Ryan noticed, stayed under the blanket.

"She says the baron would eat a little man like him," Finnegan said, gesturing toward J.B. "And shit him out for the . . . I think she means the gators." Ryan found it all like a bewildering puzzle. Gradually they were putting together some of the pieces. The whole region looked as though it had been nuked with neutron missiles that devastated people and left buildings intact. There was this mysterious Baron Tourment, who seemed to be a very big fish in a medium-size pond. Maybe used voodoo to keep his people in line. And there was this equally odd resistance group somewhere around West Lowellton, where they were heading. Led by a white wolf.

"A white wolf?" he muttered to himself.

Chapter Eleven

RYAN HAD TRULY INTENDED to let the hulking Cajun woman go free.

If he'd felt that she'd been any threat to them, then he'd have given Finn the nod to put a bullet through the base of her skull. He'd have given the word and not had a moment's unease about it. That was the way it was in the Deathlands.

But she wasn't a threat. She'd brought them through the swamps, into the pale glow of dawn, right to the edge of what had to be the suburb of West Lowellton. It didn't matter to them that she would tell Ti Jean and the other Cajuns. It was obvious that they preferred the dark, mazy wilderness to the open spaces of the town. Ryan didn't figure there was any real danger of their being pursued.

So why not let her go?

Finnegan looked at him, beneath the grove of stunted elms dripping with the leprous moss, where they waited. The woman's left hand was scratching where an early rising mosquito had raised a weal above her swollen, freckled breast. Her right hand was still beneath the torn blanket, where it had been every single time that Ryan had looked at her. That bothered him a little. Even when she'd stumbled on a couple of occasions, she'd used only her left hand to steady herself.

"How 'bout . . . ?" asked Finn, gesturing to the Cajun. His dark blue sweater and pants were splattered with mud, some patches drying, some still dark and wet. The steel toe caps of his combat boots were slick with the gray-brown slime.

"Let her go," said Ryan. "She's told us 'bout all there is. We best watch out for this Baron Tourment and the snow wolf. Tell her she can go free."

Standing beside her, virtually in her shadow, Finnegan beckoned to her. Doc grinned at the sight of the tubby little man and the looming woman.

" 'She stands like a sow that hath o'erwhelmed all her litter but one,' " he said. "*Henry Four.*" Cackled with laughter at the looks of total bewilderment on the faces of all his colleagues. "But let it pass, my brothers. Oh, let it pass."

"Hurry it up, Finn," called Ryan, staring at the oddly matched couple.

"Fucking all right," snapped Finnegan, looking away from the Cajun for a moment.

Ryan's good eye opened wide.

Just as Finnegan half turned away from the woman, gesturing with his arm toward the dark desolation of the swamp behind them, she finally began to take her right hand from under the blanket.

"Fireblast," breathed Ryan, but before the word hung in the air, the drama was played.

The G-12 coughed, the triple burst sounding like a single shot.

Finn jumped, the Model 92 Beretta pistol jerking into his fist. J.B. raised his Mini-Uzi, searching for the threat. Doc was fumbling for his Le Mat. Lori squeaked her dismay, and Krysty Wroth had drawn her H&K P7A-13 9 mm handblaster.

The Cajun woman lurched sideways as all three bullets stitched into her, all hitting within a hand's span, under the ribs on the left side of her body. Despite her great size and strength, the three bullets sent her staggering. The blanket fell away, revealing her nakedness. Blood came from the bunched wounds, dark and thick, dappling her thighs as she tottered, fighting for balance.

"Bastard," she said, in a normal, quiet conversational voice, sinking to her knees, then sliding in the dirt on her face, both hands clutched beneath her, holding the triple wound.

"Ryan! Ryan?"

"What is it, Finn?"

"You said she could go. You fucking said..." His voice was rising.

"Look in her hand, Finn."

She still lived—if the residual nervous twitching and jerking of the body could be called living. Finn kicked her over with the toe of his boot, staring down as the corpse rolled on its back, breasts sagging, blood and urine trickling across the thighs and belly.

"In her right hand," said Ryan.

The fingers were clenched, and the man bent down and pried them open. Then he stood up and shook his head at what he saw, at what they all saw.

It was an open cutthroat razor, honed down over countless years until it was only a sliver of steel, hardly as wide as a man's fingernail. The handle was of dull white bone, broken and mended with twine.

"Fucking double-poor crazy bitch," said Finnegan, spitting into the staring eyes of the dead Cajun woman.

Lori took a few steps away from the body, looking toward the nearest buildings, all shrouded with thick vegetation. "We go in there? Food? Shelter?"

"Shelter, yeah," replied Ryan. "After a hundred years or so, I'm not so damned sure 'bout any food. Let's go see. And let's take care."

THE FOUR MEN and two women moved out of the deep, lush greenery, picking their way along what had once been the farthest outpost of West Lowellton. They passed a partly completed suburban development of medium-priced housing that once pushed the sprawling frontiers of Lafayette deeper into swampland.

Nearly one hundred years ago, in the remote past.

"MOUDONGUE?"

"*Oui*, Baron. Moudongue."

"They are becoming of interest to me, my dear and loyal compatriot, Mephisto."

"We'll take them."

"Such confidence. What of the teams of sec men out in the green?"

"Pecker said they'd gone."

"Why were they not kept for me?"

"They were . . ." The sec boss hesitated, wiping a hand down the leg of his white pants. He noticed that his fingers left a sweaty trail.

"Yes?" asked the baron, his voice as gentle as a maiden's whisper. Mephisto found himself sweating a little more than before.

"They were taking a pig."

"A ritual?"

"Yes."

The exoskeleton creaked and groaned as Baron Tourment pulled himself upright, towering over the sec boss as he strode around the motel room, seeing himself reflected again and again as he passed the mirror over the oyster-pink washbasin.

"Had I given my permission?"

Mephisto had known the question was coming and had anticipated it from the moment one of the patrol teams in the swampwags had reported back to him.

"I had one in five blasted, Baron."

"Only one in five?"

"They are useful to us, so close to the part of West Lowellton where the boy runs."

The great leonine head nodded slowly, and Mephisto knew that he'd guessed right: he would live for another day.

"Truly spoken. One in five? Good."

"The outlanders took out one man."

"Who?"

"De la Tour. The one with the beard forked as if lightning had struck it."

"Was he not the one who shot the black in the buggy a day back?"

"Yes."

"Revenge?"

Mephisto nodded. "I believe so. We can ask when we take them."

"And they will tell you, my dear Mephisto?"

"They will tell me," he replied, ignoring the irony in Baron Tourment's voice.

"Where are they now?"

That was the one question that the elegant sec boss had been dreading. His patrols had returned within the hour from their search, and he knew that the baron would have heard the rumbling engines as they ground into the ville.

"One woman was missing from Moudongue."

The striding stopped, and the baron's eyes turned toward him. "Who?"

"Marie Laveaux."

"Who?"

Mephisto hissed through his teeth. "Marie. Jeanine was her younger sister, the one that you ordered to be..."

"I know. Watch your careless tongue, Mephisto. There are many who would welcome your fall. It was Marie? The large woman? I remember her." There was something that could have been a smile.

"She was..." Caution sealed his lips and made him reconsider his description of the Laveaux woman as a giantess. It would not sit well with the baron, whose head scraped the ceiling of the bridal suite at the Best Western Snowy Egret Motel.

"Was a fine strong woman. She took me and wept for more. Not like some of these fucking little tight-cunted bitches who scream and bleed, shrieking that I'm tearing them apart. No, she...she is dead, you said, Mephisto? The toll rises for these strangers."

"She was shot three times at close range. Sec-patrol leader said the slugs were strange."

Tourment sat down, the bed sinking under his weight. On the wall behind him was a painting that seemed to show a murky orange sunset and a pale blue sky streaked with fiery chem clouds.

"Strange? *Stra-a-a-ange...?*" He drew out the syllable until it almost snapped.

"Caseless small bore. High impact. Never seen anything like them."

"This was near where the snow wolf lives?"

"Yeah."

"Are they to be allied 'gainst us, Mephisto? Is this the root of the tree? The kernel of the fruit? Will the two blades be forged as one?'' He lay back, and his voice became thin and singsong. ''Shall the sky and earth wed? Will water marry fire? Will the wolf cleave to the panther?''

He was silent for a long moment, then sat up and pointed at his sec boss.

''Go get that fucking ice-suit dirty. Track 'em and take 'em. That's all. No more words, or I'll reach into your fucking chest and part the ribs and tear out your lungs.''

Mephisto carefully closed the door of the suite and stood in the narrow corridor, his eyes squeezed shut, trying to control himself. He nearly wiped his hands on his pants again. Licking his dry lips, he ran his fingers through his tight, pomaded curls.

''Mephisto, my brave and cunning friend,'' he whispered to himself. ''Best find these strangers and bring 'em here.''

He thought he heard the baron stepping toward the door inside the room, and he scampered away, set on his lethal mission.

Chapter Twelve

IT WAS THE MIDDLE of the morning.

They had walked only fifty paces into the development when they saw a large board, fixed to a triangle of steel scaffolding. It was covered in clear plastic and riveted to a wooden backing, the whole thing smeared and stained by the weather. J.B. went up to it and wiped his sleeve over the plastic, calling to the others, showing unusual excitement for such a taciturn man.

For once it would be absurdly easy for them to orient themselves.

"Come here! It's a map of where we are. A map from before the long winter!" He fumbled in one of his capacious pockets for one of his favorite long, thin cheroots, then let his hand drop as he remembered that he'd smoked the last one too many mornings and too many thousands of miles behind him.

The others gathered around, reading the notice. Doc read it aloud for Lori, rolling the prose style.

"Live Oak Crescent is a master-planned community of topclass condominiums and townhomes, set on the edges of the picturesque Atchafalaya Swamp. Affordability is our watchword. These homes are richly appointed, light, and surprisingly spacious. Each has a separate video and audio room, along with a relaxanasium in stripped afromosia teak veneer. Hot tubs are optional extras that you'll all want to add to your dream home.''

''What a load of stinking shit,'' muttered Finnegan. ''They look like little fucking boxes, right next to some more fucking little concrete boxes and some more right over there.''

Doc continued on. ''The community center at O'Brien and Stewart features Miami Beach styling with swimnasium, tennisarium, sun deck and crafted gabled shingled roofs. Live Oak Crescent is simply the state of the top art in living convenience. Realistically priced, beginning at $250,000.''

''Is that a lot of jack, Doc?'' asked J.B.

''Seems so to me,'' replied the old man. ''Upon my soul, but this must have been going on just before the ultimate madness wiped away our world. Toward the end of the year 2000. Yes, Mr. Dix, I should have said a quarter of a million greenbacks was a lot of 'jack,' even then.''

Ryan was trying to make sense of three or four lines at the bottom of the notice, set in tiny print. He read the lines over to himself.

''Qualified buyers, based on 3.2% deposit...monthly P&I payments for years one thru fifteen of...low 1.8% loan fee. The APR is 17.35. Ask our salespersons for details of zoning fees and state and federal association costings and taxes. Where applicable.''

It might as well have been written in Russian for all the sense it made to him.

''You can see where we are and where the place stretches out. There's the center of the ville,'' said J.B., pointing to where the roads seemed to converge on something called the Senator Fitzgerald Hackensacker Memorial Shopping Mall.

Most of the main landmarks in West Lowellton were on the map: the Counselor Zak Robbins Playpark, near the narrow river that wound through the ville; the Charles C. Garrett Olympic Pool and Tennisarium; the Neal R. Langholm Golf Course, straddling the river. The main shopping area was shaded with a faded purple overlay, and the location of several motels was shown, including the Snowy Egret on the far side of town, near where West Lowellton oozed out from the edges of Lafayette. A Holiday Inn was only a half mile or so from the dramatic crimson arrow with the message: YOU ARE HERE.

"First time in years I've known where I am," commented Ryan Cawdor.

The houses around them were mainly single-story, stained green with mosses and lichen. Most of their windows and doors were still intact, though several of the roofs had collapsed where damp had seeped in and rotted the supporting timbers.

"Where do we go?" Lori asked.

"I figure that one of them motels could be our prime target," replied Doc. "From the excellent state of these buildings, it's reasonable to believe they might be more than adequate for shelter."

Ryan shook his head. "I just don't believe this place. Doc, you got knowledge like no man I ever met. I never seen houses all together like this from before the long cold time. How come it . . . ? How?"

"Neutron missiles, like we figured. They seed the land with them, and the physical structures aren't hardly touched. Within about ten days, ninety-eight percent of living creatures are on their way across the dark river from which there is no returning."

"You mean they fucking die, Doc?" said Finn.

"Yes, Mr. Finnegan. That is what I mean."

"Then what's happened to all the fucking bodies?"

AS THE BRIGHT, dry summery morning progressed, they saw them everywhere. Tumbled, scattered bones on the edges of the sidewalks. On porches. In gardens. Bits of ivory among the overwhelming shades of green. Here and there some creatures of the nearby wild had feasted on the bodies, ripping apart the skeletons. There might be a single long, straight femur, its end gnawed smooth. Or a skull, grinning emptily, yards from the skeleton it had once topped.

"It's a boneyard," said J.B.

"Yeah. I seen bodies, dried up like old leather, in some of the redoubts we found over the years with the Trader. You know?"

"Sure. Like husks. Lips peeled off yellow teeth. All of 'em grinning at us. I recall that. But this is just bones, white as snow."

It was an unusually long speech for the phlegmatic Armorer. But it was a sight to stir anyone's imagination.

A century ago, the whole town had been blasted away from above. Its streets and houses had been scoured clean of inhabitants. Families had been destroyed with the demonic breath of the neutron bombs. Russian submarines off the coast had lain still and patient and received the signal that told them this was no drill. No false alarm. No testing situation.

And the people had died and the houses remained.

It was a cemetery, fifty miles wide and forty deep. Only in the swamps had people survived; many of their descendants were now muties. They avoided the ruins of the old villes, fearing the contamination they once harbored. The whole of West Lowellton was like some giant time capsule, frozen since that dread January day a hundred years ago.

Ryan was fascinated and wanted to investigate each home and shop they passed. But J.B. warned him of the need for food and shelter.

"That Baron Tourment's going to have patrols of sec men after us, Ryan."

"Sure."

"Look at 'em later."

"Yeah. Guess so."

THERE WERE surprisingly few buggies or wags of any kind. Ryan's guess was that when the alarms started to shrill, lots of folks would have headed out of town, away from the missiles they knew would wipe away their homes. But nothing had prepared them for the reality of Armageddon. All the flix that Ryan had seen in old redoubts had warned about painting windows white to cut down the flash-blast. Blankets soaked in water over doors. Sandbags. Refuge under stairs and in storm cellars. Brown paper bags over your head.

It hadn't been like that. Best way of saving your kin from the long agony of rad-poisoning was to take out the pump-action scattergun and blow everyone's head off, and finally kiss the warm barrel yourself.

Some had done that. Ryan had seen the corpses, half the bone of the head missing, the corroded ten-gauges still between the clenched jaws.

There was one saloon wagon in a side street, its tires long rotted, stripped down to metal by years of high winds, blasted by sand. The glass remained, though its surface had been hazed until it was opaque. A branch off a nearby lime tree had fallen over the hood. Krysty moved it, revealing two stickers, peeling off the chrome fenders.

One said, "I brake for children and animals and patriotic Americans." The second one said simply: "Happiness is the biggest L.R. Missile."

Doc shook his head, saying nothing.

AROUND NOON they found a street showing a full row of shops. Ryan couldn't get over the amazing sight. He'd seen old vids, flix and pix in mags. This was small-town U.S.A., standing there in front of his eyes. All that was missing was folks.

Some of the windows were broken, and there was clear evidence of looting. Also, the streets here were free of bones. As they stepped along, keeping to one side, Ryan glanced in at the storefronts.

Names clicked by, some registering, some not. Some of them had sold products he'd heard of. Some of them were obscure and incomprehensible.

What was *Alice's Tofu Joint*? What was tofu? Some kind of food, he guessed, from a placard as faded as a Brady daguerreotype.

Pick'n Mix. Garry's Auto-Tuner—best muffler service in West Lowellton. Ynez Lobos, Realtor. Ryan didn't know what a realtor was, but he figured it was someone who looked after other people's houses for a fee.

"This is fucking way-weird," said Finnegan, spitting at a red hydrant in the street.

Ten & Quarter. Circuit City. West Lowellton Estate Protection. German shepherds, man-killers. Armed patrols around the clock and back again. Save your loved ones and your possessions. Let us do the killing for you.

"Sounds like the Deathlands now," said J.B.

Guns. Guns. Guns. Guns. The storefront shouted the word again and again. The Armorer paused, wiping at the glass. In sticky gold letters, some of which were missing, the name of the ex-owner from the year 2001 declaimed itself.

Angus R. Wells. A native of Louisiana from birth. Carry arms—it's your right.

"Empty," said J.B. disappointedly. "Not a blaster left in the place."

"Guess the Cajuns must have taken 'em," Ryan said, stepping around a dead snake that must have been close to fifty feet in length when alive.

The Armorer shook his head doubtfully, swatting away a hornet with his fedora. "Guess not."

"Why?"

"This place closed up in January 2001. It would have had the best and latest blasters of the day. What they called car guns and house guns. Small caliber, pretty pistols. Berettas and Colts. Big mothers like the later Pythons and the Pumas. And hunting rifles from Spain and Czechoslovakia."

"Sure." Ryan wouldn't argue with J.B. when it came to discussing weaponry.

"I seen what them double-poor dirties had. Old blackpowder muzzle-loaders and muskets that were old before the winters came. Nothing from a store like this one here."

They moved a little farther on. Krysty stopped, tugging at Ryan's sleeve and halting him, while the others waited.

"What is it, lover?"

"I heard those swampwags again. Way off, behind us."

"That's no problem. If'n it comes to a firefight in a place like this, we could take on the whole of the baron's fucking sec-men army."

"There was something else."

"Yeah?"

"Whistling."

"I heard a whistle," said Lori, her blank face lighting for a moment.

"You did? When?"

The two women looked at each other. Lori answered Krysty, fumbling for the right words. "Soon gone. Not a long time. High and . . . weak."

"That's it. Very high frequency, Ryan. Repeated pattern of notes. Like a signal."

"Ahead or behind us?" asked J.B.

She pointed wordlessly down the street, in front of them.

"Far off?" asked Ryan.

She shook her head at the question. "Difficult, love. All these buildings. Not used to it. Even back home in Harmony it wasn't like this."

"I doubt, Miss Wroth, if there are many places like this left in the whole of the United States of America. I beg pardon. In the whole of Deathlands."

AT RYAN'S ORDERS, they spread out even more.

They covered both sides of the sunlit street, their blasters ready, their nerves stretched tight with tension. In this part of West Lowellton the greenery hadn't gained so much of a stranglehold, and the street was still fairly clear and the buildings mainly undamaged.

Ryan squinted so that the line of small stores became hazy, the outlines blurring and softening. And it became like an old vid from before the wars. All it lacked were the smiling, bustling throngs of women and children, busy at their shopping. And there were no cars. All the old vids seemed to show roads jammed with wags.

On the right was an ice-cream parlor, its sign fallen down and disintegrated into splinters of chipboard. Another realtor's sign boasted that it found houses *For the people and by the people*. There was also a store selling do-it-yourself outfits for home security, ever a barometer of social fears and neuroses.

One of the roofs that had given in to the ravages of a hundred years was composed of red shingles. It had been called the something *Hut*; the first word had vanished.

They first saw the graffiti in an empty lot next door.

It was sprayed in a shimmering white paint, in ornate, rolling letters three feet high, on the wall of a hardware store.

THIS LAND IS OUR LAND. KEEP OUT ALL LIVING DEAD AND FRENDS OF THE BARRON.

The paint reflected the sun, making Ryan blink.

"Over there," said Krysty, pointing to more painted lettering. This time it was scrawled across the main window of *T-Shirt City*.

Looking around, Ryan crossed over to examine it. TEN MORE STEPS AND YOU DEAD, it said.

He reached out with the index finger on his right hand, hugging the G-12 in his left hand. Touching the rolling letters, he stared in disbelief at his finger.

Sticky and fresh with its smear of white paint.

Chapter Thirteen

"IT'S LIKE THE DMZ in 'Nam," said J. B. Dix. "Read 'bout it. No-go region for both sides. What we heard 'bout this Baron Tourment, he controls most of the land round Lafayette. But not this ville of West Lowellton."

"White wolf," said Ryan. "Or snow wolf. Take your pick. What we heard back in Moudongue, it's renegades. Gang of wolf's-heads. Outlaws."

"Slumgullions," commented Doc Tanner.

"How's that?" asked Finnegan.

The old-timer bared his strong yellow teeth in a ferocious grin. "Good word, is it not? A cant perversion of the tongue, but it sounds like what it means." Licking his lips, he savored the word again. "Slumgullion. A rowdy fellow, living beyond the law. And as we are all aware, to do that you must be honest."

There were times when Doc simply didn't make any sense to anyone.

Bedrock bedding prices. Buy now—tomorrow may be too late.

The white lettering was inside a store window a few yards down the street. But it was obviously written before the neutron missiles were dropped over the Louisiana bayous.

"What do we do, Ryan?" asked Krysty, glancing up and down the street. Behind them, a small armadillo scuffled across the street, but otherwise the avenue was deserted.

"We could try and make it through the swamps to the gateway. But I figure them Cajuns are going to be looking for us. And there's those dead and alive fuckers to keep clear of."

"What about that warning?" asked Finn, pointing back at the first of the freshly painted signs.

"Place like this—" Ryan began, pausing as he looked around the rows of long derelict buildings, "—place like this could get you cold-cocked from anywhere. Man with a good blaster could pick us all off before we got a sight on him."

Both Ryan and J.B. had outstanding memories for trails and maps, and both had a clear sense of where they were in relation to the rest of the ville. If the Baron that everyone was shitting their pants over ruled most of the region, then West Lowellton looked like the best venture, they decided. But if there was this street-gang holding it, then they had to find some place large in which to hole up.

"Big motel," suggested J.B.

"Yeah," Ryan nodded. "Yeah. There was something called a Holiday Inn. We passed it 'bout a half mile back. Be a good place."

"There was an old vid-house near there, with a real pre-chill name. The Adelphi." J.B. shook his head at the absurdity of the names in the prenuke ville.

"Probably showing some anticommy prop-vids. I read that was all they showed round that time." Finnegan was leaning against the wall of a store, *Barney's Beanery*, that had once sold health foods. There was an addition to the sign: *and gun store.*

Faded by thousands upon thousands of days of sun and wind, there was some crude lettering on the wall of a store across the street.

"GOD WANTS YOU," it said.

Underneath it, in the same white paint as the earlier graffiti, was written: "THEN LET HIM FUCKING COMM AN GET ME."

Krysty heard the sound first.

It was a faint tinkling noise, thin and metallic, a long way from where they stood. It had an insistent rhythm, clicking away, first two fast beats, then a slow one. Two fast, one slow.

Ryan considered running for the rows of neat white houses behind the stores to lie in ambush for whomever was coming. But it didn't take a tactical genius to figure out that their attackers would have better local knowledge than they did.

"There's a chill in here," said Finnegan, flattening his snub nose against the dusty window. "Just bones heaped together."

"Nothing else? No blasters?" asked J.B.

"No. Big poster on the back wall, half-torn. Says, 'Brownsville Texas is the fucking pits.' Oh, and one other over a door. Big heart with the words 'I love Lafayette.' That's all they wrote."

The chinking sound was growing closer. Krysty looked at Ryan. "You know there's two, mebbe three of them doing it?"

"I can hear that."

"So?"

"Let's go find us that Holiday Inn place we saw on the map."

Grimacing, Doc straightened, pushing at the base of his spine with his right hand. "I fear I am not so supple as I once was. Did you say we were all going to seek out a Holiday Inn in which to rest?''

"Yeah, Doc."

"Then let us trust that the best surprise we get will be no surprise at all.''

"Sure," replied Ryan, wondering what the old man was babbling about.

THE LARGE SIGN that had once welcomed Kiwanis, Elks, baseball teams and homecoming queens had rusted and fallen to the dirt, probably half a century ago.

"What the fuck is a Kiwanis?" muttered Finnegan, not really expecting an answer and not getting one.

As they left the shopping street on the edge of West Lowellton, the metallic drumming seemed to fade away. Krysty swore she heard someone laughing, crazed and long, but she might have been mistaken.

Ryan led them at a brisk pace, with the Armorer at the rear constantly checking that they weren't being followed. Here the streets were narrower, with older properties built on either side. Most had rickety mailboxes, many still showing the dragon's-head logo of the West Lowellton *Comet and Advertiser*. Off the main drag they saw more sun-bleached bones scattered here and there. On a wooden porch several skeletons were jumbled together as if a family had chosen to die together.

The sun shone through the long branches of the whitebeam trees that lined the dappled suburban streets. Intermittently they came upon the rotting remnants of automobiles, their tires long gone, settled on their hubs. They were overwhelmed by the visible tragedy of the Big Chill of 2001. It wasn't like just reading about it, or hearing from some old tapes. This was *now* and this was real.

The Holiday Inn stood on a slight mound in the center
of a maze of small waterways. Some had silted up; some
had dried to lush valleys of moss; some still flowed with
gurgling muddy water. The motel itself was a sprawling
single-story structure, originally painted white and built
with central pillars and columns in the American Colonial
style. On its western flank a tall sycamore had died and
fallen, breaking three windows. The flowering shrubs that
once had been carefully tended now ran wild, with azaleas
and bougainvillea rampant, clear across the circular drive
and parking spaces, flooding into the railed swimming
pool with its turquoise slide. The permanently green As-
troturf was covered with lichen.

The six of them stood and stared. Finn spat onto the
dusty road, then started and peered down by his boots.

"Fucking tracks, Ryan."

Ryan mentally cursed himself for being so careless. He'd
been so interested in seeing this motel, preserved like a fly
trapped forever in yellow amber, that he'd been ignoring
basic safety. Like keeping his eyes open.

Finnegan was correct. The thick dust on the blacktop
was overlaid with the familiar tracks of the swampwags.
He knelt down to run his fingers lightly over the marks,
then stood and scrutinized them from a different angle. He
walked a few paces toward the imposing bulk of the motel, looking back at the tracks.

"They all turned here, J.B.," he said. "They come this
far, then they go right around and head back toward the
main part of the ville."

"Yeah. I read it that way."

"Mebbe this Holiday Inn place marks the edge of Baron
Tourment's secure territory."

Ryan looked at Krysty. "Could be, lover. This gang runs part of West Lowellton. This baron maybe hasn't enough sec men to come clear out the nest of rats."

That made sense.

They could imagine no other reason why the tire tracks should stop so abruptly about a hundred paces before the tangled skein of waterways and narrow bridges that circled the building.

From the south came the sullen rumbling of thunder. A deep purple cloud moved menacingly along the southern fringe of the sky, its upper edge touched with vermilion.

"Nuke storm on the way," said Finn.

"No," said Doc.

"What?"

"Not a nuke storm. I spent a summer here, way back in . . . my mind sort of trembles when I try and recall dates and places. I spent a vacation with Emily . . . Was that her name? Emily?"

Only once since Ryan Cawdor had met Doc Tanner had the old man mentioned Emily. It was just another ill-shaped piece in the jigsaw puzzle of the man's mysterious past.

"Go on, Doc," urged Lori. "Please."

"It was out near Baton Rouge. Rained, so we got busted flat, roads turned to rivers. Dark at noon, so's you couldn't see a hand before your face. Lord, but that was a time. Emily cried on my shoulder, and she lost her kerchief that day. Lace-trimmed. Sky like this. But there was a pool of clear gold light, straight over our heads—we saw it. Looking up, like a road to the throne of the Lord Himself. Emily wasn't much on religion. . . . She . . . seen an eagle in that light."

The voice was fading, as it often did during Doc's recollections. This one had gone on longer than most. Ryan prompted him gently.

"And the sky was like that? Purple and red at the edges?"

"All around. This eagle. Emily... was it with her? Or later, after I'd... they trawled and... I recall a line or two of verse by..." The brow furrowed with the effort of concentration. "By Oliver Makin. 'The bird that flies above the clouds knows only the sun, and his storms are sunstorms.' Yes, that was it, I believe. I always thought that a pretty conceit. I'm sorry, I fail to remember why..."

Lori squeezed his hand. Ryan was struck by the way Doc Tanner mixed moments of the highest intelligence with long hours of near senile meanderings.

"So, it's not a fucking nuke storm," said Finn. "Least that's good news. But it still looks like the skies are going to fucking piss all over us."

"Best get inside the building," said Ryan. "I'll go first. J.B.?"

"Yeah?"

"Bring up..."

"The rear. I got it, Ryan."

THE RELICS of several automobiles were parked in the overgrown lot at the side of the building. Over the main doorway there was a kind of archway. Beyond it was a pair of double doors, one with the glass cracked clean across from corner to corner. Ryan, the G-12 at the ready, stepped lightly toward the entrance, sniffing the air like a prowling panther. The green scent of the luxurious vegetation filled his nostrils.

"Should we go in, Ryan?" asked Finnegan.

"Fireblast! Why not?"

The door was stiff, creaking on dry hinges. Ryan kicked away a pile of desiccated leaves heaped in the entrance; they rustled loudly. With the sun behind them, the group filed through the door one by one into the cool dark vestibule; the air felt almost clammy on the skin. Last to enter, J.B. pulled the door shut.

"Shall I stay here and cover our asses?"

"No. If'n there's hunters after us, this place is too big to cover until we've checked it out. Safer to keep together."

The Armorer nodded.

"Be quicker if we split up," suggested Finn. "Mebbe me, J.B., Doc 'n' Lori could go one way, you 'n' Krysty go the other, and meet up back here in the . . . what the fuck is this big room?"

"Called the lobby, my dear Mr. Finnegan," replied Doc Tanner. "By the three Kennedys! This place brings back such a flood of memories."

"Tell us 'bout them, Doc," said Ryan, but the old man was already going on ahead, pushing through a second set of glass doors, with ornate brass handles shaped like the heads of twining alligators.

The rest of the group followed him into the cavernous lobby. It was a place of deep and swimming shadows, with large chairs and sofas set about circular tables. The walls had paintings of the bayous, streaked with dark and light greens. To one side was a long desk marked Registration; across the lobby two passages led off to the left and to the right. The one on the left carried a sign in a sinuous gold script: Cajuns' Bar & Atchafalaya Dining Room.

Ryan inhaled deeply, tasting old, old dust, stale and flat. He closed his eye and licked his dry lips, savoring the feeling of being inside a creature dead a hundred years. It was a feeling he'd known before, when he and the Trader had first discovered the sealed entrances to a redoubt, locked away since before the big winter. But this was different. This was not an arid military storehouse but something that had lived and bustled with activity.

"Okay, Finn. Krysty and me'll go left. Rest of you go right. Meet back here in—" he glanced down at his chron "—in 'bout an hour. Watch your triggers. Don't want to chill each other."

Their boot heels muffled by the thick pile carpets, four of them went cautiously off, vanishing around a corner. Ryan turned and grinned wolfishly at Krysty, noticing that her long scarlet hair was shimmering and moving gently on its own, though there was no draft to stir it.

"Hear anything? Feel anything?" he asked.

"Just a lot of love for you," she whispered, her voice almost vanishing before it reached him.

"Nothing living?"

She shook her head slowly. "Smell reminds me of how Mother Sonja used to take out our winter clothes, back in Harmony. She'd open up the closets that had been shut tight all summer, and the smell . . . it was kind of like this. Dry and musty."

Ryan walked to the long desk. There was a notice neatly printed on a board. "Jerry Suster call home soonest." Under it, hastily chalked, was the single word: "No-show."

The place showed every sign of a rapid and disorganized withdrawal, with clipboards, pens, cards and small change scattered everywhere. At the far end of the desk Krysty found a round metal drum, with a printed label behind clear plastic. "How far to your next Holiday Inn destination? Allow us to make your reservation."

"See how far we come from Alaska," said Ryan.

Krysty flipped open a slot on the front of the drum, revealing hundreds of alphabetically arranged rectangular cards. As she began to turn the drum, the cards quivered and began to collapse into tiny shards of dry paper, disintegrating in her fingers.

"By Gaia!" she exclaimed. "All rotted away."

"Figure there'll be a lot of that. We found that natural materials like wool and cotton all rot in a few years, and artificial materials like plastic last longer."

"Look." She pointed to a rack of colored cards with shiny, laminated faces, hanging on the wall.

They carefully examined the curling pieces, feeling how brittle and fragile they were, like some ancient manuscript discovered in a cave. These were brochures that described tourist attractions within a reasonable drive from the motel. Ryan had actually heard of some of them, like Disneyworld and Epcot. Many featured smiling families on holiday, wearing bright shirts and shorts.

"Bayou buggy trips," said Krysty. "In swampwags."

Another card showed some caves, eerie and dank, with an official of some sort in a buff uniform and wide-brimmed hat pointing out a massive stalactite. "Tuckaluckahoochy Caverns, only thirty miles from Lafayette, first discovered in 1996," read the caption.

"Mebbe food in the kitchens," suggested Ryan. "We found lots still usable. If'n it's tinned or freeze-sealed, it's edible."

They found a corpse in the Atchafalaya Dining Room.

Sinews of gristle still held most of the skeleton together. It sat at a table near the door, the skull rolled forward, resting against an overturned green bottle. The left leg had become detached, and the left arm was loose, the fingers stiffly penetrating the maroon carpet. The right arm was on the table, the calcified fingers clutching a shot glass with a dried brown smear at its bottom. There was nothing apparent to indicate how the person had died.

A long plastic-coated menu rested against a glass candlestick, and Krysty picked it up. Angling it to catch what little light there was, she showed it to Ryan.

"'A prime rib of beef, one of our forever and a day favorites, with choice of rice or potato, our crisp'n fresh house salad, bakery rolls and whipped butter.' Sound good, lover? Guess I'll have that. Or maybe 'the shrimp platter, out of the bay yesterday, served with toasted almonds and pineapple rings.'"

Ryan looked over her shoulder. "I'll take the deep-fried breaded cheese sticks for a starter, or the egg rolls and mustard sauce. The chef's salad with . . . what the fuck's a julienne of ham? And what are olives? Never heard of 'em. A stuffed flounder and crab meat stuffing. Heard of a crab but not a flounder."

"It's a fish, I think."

"Right now I'd settle for anything."

"How 'bout bird shit on rye?" asked Krysty.

"Sure. As long as it's *good* bird shit."

"Let's go look in the kitchen."

They couldn't believe their luck in the back. Right by the bat-wing doors was an open closet door. Inside, a dozen hand-torches hung on hooks next to a push-button power pack. Ryan pressed the red switch a few times, and the bulbs began to glow, brighter and brighter.

"Solves a problem. Take one, and we can come back for the others."

The torches threw a bright narrow beam that lasted about ten minutes before needing recharging. The light was reflected off the polished metal of pots and pans sitting neatly in racks. The shelves at the far end of the kitchen were stacked with all kinds of tins and packets. Krysty let her light explore them.

"The packets have probably gone off, but there's plenty of tins. Ready meals in sealed cartons. Gumbo...what's that?" She peered at the label. "Oh, yeah. Freeze-dried collard greens, fatback and chili. Irradiated and reconstituted pulk salad. Sounds like enough. What d'you say, lover?"

Ryan shone the torch on his own face, the harsh beam highlighting the sharp contours of his cheeks and mouth. "Don't you see my tongue hanging out? We'll look round some, then meet up with the others. Bring a spare light with you."

MANY OF THE DRAPES were still drawn, letting in only a murky, filtered sunlight. Here and there doors to rooms stood open, with sharp-edged bars of brightness thrown across the corridors.

"Why the dead not smell? Quint chilled the dead. Some days he did not, and the dead smell." Lori wrinkled up her nose in disgust at the memory.

"Too long a time has passed, dearest," replied Doc Tanner. "The flesh rots slowly, and mortifies. Gradually it all dries, and the maggots feed on it. After a few years slip by, there is nothing left for the maggots, and they too die and rot. Slowly and very quietly the corpse becomes sinew and bone. Nothing else remains. Nothing to smell anymore."

"Guess for a few weeks West Lowellton sure must have fucking stank like a summer slaughterhouse," added the sweating Finnegan.

J. B. Dix, hefting the Mini-Uzi, stepped into one of the rooms on the right of the corridor. The drapes were half open, and the waves of light illuminated countless motes

of dust suspended in the air. Beyond the window, greenery was pressed against the glass. In a corner, termites had
evidently worked their way in, destroying some wood at
floor level.

He looked around. Two double beds, huge by compar-
ison with all the other beds the Armorer had ever seen. It
looked like neither of them had been used, the covers as
tight and square as when they had last been made up in
January 2001, probably by some Puerto Rican maid.
There were lights mounted on the wall above each bed, and
a painting of a cowboy riding a spirited Appaloosa stallion. A low bureau faced the beds, with a polished black
vid set upon it. A round table with two chairs in dark
plastic hide stood against the window in an ugly little
grouping with a spidery lamp.

J.B. walked over the carpet, breathing slow and easy,
seeing his reflection approach a massive mirror screwed
over a washbasin in pastel pink. Glancing around to make
sure the others hadn't followed him in, the Armorer
winked at himself and tipped his fedora.

There was a long pink bath and a pink toilet, sealed in
some kind of clear plastic. A small label pasted to it read,
"Sanitized for your protection". Beneath it the water was
long gone.

Drinking glasses on the basin were also sealed tight. J.B.
reached over and turned one of the chromed taps, not
surprised to see that nothing happened. No leaking drops
of rusty water. No hissing and gurgling in the pipes. No
skittering insects.

"J.B., come look in here!"

Quick and light as a cat, the Armorer darted across the
corridor. Finn was in the doorway of an identical room,
with Lori and Doc at his elbow.

"What?"

"Couple of chills. In the bed."

J.B. stepped past him, his eyes surveying the place. The thick shades were down almost to the bottom, letting in little light. But there was enough to see the two leering skeletons in the bed on the right. There were a couple of open valises on the floor and several empty bottles on the table, two glasses next to them.

Doc pushed past the Armorer, straight to the smaller table at the head of the bed. He picked up a white plastic container and shook it to show it was empty. Peering at the label, he replaced it where it was.

"What is it?" asked Lori.

"Morphine derivative. Very strong sleeping tablets. There were some fifty or so, I would hazard a guess. Now there are none."

"They chilled themselves?"

"Yes."

Finnegan whistled. "I can't ever figure someone doing that."

The old man patted him gently on the shoulder. "That is a sad comment on the times in which we live and the life that you must lead, my dear young friend. You must be aware that when civilization ended, it was not utterly unexpected. There was a time of warning for some. Only for some."

"Some ran," said J.B.

"One day, Mr. Dix, I shall entertain you with the tale of the man who had an appointment in Samarra. You can run faster than the wind, but Death will always o'ertake you. These two had warning, and they chose to die together, in each other's arms, perhaps with some good corn liquor to warm their passing. It was a more dignified departure from life than many enjoyed."

"That is sad," Lori said quietly.

"Yeah. Let's leave 'em," agreed Finnegan, leading them out of the suite of death.

RYAN AND KRYSTY found bodies in half a dozen rooms in the Holiday Inn of West Lowellton. Most were in the beds.

Not all.

One skeleton was in the bathtub. The pale pearlized sides were streaked with clotted black marks, thick around the top. In the bottom, almost hidden by the slumped pelvis, was a slim razor blade, its edges dulled with the long-dried blood. The skull hung forward, drooping in a final disconsolate slump. Shreds of long gray hair were still pasted to the ridges of the head.

The right hand, which had been dangling outside the tub, had become detached and lay in an untidy heap of carpals and phalanges on top of an open book.

"What is it?" asked Ryan.

Krysty stooped to pick it up, keeping her finger between the open pages. "The Bible. Whoever it was got in a warm tub and opened up his or her veins. Uncle Tyas McNann told me it was how the old Greeks and Romans used to take their lives."

"What chapter was he or she reading?"

Krysty examined the heading that the dead fingers had marked, stumbling over some of the unfamiliar language.

"It's from the New Testament—the First Epistle of Paul the Apostle to the Corinthians."

"Who were they?"

"Some old Romans or Greeks, I guess, lover. It's open at chapter thirteen."

"Read a little, Krysty."

The girl began, her voice rising with the mouth-filling phrases of the King James text. "'But when that which is perfect is come, then that which is in part shall be done away. When I was a child, I spake as a child, I understood as a child, I thought as a child: but when I became a man I put away childish things. For now we see through a glass, darkly.'"

She stopped there, turning her face to his, and he saw the tears streaking her cheeks.

"One day, Krysty..." he said.

THEY MET UP AGAIN in the lobby about half an hour later. All were subdued by the macabre experience of touring the luxurious mausoleum. Lori had been crying, and Doc Tanner was showing worrisome signs of retreating once more into a catatonic madness. His eyes had become hooded, as if they'd been painted with a thin veil of beeswax. Occasionally he would mutter. "Madness," or "Oh, the horror of it all.... The bastards! Insane, criminal bastards!"

Ryan took them to the kitchen, gave everyone a torch and showed them how to prime them with the push-button. He and Finn and J.B. took a spare light to hang on their belts. He and Krysty also showed everyone the supplies of food.

It seemed like there'd be no way of heating anything up, but Finn went fossicking around the storage closets, emerging with a red cylinder of camping gas. Lori teetered off and brought in pans of discolored water from the streams around the motel, heating them and tipping in the unappetizing powders, stirring them to form a bland thick soup. Krysty added some salt and pepper from the metal condiment containers on the tables in the Atchafalaya Dining Room.

Finnegan disappeared through the heavy doors of the Cajuns' Bar, which were covered with shreds of rotted maroon velvet. He returned with a dozen bottles in his arms.

They sat and drank, mostly in silence. Some of the wine was still drinkable, despite having stood untouched on shelves for almost a century. Best was a couple of quarts of imported French brandy, thick and sweet, to be savored on the palate, with a fiery kick that didn't register properly until it was well down the throat.

"Bar was filled with bones. Must have been the best parts of ten to fifteen people all jumbled in the joint. Some was women. Remains of some fancy shoes in among the ribs and skulls."

Ryan stopped spooning up the reconstituted mush to look at the chubby gunman. "What's that, Finn? Bones all jumbled up?"

"Yeah."

"Then someone had been in that part?"

Finnegan considered the question, belched and took another sip of the brandy. "Got to be right. Fucking right, Ryan. Only place in this gaudy that the chills had been moved at all. Yeah. Looked like bottles were gone. Gaps on shelves."

It was late afternoon.

The sun that had shone so boldly through the morning had vanished, drifting away under a leaden-gray cloud cover.

Through chinks in the faded drapes, the lights from the torches flickered and danced. They could be seen outside, across the waterways.

They could be seen by the crouching figure in ragged leather breeches and jerkin. A figure with eyes like fire and hair white as snow.

Chapter Fourteen

THE RAZOR-EDGE OF THE DAGGER methodically chopped and cut the crystalline powder. The chopping made it as fine as ground flour, separating it into narrow lines no thicker than a stalk of wheat, no longer than a man's middle finger. The surface of the mirror was dulled and scored with a thousand tiny scratches, from years of use. It was an artifact that predated the short war, brought in by one of the sec patrols, handed first to the sec boss, then on to the baron himself.

The drug, a powerful hallucinogenic mixture of cocaine, heroin and mescaline, had been brought by swampwag to the baron's headquarters from a tumbledown dock a few miles from Baton Rouge. It had been part of a shipment carried by a battered clipper ship from Trinidad. Its country of origin had once been called Colombia, but now had no name at all.

The Baron knelt beside the glass-topped table, his legs stuck awkwardly behind him, his great head lowered over the mirror. In his right hand he held a thin tube of beaten gold, made for him deep in the swamps by one of the living dead who had an unusual skill with metals.

The tube traveled slowly along the line of the drug, known as "jolt," from its sudden and strong effect on users. Baron Tourment snorted at it, the powder disappearing as the tube went along one line, then down the next, taking four lines in total.

Immediately shutting his eyes, holding his face between his two huge hands, he waited for the rush. In the whole of Deathlands it was doubtful that there was a single man of science with the pharmacological knowledge to understand how jolt worked. But its effects were always the same.

"Uh," grunted Tourment as a kick of pain speared through his sinuses, bursting behind his eyes. His head shook uncontrollably, rolling from side to side. He tried to keep his eyes squeezed shut, but the force of the spasm jammed them open, the pupils rolling sightlessly. His fingers grasped convulsively and his toes drummed; his walking frame clattered on the wooden floor of the suite.

After the first spasm of pain, the drug moved differently, attacking the cortex, closing down on the short-term memory of the frontal lobes. The power of a shot of jolt lasted from three to five minutes, depending on its purity and on the strength of the user. Baron Tourment could afford to pay for the best, but his giant body absorbed the drug too fast for his own pleasure. Its effects rarely lasted for more than about three and a half minutes.

But what a two hundred seconds they were!

A tumbling passage through time and memory and imagination, into scenes of desolation and horror. Scenes of horrific violence that made the giant black man press his fingers against his swelling erection. Twice he laughed loudly, making the guards outside the door shudder and glance fearfully at each other. When the Baron was jolting, his mood was even less predictable than usual. A sec man who'd once entered at the wrong moment had been taken out, clutching his own spilled intestines. The baron had laughed then.

But Tourment used the jolt for one special reason. In the last thirty seconds or so, it clouded the mind, and a form of madness followed. The Baron was the seventh son of a seventh daughter, and had always had a little of the power of seeing. As the jolt worked its way into the abandoned corridors of the mind, it sometimes increased his precognition, his powers of doomseeing. Sometimes it granted him remarkable insight into a potential advantage.

Or a potential danger.

Since the strange death of the auguring bird and the passing of the old woman, Baron Tourment had been uneasy.

Outsiders had come into his demesne. He still believed in his heart that the strangers must be mercies: hired guns from outside the ville. Maybe from the north or farther east. Mercenaries! Brought in by the young boy in West Lowellton.

"Should have purged 'em," he muttered, his voice thickened by the jolt.

How could they have afforded it? Mercies, to go against him! It must have been his generosity in leaving them with a little in previous years. That was his mistake, and they used it to hire blasters.

Now the jolt was cartwheeling through the ridges of his skull. He lay flat on the floor, which was the only safe place to be after snorting several lines of jolt. The eyes were open, staring wide and blind, the hands so contracted that the nails drew half moons of blood from his pale palms.

"Ten thousand doors to death," he whispered, his sibilant voice dying against the velvet drapes that covered the doors and windows.

He was in the bayous. Naked and alone, beneath a sky that was slashed with green clouds. The mud rose to his groin. He tried to run but without his prosthetic aids he kept falling. His face was vanishing beneath warm, clinging mud that filled his ears and nose and eyes and open mouth. He tried to scream, but the slime choked him.

Someone was pursuing him, someone who always dodged aside when the baron tried to look behind him into the gathering darkness.

As he rose from the wallowing sludge, he glanced down. Saw that his penis was covered with big scaly leeches, drawing a million specks of bright blood that dappled his thighs and matted in his pubic hair.

On the floor of the Best Western Snowy Egret, the huge man arched his back; openmouthed, he silently screamed his terror. Sweat burst from his forehead; sweat soaked his shirt.

The person behind him was approaching. He could almost feel his hot breath on his naked back. His ears caught the scraping sounds of horns and claws against the branches as his pursuer pushed through, struggling toward...

Toward...?

The jolt was bringing him to a violent mental climax. The vision was nearly there, as he'd hoped. The truth about the strangers might be revealed to him in a moment of vivid revelation.

He was exhausted, panting for breath, his whole body now coated with the blood-sucking leeches. The experience was so appalling that he wanted to fall to his knees and vomit. But then he might get caught by...by what was closing in on him.

It was near.

The sec guards outside the suite heard moaning and panting through the thick door. Then an agonized scream of chilling horror, and Baron Tourment's voice, shrill and strained, barely recognizable. The same phrase, over and over.

"The one-eyed man kills me! The one-eyed man kills me! The one-eyed man kills me!"

Chapter Fifteen

RYAN'S SUSPICION THAT others had been in the Holiday Inn within the past few months were reinforced when it became apparent that the slogan painter had been at work. The white letters were dry, but from their condition it was obvious they hadn't been there long.

They were on a wall that ran from the back of the restaurant toward the abandoned swimming pool, with its crust of dried leaves and moss.

The message was simple.

"COME HERE AND YOU DIE."

Ryan picked the best place he could find from which to mount a defense. It had once been a games room with all manner of vids and pinball machines decorated by archaic and oddly beautiful artwork and names like Redzapper and Wackamole. There was also the yawning maw of a cracked, dust-filled Jacuzzi.

The room had only two doors, one of which had strips of reinforced steel across it, and could be locked and bolted. J.B. studied it, puzzled about the necessity for that kind of security in a games room. He liked the fact that since the room overlooked a deep waterway, there was no way an attacker could sneak through a window. From the swirling disturbances in the gray water, it looked like it was well-stocked with piranhas.

Ryan organized the group into pairs for guard duty, and with help from J.B. and Krysty, arranged a rotation of shifts. They decided that since they could easily lock one of the doors to the games room, only the other one had to be guarded. After some consideration, Ryan said, "We need another guard farther down the corridor that leads to that place where we first came in. What's it called? The..." He glanced surreptitiously at Doc.

The old man responded as Ryan hoped he would. He was evidently recovering from his earlier gloom.

"The *lobby*, Mr. Cawdor."

"Thanks. We'll split up like this." He stopped. "Doc, I don't want any shit from you. I know you want to be with Lori. But we've got only three trained guns now—me, J.B. and Finn here. So, Doc, you go with Finn; Lori with J.B.; and Krysty with me."

"All right" was all the old man said, removing his dented stovepipe hat and dropping Ryan a low courtly bow.

Krysty offered to heat up more of the gooey green-gray collard greens, pulk salad and gumbo, but there were no takers.

"Must be gooder...better food in houses we see. Not this..." Lori couldn't find a word for it.

"Mebbe," said Ryan. "In the morning, you two girls could go out with Finn and scout around some. See what you can dig up."

The fat man grinned, licking his lips. "You got a deal, Cap'n Cawdor. You got yourself a real fucking good deal."

THE NIGHT PASSED UNEVENTFULLY, apart from the noises from the swamps and streams.

During their first break from guard duty, Ryan and Krysty found themselves a room down the corridor from the games area, one with no heaps of bones in it. Tugging back the covers on the king-size bed, they cosily snuggled into it.

Wary of intrusions or disturbances, they removed only a minimum of clothing.

Ryan had deliberately split the bottoms of his dark gray pants so that he could pull them off over his high combat boots. He kept on the brown shirt, still stained with mud and with Henn's blood. The G-12 went on the floor beside the bed, the SIG-Sauer P-226 9 mm pistol beneath one of the two pillows.

Krysty kicked off the magnificent cowboy boots she'd found in the cold redoubt only days back. The chiseled silver points of the toes gleamed in the pale moonlight that filtered through the rotting drapes; the moon also brought the silver spread-wing falcons on the sides to a cold sheen. Krysty rolled down the khaki coveralls, sliding her thin panties to her knees.

Entwined, they abandoned themselves to their passion. She sighed once as he entered her, her eyes wide open, looking directly into his face. In the moonglow the hooked nose and narrow cheeks made him look almost like some ferocious bird of prey, hovering above her, about to rend her.

It was an exciting thought.

THEY WERE AWAKENED during the night by a brief, vicious thunderstorm. Only Doc Tanner slept through it. He lay on his back on the floor of the games room, his mouth hanging open, snoring stentoriously, almost drowning out the howling wind and the pounding rain.

All of them were awake, up, and dressed by six in the morning.

"What the fuck is there to eat?" asked Finnegan. "Not more of that doomie shit! I look at it in the fucking bowl, and I can't recall if'n I'm just going to eat it, or if I've already eaten it and barfed it back up."

"I farted all night," said Lori, smiling in her simple way.

"Ryan, me and the girls'll go explore some of the houses we passed. Didn't seem too badly damaged or nothing. Got to be tins and bottles. Anything's better than this stuff."

Seeing that both Lori and Krysty were willing, Ryan nodded his approval. "Sure. Take care. Watch out for any gangs and the baron's sec men. He sounds a mean mother." Ryan consulted the chron on his left wrist. "It's nearly six and a half. Leave at seven. Be back by...by eleven. If you run into trouble, fire three spaced shots, and we'll come running."

JUST BEFORE SEVEN, Ryan found Krysty in the suite where they'd made love the night before. She was pulling the sheets across the rumpled bed.

"Fireblast it, lover! No one's going to complain that we've messed up their room!"

Krysty smiled, shaking her head to tumble the unique hair out of her eyes. "Guess not, Ryan. But Mother Sonja brought her daughter up proper."

Slumping into a well-padded armchair, he watched her gracefully move and his eye was caught by something white beneath the bed. He knelt down, peering at it, giving a sudden, barking laugh.

"What is it?"

At his beckoning finger, she joined him on the floor; saw what made him laugh, and laughed also. It was a neat square card, the printing hardly faded in a hundred years. It read:

"Yes. We have even dusted under here."

AFTER FINN AND THE GIRLS left on their foraging expedition, the others passed the time in their own ways.

Doc browsed among the postcards in the dusty lobby. Picking up one from a pile of leaflets, he took it to Ryan.

"Attractions in West Lowellton and nearby Lafayette," he said. "What a center of activity this must have been before it became a gigantic catafalque."

"What's that?" asked J.B. "Sounds like some old siege weapon."

"A building to house the dead, Mr. Dix. Like this entire continent. Oh, but if I had known then what I know now."

"What's that, Doc?" asked Ryan, sensing a chance to uncover whatever bizarre truth lay behind the man called Doctor Theophilus Tanner.

"Ah, no." Doc wagged his finger. "One day, perhaps, my dear young man. But not now."

"When? You know my past, Doc. How 'bout yours? Come on. It can't be that mysterious."

Doc fumbled with the lion's head atop his ebony sword stick and coughed. "If I were to tell you, Ryan, then I vow you would not believe it."

"I would, Doc. Come on. Now's a good time. Just you, me an' J.B. here."

"I'm sorry. 'We must fight on the darkling plain, swept with confused alarms,' Ryan."

"How's that?"

"A great singer once sang that we must keep our dreams as clean as silver, for this may be the last hurrah. Oh, had he but known the truth of that, so few years later."

"Doc," said Ryan. "Tell us."

The old man ran a hand through his long gray hair, flipped through the leaflet in his hand, then blandly changed the subject of their conversation.

"I see we are but six miles from Interstate 10. Nine miles from the Evangeline Race Track. Once I visited the Kentucky Derby. Such a day, Ryan."

J.B. shook his head and walked away, checking the perimeter of the Holiday Inn. Ryan knew that Doc wouldn't open up until he was good and ready, or until some freak of chance broke the crystal goblet of his secret.

"A mere thirty miles from Longfellow's Evangeline Oak. That would be a national treasure to behold. Probably there are few such left in the Deathlands." Ryan couldn't be bothered to ask what this oak tree was, guessing that any explanation would only increase his confusion.

"Does that say anything about where you can find food hereabouts?"

"No. It tells us that this establishment had kennels, but that dogs were not allowed in the 136 rooms. Also that we are but fifteen miles from the campus of the University of Southwestern Louisiana. Their library would be a trove of interest, Ryan. It is probably intact, if vandals have not destroyed it."

"You can't eat fucking books, Doc."

"There is a witty response to that rational observation, Mr. Cawdor, but it escapes me for the moment."

He opened his hand, allowing the booklet to flutter to the carpet like the last dead leaf from an irradiated tree.

THE MORNING PASSED.

Doc went and curled up in a corner, sleeping like a child.

J.B. vanished for an hour and returned to tell Ryan that he thought it might be possible to start an emergency electrical generator. "Better than the hand-torches. Shall I try?"

"Why not?"

Ryan wandered the deserted corridors, encountering the occasional skeleton, and tried to fathom what it must have been like back before the nuke winter.

In the corner of the motel where the fallen tree had hit, termites had tunneled in, undermining the foundations and making one entire wing dangerous; there were huge cracks in the walls and ceilings. Ryan gazed out through the glass, which had been dulled over the hundred years of the scouring action of the wind. He looked across the oily waters that snaked around the building to the towering live oaks that obscured the nearby road.

The sky was clouding over again. From old books Ryan had learned that in olden times the weather was often the same for days on end. Bright and sunny through the summers, clear and crisply cold through the winter. That was hard to imagine. Ever since his youth at his father's ville of Front Royal back in Virginia, he'd known the weather only to change rapidly, within hours, perhaps a dozen times in a single day. A sunny sky would be soon overtaken with chem clouds, and violent storms would soon erupt, quickly flooding rivers and canals. In parts of the Deathlands, the winds and acid rain could strip the skin from a person in minutes. There might be snow in July in what had been called Arizona, and blistering heat around the sculpted peak of Mount Washton, in the far north, on a January morning.

Here, deep in the South, humidity and a clinging, sweating heat seemed the order on most days. Fortunately, it was cooler inside the motel. Looking out the window, Ryan saw huge insects, wings iridescent, dart over the warm streams. Far to the north, there was the familiar jagged lace of purple lightning. The rumble of thunder never reached him.

Realizing that the double-paned windows might also prevent him from hearing warning shots from Krysty and the others, he moved quickly to the main entrance, pushed open the stiff glass doors and emerged into the warm damp morning. Immediately he heard the harsh sound of swampwag engines. It came from the suburb of West Lowellton, not too far away, where his three companions had gone scavenging.

He spun on his heel, sprinted into the echoing lobby and shouted for J.B. and Doc. Returning to the arched entrance, he flattened himself against the red brick wall.

"What is it? Shots?"

"No. Listen."

"Wags. Those swamp buggies. Real close. Half mile, mebbe less."

Doc Tanner approached briskly, his cane clicking on the stone floor. His Le Mat pistol was tucked into his belt in a piratical manner, and his hat was at a rakish angle.

"I fear I slumbered, and...I can hear engines. It sounds like those—"

"Swampwags, Doc. Yeah."

"Go or stay?" snapped the Armorer tersely.

"Stay," was Ryan's immediate response. "It figures they're mebbe searching for us. With six of us running round, they double their chances of getting us."

"And halves the odds," said J.B.

"Yeah, it does. But we stay."

"Should we not be looking for a defensive position?" asked Doc. "In the event of their coming here?"

It was a difficult decision. Judging by the noise of the engines, there were at least a half dozen of the floundering buggies in the vicinity. That could mean thirty or forty men, maybe more. It didn't much matter if they were Cajuns or the baron's sec guards. A firefight out in the open would have only one ending. But if they waited in the motel, they could cause untold havoc among any attackers, perhaps stand a better chance.

Overlaying the rumbling of the swampwags was the noise of gunfire. It sounded like thin material ripping as the high velocity bullets exploded in short bursts. J.B. looked at Ryan.

"If they got 'em cold, they're chilled by now. If not, they'll make it out of there. Best we can do is wait and see."

"That's how I see it, too."

Doc Tanner pounded the stone wall. "Those young girls! Stouthearted Finnegan! By the three Kennedys, gentlemen! Can we stand here and allow them to be slaughtered?"

"Yeah, Doc, we can," replied J.B.

"Yeah, Doc, we can," repeated Ryan. "We go after them, and we're there with too little, too fucking late. Don't think I don't care about Lori or that fat tub of guts Finnegan. And you know how much I care 'bout Krysty Wroth. But in this life there's only one real certainty. Fuck up and you lose."

"But they may have died."

"We all do, Doc," said J.B. quietly.

GUNFIRE CRACKLED for about two and a half minutes. Then came the unmistakable sharp cracks of a couple of stun grens, then more gunfire for around a half minute.

Then just the swampwags' throaty roar and the shouting of a confusion of orders.

"Best find a place where we can blast 'em if'n they come this way," suggested Ryan.

"You think they might have been . . . killed, Ryan? Or taken?"

"Yeah. Mebbe they'll take what they got and pull out. Mebbe not. All we can do is listen and wait. If they aren't here in an hour, then I guess it means they're not coming. Not yet, anyway."

RYAN CHOSE THE KENNELS. Partly outside, they were connected to the motel and also gave them access to some low scrub that concealed a dry river bed stretching southwest. The three of them went there, waiting and listening, their blasters cocked and ready.

There was no further shooting, and the shouting faded. Soon the buggies could be heard drifting away, seemingly toward the main part of the swamps.

Within half an hour, the natural sounds of insects and the wind in the live oaks had resumed. The clouds that had threatened rain earlier in the morning had broken up, leaving only a veil of high thin mist that filtered the sun into an orange blur.

"Ryan? Let's go see what happened."

"Wait, Doc. Keep quiet and wait. Don't move or speak till I say so."

Time crawled by. Ryan tried to keep his mind off Krysty Wroth. Her face, voice, body. The only woman who'd ever meant more than a fleeting fuck to him. Common sense told him that along with Lori and Finn, she had probably been chilled. The sec men of the baron, with their superior firepower, had sent them all to buy the farm.

Unless . . .

"Unless he wanted prisoners," he muttered to himself, hardly aware he'd spoken at all.

It was a hope. Best he'd got.

IT WAS SEVEN MINUTES past noon, by his wrist-chron. At twelve he and the others had decided to go and find out what had gone down on the edges of West Lowellton.

And to bury their dead.

If Krysty, Lori and Finn had been taken, it wasn't going to do them any good to rush in like a blinded steer charging into the shambles.

It was still seven minutes off noon, by his wrist-chron, when he caught the whisper of stealthy movement somewhere behind them, inside the motel.

He shrank back into the narrow stone kennel, fingering the trigger of the Heckler & Koch. The noise sounded like the plastic end of a blind-pull, tapping on glass in the wind. But the wind had fallen, and the air was still.

The tapping came again. Three, spaced out, then two, closer together. Then more tapping, repeating the same pattern.

"It's Finn," Ryan whispered, warning Doc and the Armorer. "Cover me, J.B., while I make a run for the door. Then Doc, then you."

In thirty seconds they were all safe inside the motel, the security door locked behind them, the steel bolt thrown across it.

"Finn!" called Ryan. "Finnegan, we're here."

They heard footsteps, dragging a little, moving slowly toward them along the corridor, from the direction of the games room and the main entrance.

"That you, Finn?" There was a note of tension in Ryan's voice. "Speak up."

"It's me." The words sounded as if they'd been uttered by someone who had witnessed an unspeakable horror. At Ryan's side, Doc shuddered convulsively. "Yeah, it's me. Only me."

FINNEGAN WAS ONE of the toughest of all of the Trader's longtime blasters. He'd been in more firefights than he'd spent night in beds. He drained most of a quart of Jim Bean, spitting on the floor, wiping the back of a blood-stained hand across his mouth.

"Now?" asked Ryan.

"Sure. Heard 'em coming. Krysty heard 'em first. But there was a lot of the fuckers. Ten or more of those fat-tired mothers. Looked like someone seen us. Told the baron. Sent out the sec men. We holed up in a square of houses. Pretty little places, I guess. If you like fucking pretty. Lot of bones round there. We'd got us some tins and packets of freeze-dries. Real nice. Shrimps and sauce and all."

He took another swig from the bottle. Doc looked as though he was going to interrupt him, then changed his mind and reached out for the bottle to take a pull on it himself. He passed it on to Ryan, who shook his head, and J.B. took a single mouthful, rinsed it around and spat it out.

"I took the front, Krysty on the flank. Put little Lori safe as I could round the back." He glanced at Doc. "Best as I fucking could."

"How many men? What blasters they carry?"

Finn sighed, looking at J.B. through narrowed eyes. It was obvious he was ragged, near exhaustion. "Some of the swampwags were bigger. I guess mebbe fifty or more of the fuckers. Most got old M-16s. Carbines. Some got Browning pistols. Nothing big. Two of the buggies had gren launchers. They were good. Smart fucker in a white suit giving the orders. Had a couple of shots at him. Made him duck. Got mud an' shit all over him.''

"Go on," said Ryan.

"Not much to tell. Too many of 'em. Figure I chilled seven or eight. Not great at street firefighting. Kept moving. They made a rush, got between me and the girls. No way I could get back. No way."

"No way, José," muttered Doc mysteriously.

"Dead or taken?" That was the big question. Would there be burying and revenge, or rescue?

"I figure taken. You hear a couple of stun grens go off?"

"Yeah," said Ryan.

"That was it. I went in the front and out the side of a house, doubled back to kill whatever moved. Fucking weird. Put out a triple burst from the old H&K here." He patted the silenced gray submachine gun on his lap. "All hit him in the throat. Fucking head fell right off. Never seen that before. Clean as a big axe. Rolled round my fucking feet and fucking near tripped me over. That was when I heard the stuns. Ran up into the loft of an old frame house. Looked down. They were loading the girls into one of the wags. I had a go, but it wasn't no good. Near got caught. I tried."

"Sure. Never thought any different, Finn. You couldn't save 'em, then no man could."

Finn nodded, taking another long, bubbling draw at the bottle, draining it dry, then let it drop from his hand with a dull clunk.

The room was silent. Ryan wondered when the sec men might be back, guessing that they'd be reporting to the sinister Baron Tourment with their prizes. They'd interrogate Krysty and Lori to find out all they could about how many there were, about arms, strength. And if the girls didn't cooperate, they'd use stronger measures.

"Time's wasting," said Ryan. "They'll guess we might come in after them. Be ready."

Never for a moment did Ryan, J.B. or Doc consider just walking away. It would have been easy to head for the gateway and shut the door. Move somewhere else. And with the unreliability and random quality of the mat-trans systems, there was no way they'd ever come back to Louisiana. It wasn't like it used to be with the Trader.

Back then, with a small army traveling together, if you got left, then you got left. It was the survival of the mostest that counted. That was the rule, and every man and woman with the warwags knew that. You lived and you died by those rules.

Now there were just the six of them, moving together through an alien land where hostility was the norm and friendship was suspect. That meant you went out on the edge for one of the others.

One of the codes was a man didn't just close his eyes and ride around.

The three men looked at each other in the dusty, dimly lit room, each absorbed with his own private thoughts.

The stranger's voice, coming out of the darkness by the door, made them all jump.

"You 'gainst Baron?"

Ryan answered. "Well, we ain't fucking for him."

"Then we ought talk."

In the dim light, the newcomer's white hair flared like a vivid magnesium torch.

Chapter Sixteen

MEPHISTO WAS THOROUGHLY pissed off with what had happened.

His best ivory suit was ruined. Soaked in salt water, sodden with orange-gray mud, and liberally smeared with gator shit.

Baron Tourment wasn't that concerned for the health and well-being of his sec men. But to have eight corpses to dump into the bayous in a single day couldn't just be overlooked—and there were four more men with serious gunshot wounds to tend.

All that lay on the crimson debit side of the day's accounting. But there was an entry to be made on the credit side.

He had two prisoners, both fairly unhurt. And as a bonus, both were female, and both young and attractive.

They had a few cuts, bruises and scratches, nothing worse. Except that the stun grens always left victims partly deaf for a couple of hours, often caused a little bleeding from the ears and nose and mouth, and frequently burst tiny capillaries in the eyes, making them pink and sore.

Mephisto was in the storage room in the basement of the old Best Western Snowy Egret Inn, only a few miles away from the Holiday Inn in West Lowellton. Half a dozen of his best men were stationed in the corridor, and the guards around the perimeter had been doubled. The Cajuns had spoken of six people: four men and two women. Mephisto had very nearly gotten himself chilled by a fat man in what looked like a dark blue uniform. The zipping burst of lead had missed him only by a fraction of an inch and had actually torn a hole through the padded left shoulder of his suit.

It was rare that his verbal exchanges with Baron Tourment involved any humor. Even grim humor. But after he had made his initial report, the baron had looked at the state of his beloved suit.

"It looks to me, Mephisto, like you got yourself elected out there."

He'd replied, "No, baron, but I surely got nominated real good."

His lips curled into a smile at the memory. The deaths of the men had creased Tourment's heavy brow, but the news that two women were bound and unconscious in the basement had brought a flash of white from his excellent teeth.

Now Mephisto waited for his lord and master to arrive to inspect the prisoners.

The rooms had two tables; the tops were scored and scarred, even scorched in places. The floor was blood-stained. Being questioned by Baron Tourment was not a gentle experience.

One table held the blonde. A tasty dish for the baron. She was very tall—close to six feet was Mephisto's guess. Her long hair was the color of summer corn in the old vids, and her red skirt, topped by a red blouse, showed most of the smooth thighs. Boots in crimson leather reached way over her knees, with high heels that must have added five or six inches to her stature. The boots had tiny silver spurs that made a delicate tinkling sound as the girl struggled with her bonds, moaning and clawing her way back toward consciousness.

"Delicious," whispered the sec boss. But the other woman was even more amazing.

Though an inch or two shorter than the blonde, she was beautifully built, with firm thighs and fine, proud breasts. Mephisto glanced toward the door, wondering whether he dared risk being caught stripping either of the women for his own pleasure; he decided immediately that he didn't dare. This girl wore coveralls streaked with drying blood from when she'd taken the neck out of one of the sec men who tried to close in on her before they used the stun grens. She still had on the most amazing pair of boots that the sec boss had ever set eyes on.

But it was the hair...

Hair that was brighter than any fire. Redder than a chem cloud sunset across the bayous. Long and thick tresses, clotted with mud, tumbled over the girl's shoulders. Mephisto moved closer, extended a hand tentatively to touch the hair.

"Lord Jesus!"

He spun on his heels, his eyes wide with panic, face pale with terror, afraid that his forbidden Christian oath might have been overheard. If it had, then he was a dead man. Although standing up and breathing, he'd be as dead as a pair of gator-skin boots.

But the hair. It had *moved* under his fingers. Moved and tangled itself around his palm with an infinitely gentle slowness.

The silken hairs had actually responded to his touch.

Mephisto again looked over his shoulder and hastily crossed himself, whispering the words "Sweet Jesus."

These strangers weren't ordinary mercies, hired from some frontier ville farther west in Tex-Mex. They weren't drunken outlander pistoleers who'd slit a throat for a handful of jack and a gaudy whore.

Then who were they?

Behind him the door swung silently open on its oiled hinges. Mephisto heard the creaking of the baron's leg-supports. His ears caught the rhythmic chunking of one of the ice-making machines out in the kitchen units beyond.

"Are they awake, Mephisto?"

"Coming around."

"And we know nothing of them?"

"Nothing. Fine clothes and boots."

"Weapons?"

"Yeller hair had only a small pearl-handled PPK. Slut's blaster, .22. Nothing else."

"Red hair?"

"Pistol. But a man's gun. Real stopper. Name on it's Heckler & Koch. Real handsome pistol. Silvered finish. Holds thirteen rounds of nine mil."

"The fat man who clipped you?"

Tourment loomed over the helpless women, his giant shadow stretching across the floor and onto the far wall of the underground chamber. He leaned forward, stumbling, steadying himself on the shoulder of his sec boss; he winced at the frightening power of the pincering hand.

"He . . . he had a sub, firing triple bursts. I guess a big handblaster as well. He was good. Most of the dead were on his sheet. But both of the women also blasted men forever into the dark night."

"The big, big question, Mephisto, is: who are they? And where do they come from? Are they friends come to aid our snow wolf? That most of all. Six was the word from the village?"

"One was shot. Six left."

"Where, then, are the other three?"

"In hiding. I figure that they're with the West Lowell-ton gangs."

Tourment laid a hand on the thigh of Lori Quint, just above the top of her high boots. She stirred but still didn't come round.

"I should have known, Mephisto. When my men didn't return . . . I should have known that this was bad."

"Shall I stay while . . . ?" He hesitated, knowing what slippery ground this was.

"While I talk with these two little peaches? No. Go now. Wait, and I'll call you when I'm done, and you can come back and . . ." The sentence drifted away into a menacing silence. The sec boss left the room, shutting the door firmly behind him, glad of the chance to go to get washed and changed. He knew that Tourment wouldn't be wanting him for some time.

KRYSTY WAS REGAINING CONSCIOUSNESS. From the long years of her mother's training, she knew how to control her body: keeping still, maintaining a steady breathing, keeping her eyelids from fluttering. Giving no clue at all that she was reawakening.

It had been clear almost as soon as the swampwags came thundering in from every quarter that the three of them were in deep trouble. The fight had been short-lived, ending with the gray stun-grens sailing toward them. Now her wrists and ankles were tied, her body strained into a cross. Her hearing and sense of smell were extremely acute, and she lay very still, listening, trying to work out where she was and who was there.

Lori had a distinctive smell, just as Ryan did, and Doc. Krysty knew that she was there, close by. Finn carried the characteristic smell of a fat man who sweated a lot. He wasn't in the room with them, but that didn't mean that he was safe. Maybe the baron's sec men had him somewhere else; maybe he was dead.

There was a strange creaking sound, like metal and leather under stress. And another smell. Sweat. But it was hardly human. A sour, feral scent like an animal's, overlaid with some sort of perfume. Heavy breathing, like that of a ponderous old man laboring to climb steps.

Krysty cautiously opened her eyes. She saw a giant black man who supported his bulk with a metal frame, leaning over the sleeping Lori at a table only a few feet away.

The man wore a fine midnight-blue suit, clearly hand-sewn. A wide leather-and-silver belt around his stomach supported twin holsters, the flaps buttoned down; she couldn't tell if he were carrying blasters. His back was half turned, so all she could see was his short neatly-trimmed curly hair.

The chamber was underground. All her wakening senses told her that; besides, it had no windows. There were white strips of light in the ceiling, and serpentine protrusions of different-colored pipes. The room was about forty feet square, Krysty judged. She closed her eyes again as she suddenly, overwhelmingly, caught the stench of fear that permeated the cellar. There was blood there, as well.

Her heart sank.

PRECISELY AT THE MOMENT that Krysty was recovering from the effects of the stun grens, Ryan Cawdor, J. B. Dix, Doc Tanner and Finnegan were staring at the peculiar apparition that suddenly stood before them, leaning against the frame of the door.

"We ought talk."

Ryan, like the others, had immediately swung his gun toward the stranger, who showed no awareness of his own vulnerability.

He was the strangest person that Ryan had ever seen, even in ten years of traveling through the Deathlands, with its many nuke-ravaged muties.

Around nineteen years old, Ryan guessed. Very short. Barely five three, weighing around 120 pounds. But "thin" wasn't the right word; "lean" was a lot better. The lad looked well-muscled and powerful. He wore pants and a vest of leather and canvas, dyed in irregular patches of brown, gray and green, giving a camouflage effect. Ryan had a keen eye for a fighting man, and he instinctively felt that, despite the boy's slight stature, he was someone to be reckoned with. He held himself well, leaning against the door, his body tensed like a steel spring. Ryan also noticed that the thick material of his clothes glittered here and there, and he guessed there were small pieces of keen-edged metal sewn in. There was no sign of a concealed blaster. But Ryan's intuition told him that the stranger would be a knife-man.

But above all it was the head and face that drew attention.

The face was thin and pinched, like a starved rat's. The nose was narrow, with a crooked scar sliced across it. Another jagged cicatrix seamed the left cheek, tugging the corner of the mouth upward in a crooked smile. The most startling feature of the face was the eyes. Set in caverns of wind-scoured white bone, they were a brilliant glowing red. Like twin rubies set in ivory. The lad's skin was pallid beyond belief, like some creature that had spent its existence beneath a damp stone.

And the hair.

A tumbling mane of purest white, fine as spun silk, dazzling in the dim light.

"You're the snow wolf," said Ryan.

"That question?"

"No."

"Yeah. That's what call me." He seemed more economical with words than even J. B. Dix.

"Spray painter. Run West Lowellton."

"Yeah."

"And you are no friend to Baron Tourment?" asked Doc Tanner.

There was the first sign of a smile. "If'n he was drowning, I'd piss in his face. That answer it?"

"Why are you here? And what's your name?"

"Jak Lauren. I'm here 'cause sec men taken women. See why you're here. See if you help us. We help you."

"My name's Ryan Cawdor, Jak. This is J. B. Dix, Finnegan, and Doc Tanner."

Each of the party got a long blank stare from the penetrating eyes and the briefest of nods.

"Where from, Ryan?"

The answer was a finger, pointed roughly north.

"Going?"

The finger swiveled and pointed roughly south. The gesture got a snatched grin.

"Want help?"

Ryan glanced at the others, seeing the faint gestures of agreement. "Could be, Jak. First we talk some."

"Sure."

LORI AWOKE, already struggling against the tight cords that bound her to the table. She realized immediately that it was useless. The monstrously tall figure of Baron Tourment loomed over her, his right hand between her spread legs.

Before she could speak, the girl saw Krysty staring intently at her from the table at her right.

"Try not to tell him anything," hissed the flame-haired girl.

"No," replied Lori, her voice trembling as she fought against nausea from the hangover of the grens that had scrambled her brains.

Tourment turned to look at Krysty, his voice calm and serene. "Open your mouth again, slut, and I'll rip your tongue out from its roots."

She closed her eyes again, using all her self-control to maintain her breathing and not panic. Maybe Finnegan had escaped, she told herself, and Ryan would find some way of rescuing them.

Krysty swallowed hard at the realization that she had never felt so frightened or so helpless in her entire life.

RYAN AND THE OTHERS listened to the albino boy rattle off his account of life in West Lowellton. How Baron Tourment controlled the whole area, apart from a section of West Lowellton. Some of what he told them they already knew, or had guessed. The baron made his headquarters in another big abandoned motel, not far away. Jak Lauren's gang consisted of about forty fighters. Most of them men, was all he'd give out. He was also careful about his weapons.

"Broke in armory year back. Baron knows what we got. Knows we got enough to stop him looking for firefight. Mebbe beat us, but take knocks that'd cripple him. So it's a standoff."

Ryan was fascinated by the boy's talk about his plans for West Lowellton and Lafayette, once the tyrannical fist of Tourment was removed from the land.

It revealed a spirit that somehow reinforced all the good things he and Krysty had talked about. Why it was important that they didn't give up. Why there was a point in going on. Because there was already a kind of future. All a man could do was strive to make it better. Move on through the land and leave it just a little cleansed.

"Lafayette's got big library. Lotsa books. Old vids. Got the viewers working again. We got big plans, Ryan. Set up windmills to bring power. Got some gasoline, but not enough. Baron don't have that much gas. We can make 'lectrics with wind. There's ways using tides and all. We gotta try."

"Sure," interrupted Doc. "What you say, young fellow, is feasible. Can be done. Only if you got peace."

Jak nodded his head, the veil of fine white hair floating about his narrow face like a drift of snow.

"Sure. That's it. But we can't beat Tourment. Less'n we got help."

"From us?" asked J. B. Dix.

"Yeah. We help get women back. You come in with us and wipe out the giant."

"And set up your windmills?"

The lad shook his head angrily. "That's not all. You outland stupe! Drain the bayous. Bring back good land for crops. Stop the way we live. Moving and blasting and eating and moving on."

Doc Tanner coughed. "Classic piece of optimistic sociological growth, gentlemen. Boy wants his people to have time and freedom to make the quantum leap from being primitive hunter-gatherers to having a settled agrarian culture."

"That's what we want, old man?" asked Jak. "You understand all them words. I read 'em. Taught myself. I heard them words. Yeah, that's what we want."

Ryan sat quietly, listening and thinking. This raggedy kid, not yet twenty, had plans and ideals like nothing he'd heard before—not in all his time in Deathlands. If ever they had found a case, a reason to live, this could be it. He blinked his good eye as he realized that for a moment he'd forgotten about Krysty and Lori, so deeply had he been affected by this broad picture of purging the area of Baron Tourment and his evil.

"You help us with the women, and we'll help you? That the deal?"

"Sure. We got a base in an old vid-house a mile from here."

"Kid?" said Finnegan.

"Yeah?"

"You run this pocket army? You run it?"

"Me."

Finn sucked at his teeth. "How come a kid like you is boss blaster?"

"I killed more sec men than anyone else."

WHEN BARON TOURMENT unzipped his pants and unpeeled his cock, holding it in his right hand, standing near the head of the table where Lori was tied, the girl screamed.

Once.

Krysty winced as the massive man slapped Lori across the face, the blow as sharp as thunder. The girl's cheek reddened, and blood trickled from her nose. Her eyes rolled in their sockets, and she moaned, knocked stupid by the force of the blow.

"Keep it quiet, whore," he said, still showing no anger in his voice. "I'll have every tooth in your jaw knocked out with a hammer. Then I'll fuck you in the mouth so hard you'll feel it in your fucking guts. It'll choke you to death if I don't drown you when I come. So why not be good?"

Krysty started to flex her muscles, ready to draw on her secret power, knowing that she could snap the cords, and maybe even take the towering baron. And after that?

After that, they'd be alive, and he'd maybe lie iced on the floor.

But the baron stepped away, pushing his erection back out of sight. "Later. Right now it's questions and answers. Then it can be pleasure."

Lori still sobbed quietly.

JAK REFUSED FINN'S OFFER of a slug of thick, sweet brandy. "No. Best we go and meet others. Talk battle plan. Not much time. Baron has a way with women that's fast and ugly."

Ryan stood up, stretching, holding the G-12. Jak Lauren glanced at it. "My eyes saw that. Said it wasn't like any normal blaster."

Ryan held it out. "Fifty-shot automatic. Caseless bullets. Carry 'em in pockets." He didn't mention their reserves of ammo back with their clothes and supplies at the gateway. "Four point seven by twenty-one mil. No recoil, and it's real quiet. Single, triple burst or continuous. Night sight. Nice gun."

The boy looked at it enviously. "Ten of those, and we wouldn't need your outland help."

A question came to Ryan. "Jak? How do you know where we come from?"

"Out the swamps. The old secret place. There's stories our fathers told that one day folks'd come from there and help us. Has to be you."

Ryan nodded. "Let's go then. One other question?"

"What?"

"How old are you, Jak?"

"Fourteen last midwinter."

THE BARON SWAYED on the tensioned struts and webbing that enabled him to stand upright on his weak legs. His fingers on the aluminum handle of the door of the cellar, he looked back at the two women, helpless on the tables.

"Later," he said.

Lori's left eye was closed shut, purpled with a deep bruise. Her panties were around her knees, and her thighs were both scratched and bitten. The blouse was torn open, baring her breasts. Her pale skin showed bloody furrows, narrow as coffin nails.

Krysty was untouched.

As Baron Tourment had loomed over her, grinning, his hands working like steel traps, she had looked directly into his eyes. "I have the Earth power, and I swear by Gaia that if you harm me I'll kill you."

He had straightened and left her, staggering clumsily on his steel-bound legs.

"You threaten me!" He was unable to hide his shock, and also, she noticed with a grim satisfaction, unable to conceal the touch of fear.

As he paused on the threshold, he looked venomously at Krysty Wroth. "Later, firehead. You'll beg for death after...after you tell me."

"Tell you what, cripple?"

The taunt failed to rile him. He even managed a laugh that echoed hollowly. "Tell me all I want."

Krysty had a little of the gift of doomseeing, and she realized that Tourment also had something of the gift. Or the curse. He must know about them. That was partly how he'd got to them. But if he had questions, then he had only some of the answers.

"You know nothing," she mocked. "Nothing. You would torture women to pierce your own blindness."

"What?"

"You fear the snow-wolf boy. And now you fear all of us."

"No. I have you and her. Soon I will have the other four."

So Finn had escaped. That in itself was a small victory for Krysty.

"A mouthful of dirt and slime is all you'll have. A gift."

Baron Tourment laughed. "Who makes me this gift, you gaudy slag?"

"The one-eyed man," she replied.

The door of the cellar slammed with such crazed violence that the lock splintered apart as the Baron burst out, away from the girl.

Krysty and Lori were left alone to wait.

Chapter Seventeen

ONCE INSIDE THE DOORS, Doc Tanner closed his eyes, standing still, hands folded in front of him. Like a pilgrim reaching the shrine of a blessed saint, he seemed transfixed with a deep religious awe.

"Lordy," was all he said.

"What is it, Doc?" asked Finnegan.

The old man smiled with an infinite gentleness so unlike his frequent grouchiness that Finn took a startled step backward. "Should have said to me, 'What's up, Doc?' That would have been right. But forgive me, Finn. I know I ramble on."

"Tell us 'bout it, Doc," urged Ryan.

"Something wrong with him?" asked Jak Lauren, who'd been leading the way.

"Nothing's wrong, young man. Nothing. It's just that I can recall things you..." He shook his head, rubbing at his eyes. "Got a speck of dust in 'em. No, it's just walking in this establishment brings back such a flood of memories. Oh, my dear Emily! How she... Give me pause, gentlemen!"

Ryan, J.B. and Finn looked away, embarrassed by the old man's weeping. Jak Lauren and several of his tatterdemalion gang looked on, bewildered.

All around them, the dusty lobby of the Adelphi Cinema, West Lowellton, silently waited.

Doc pulled out his kerchief with the swallow's-eye design and raised it to his beaky nose to snort into it with a
bellow of noise. Sniffing, he looked around at the others.

"Your pardon, gentles all. You cannot possibly imagine how, after all this time... Oh, such an eternity! It still
has that flavor. Warm velvet plush, overlaid with dust. A
little sweat. Darkness and flickering lights. Laughter and
tears. Popcorn and Babe Ruths. And magic. That above
all. I can still savor the magic."

"You remember vid-houses, Doc?" asked Ryan. "There
hasn't been one open in Deathlands that I know of in a
hundred years."

"I heard of one up in Jersey," said Finn. "Then I heard
it was a gaudy porn-place."

The interruption gave Doc a moment to recover. He
looked sideways at Ryan. "Very nearly, my dear Mr.
Cawdor. But shall a butterfly be broken on a wheel or an
old dog taught new tricks? No."

"Time's wasting," interrupted Jak Lauren. "Blood's
flowing and there's dying."

He led the way into the interior of the building. As with
the motel, Ryan was fascinated with this living artifact
from the prenuke past. A pinhole glimpse of the dead
America.

Ryan had noticed a small plaque on the outside wall,
telling the world that "The Adelphi Cinema was opened
officially on September 24, 1989, by Senator John J.
McLaglen."

It was a squat, rectangular building, with a faintly
Spanish or Moorish look to it. Pale fawn stucco had
weathered down to near white. A marquee awning, with
vertical slit windows above it, had once held news of
forthcoming attractions. On one side Ryan had seen a glass
cubicle where he guessed tickets and food and cigarettes

had once been sold. A peeling, faded notice warned, "The Surgeon General has determined that the more you smoke, the faster you die."

There were around thirty of the gang around the building. Ryan had been impressed with Jak's grasp of military security. They had been escorted back from the Holiday Inn, with guards ranged on either side of them, covering a couple of blocks in each direction. They carried a bewildering range of battered blasters, most of them either handguns or old hunting rifles that had their origins in Spain or Czechoslovakia. Pistols came in all shapes and sizes, virtually all showing signs of having been welded or having the bore enlarged. In the first couple of minutes Ryan spotted Colts, Pumas, Pythons, Brownings, Enfields, Webleys and Smith & Wessons, with a few Russian Stechkins and Makarovs. Predictably, because of the comparative ease of making ammo, there were some very old Colt Navys and Walkers.

Lauren's renegade unit was comprised mainly of men and a lesser number of women, between the ages of fifteen and thirty, with some of them older. They all looked scruffy, in patched clothes. And all of them looked as though they never quite got enough to eat.

The one characteristic that they shared, and that set them apart from most of the population of Deathlands—those that weren't muties, that is—was an alertness, a hair-trigger readiness; jumpy and sharp, their eyes were constantly on the watch. They were a bunch of ordinary people doing the best they could. Ryan thought then about what Jak had told them about his hopes and plans, and once again felt how much he wanted to help the snow-haired lad.

But still at the core of his heart was Krysty Wroth. As he followed the slight boy through the swing doors into the auditorium, he was already calculating. How many men? Day or night? Frontal raid or try to sneak in? Whatever happened, there were men and women in the old cinema who would be dead within twenty-four hours. You didn't slice through someone's carotid artery without some of their blood splashing all over you.

"Quiet!" yelled Lauren, holding up a hand for silence. "These them. Got good guns. Help, we help 'em get women away baron. This is big one, friends. We hit hard and mebbe win forever."

There were about a dozen of what Ryan figured were the top hands in the outfit. All had the killer look around the eyes and mouth. It was immediately obvious that they didn't much care for having four strangers suddenly in their midst.

"Why the fuck we need 'em, Jak?" asked a tall woman whose lower jaw was disfigured with a livid scar zagging across her neck.

"You don't need us, lady," replied Ryan. "Way I see it, if you keep alive and Tourment doesn't get no stronger, in about fifty years you might be able to put a real fucking fright up him."

There was a general relaxing of tension, and some of them laughed openly. The woman spat on the floor and turned away in obvious disgust.

"I don't like a bad winner, lady, but I sure hate a fucking sore loser," added Ryan, pushing it deliberately, knowing that this wasn't a place to back off even an inch.

"Let it lay, Zee," snapped Jak. "We voted and they're in."

"These women he got . . . mean a lot to you, brother?" asked the woman, still not beaten.

"Do muties shit in their pants?" he replied, getting a bigger laugh and even a grudging half smile from Zee.

Jak shook his head. "That's enough. There's some serious talk to go down. We know his place. Even got plans from city files. What we didn't have was blasters and mercies. Now we got 'em."

Finnegan didn't much like that. "Not fucking mercies, kid. We go where we want and chill who we *want* to chill. You need us more'n we need you, kid."

Suddenly there was a flicker of light, and Jak was in a classic knife-fighter's crouch in front of Finn, the blade dancing from hand to hand, faster than the eye could follow.

"Don't call me kid, fatso."

Ryan knew better than to try and step into a scene like this. Finn, despite his chubby, amiable exterior, was a bloody-handed killer and was quite capable of drawing on the boy and spreading him all over the far wall. If that happened, things would get hot.

"Don't call me fatso, kid."

Jak was balanced on his toes like a wind-blown feather, watching Finnegan, red eyes locked on the older man's face. "You got balls, fatso."

"Kids like you, they got lotsa gall but no fucking sand. I could drop you before you could use the knife, kid."

Lauren grinned wolfishly. "Sure you could. You're here 'cause you're good, fatso. Heard you chilled some sec men this morn. You draw, you mebbe hit me, but you're on your fucking back looking up at sky, wondering why you wanted to be a prick."

Ryan could see a real risk, after the first combustible moment, that they might talk each other into killing each other.

"That's it," Ryan said, feeling the ripple of disappointment around him. For a kid of fourteen, Jak Lauren had some serious respect from his people. They really thought he could take Finn.

Maybe he could. Ryan wasn't going to find out.

"It's gone noon," he said, showing his chron around. The place was badly lit, with a row of flickering lamps, in glass bowls with swimming fish engraved on them. At one end of the sloping room was a massive maroon curtain with golden tassels draped across it. From what he recollected, Ryan guessed that there would be a screen behind it.

"Sure has. You're right, Ryan." The slim knife disappeared as quickly as it had sprung to his hand. Though Ryan was watching him intently, he hadn't seen where the boy had hidden it.

"We talk about how we do this?" asked J.B., moving casually against the right-hand wall. It was second nature for the Armorer to seek out a position where he had his back against something solid.

Jak half bowed to him. "Sure. Talk plan. Can't go until after dark. They're too ready. Tourment's no fool. Before talk, we'll show something to you. Rare. From before the quick sick came."

"Food?" asked Finnegan, omitting the "kid" this time.

"Sure. Always ready. Talk. Then go in and get the prisoners."

Ryan spotted something in the use of the word. Something that meant more than just Lori and Krysty.

"How many prisoners, Jak?" he asked.

"Three."

"Three?"

"Yeah. Night 'fore last. Mephisto sec men snatch squad got lucky. Picked up my father. This time tomorrow Tourment'll have killed them all."

"Then let's get to it," suggested Ryan.

The boy nodded, solemn-faced, the cascading white hair framing his skull like a silver halo.

Chapter Eighteen

KRYSTY WROTH WAS ANGRY with herself. Angry that she'd let her emotions govern her good sense. Mother Sonja's often repeated motto, Strive for Life, had been momentarily forgotten.

It was scant consolation that Baron Tourment's evening roll call would be two sec men short.

THEY'D COME IN a couple of minutes after the giant ville chief had lumbered clumsily out. They were both small, with sallow complexions, looking as though they'd been standing out in the rain for too long. When they spoke, she heard the nasal tones of the bayous and guessed they came from Cajun stock. The one with a small mustache looked around thirty; the other, with a three-day stubble on his chin was nearer twenty. Both men carried greased M-16 blasters.

There hadn't been time for Krysty to do more than hiss a warning to the sobbing Lori to try to hold out and tell the baron nothing. Then the sec men were walking cockily to stand between them.

"Yellow hair or red?" one said.

"Yellow."

"Why?"

"Already got her snatch warm and waiting. Red's got hers sewn up in her pants. Baron might guess if'n we cut her naked."

The one with the mustache, called Neal, ran a hand under Lori's disarranged skirt, giggling as she wriggled at the touch. "Warm and wet, Alain. And yellow as a possum's guts."

Krysty had tried. "You do that one more time, you sack of cancerous pus, and I'll snake on you to the fucking baron."

"He don't care," said Alain, rubbing a hand thoughtfully over his rough chin. "Long as we don't do no mortal hurt. He don't give a fuck."

"Why not do yellow first? Then fuck red in the mouth, and see how she likes it."

"I'd bite it off, if it's big enough to get my teeth in."

Both guards laughed. "First off, Alain here'd push the muzzle of his old blaster half a foot up your fucking nose, bitch. You even set your fucking teeth in me, and they'll be wiping your fucking brains off the ceiling."

It crossed Krysty's mind to let them. Lie there and blank her mind clear of what was happening to her. She could do it. She'd done it before, back in Mocsin with the sec boss there. Kurt Strasser. Before she'd met Ryan Cawdor.

But there was Lori.

The girl, despite her bizarre upbringing, had an oddly unflawed innocence. If Krysty lay there and allowed these two brutish pigs to do what they wanted, she knew they wouldn't stop at a simple fucking. That would just set them on other ways of humiliating and hurting them both.

"Gaia, help me," she whispered, closing her eyes, trying to relax and draw on the immense power of the Earth Mother. Part of Krysty's mind told her this would be futile. But she recalled what Ryan had said about leaving a place a tad cleaner than when you came to it. That she would do.

The cords that bound her ankles and wrists were made of waxed whipcord, tied so tightly that there was blood seeping from under the nails of her fingers and toes, burst from the swollen flesh. The pain had been easy to control, but she worried that she might not be able to function well in a fight.

"Help me, help me, help me," she repeated, drawing on the strength in the way that her dead mother had taught her, way back in Harmony.

"Be real good fucking this. Better'n that 'fayette slut with boils on her tits," sniggered Neal.

"Yeah."

"Me first."

"Sure. Like my bun well buttered," cackled the younger man.

Drool hung from the corner of Alain's narrow mouth. He put his head back and laughed again, and Krysty saw the way the cords of his neck stood out like strips of thin iron.

The girl took a deep breath, her mind wandering back unbidden to a fine summer's day in Harmony. She would have been around sixteen years old then and filled with devilment. Carl Lanning, a fresh-cheeked boy who would pluck her cherry, was the son of the blacksmith, Herb. The lad had teased Krysty about her powers, challenging her to show him. The forge had been deserted; the fires had slumbered with a dull red glow, and the hammers were ranged on the walls. She'd picked up a freshly hammered iron shoe, the holes rough-edged and silver. "Go, Krysty," Carl had encouraged her, watching. He'd fallen silent, unbelieving as she'd gripped the horseshoe, putting a surge of incredible strength into her hands and wrists. She twisted it as though it was saltwater taffy, then dropped it to the floor of the forge where it rang like a bell.

Peter Maritza and Uncle Tyas McNann had learned of her trick, taken her into the smoke-scented parlor and sat her beneath the framed picture of a racehorse called Sky-rocket. They had taken her to task for abusing her unique gift, warning her she must use it sparingly and wisely. "Only when you must, girl," Peter had said.

Now, watching the two men prepare for their corrupt sexual pleasures with the helpless Lori, Krysty's lips moved.

"Now I must, Uncle."

Both men had their backs to her, fumbling with their trousers, their blasters laid on the stone by their feet.

"Gaia, help me," whispered Krysty, feeling her energy increasing until it seemed as though her body might burst with it.

The cord around her right wrist snapped with a sharp sound, like a metal spring failing. The left followed only a moment later. She began to sit up, the bindings breaking together as she flexed both legs.

"What the fuck!" said Neal, looking around. Alain hopped off balance, his eyes wide as saucers in his pinched face.

Even Lori, lying still, opened her eyes at the crack of the cords disintegrating, unable to believe what she saw.

Gripping the table's edge with both hands, Krysty pushed herself off, aiming her feet toward Neal's face; the tapered heels of her boots sledgehammered toward his mouth.

"You..." he began, the word rammed back into his throat as Krysty's boots struck.

The power of her attack was utterly devastating.

The silver-patterned leather heels hit the sec guard plumb in the center of his gaping mouth; the blow tore his lip into tatters of bloody flesh, splintering his few remaining teeth into shards of bone. His lower jaw cracked like a dry twig, dislocated, the awesome force actually ripping it from its socket so it flapped loose as he staggered backward. He was momentarily lifted clear off his feet.

But the effect of the kick didn't stop there. Krysty pushed off like a gymnast, her boots crushing Neal's nose, destroying both cheekbones, pulping the left eye to watery jelly. Fragments of bone were driven upward through the soft palate into the lower part of the brain, beginning the irrevocable process of death.

Alain was still teetering, his trousers falling to his ankles and revealing a shrinking penis and sagging balls. Had his reflexes been honed, there was a split-second when he might have gone for his blaster and shot Krysty, while she was still recovering her balance, nearly slipping in Neal's spouting blood. But his hands went in panic to his groin as his eyes searched for a way out. His mouth opened with the beginnings of a request for mercy.

"Lady..." he began.

"I don't have the time," she hissed, swinging around, pivoting on the right foot, the left lashing out toward his abdomen.

This time it was the toe that did the damage. The craftsman who had worked away, chiseling silver into points to ornament the western boots, could never have dreamed a hundred years ago how lethal those elongated tips could be.

Though Alain tried to fend off the kick with his hands, he might as well have tried to throttle a cyclone. Three fingers were crushed and broken, the thumb on the right hand agonizingly dislocated. The foot powered on, puncturing his scrotal sac, transforming his testicles to crimson rags of gristle, nearly severing his penis. With the cracking of bone, the entire pelvic girdle opened up. The guard staggered back, banging against the table, his face as white as parchment, a mask of silent pain. Falling to his knees, he collapsed, blood fountaining from his ruined groin, legs kicking and jerking spasmodically under the colossal shock.

Turning from the dying men, Krysty effortlessly snapped the cords at Lori's wrists and ankles.

"How did you kill them like that?" stammered the blond girl, instinctively hoisting her panties back to their rightful position.

"I guess it's 'cause I'm a fucking mutie, girl."

"Can you open door?"

Krysty shook her head, feeling the familiar wave of weariness touching her temples. Using the powers always left her drained and enfeebled. It was the price that her mother had warned her that she must pay.

"Too tired. Must sit down, or I'll..." At her feet, the body of the younger sec guard finally ceased thrashing. Blood oozed silently across the floor. There was no sound from beyond the bolted door to indicate that anyone had heard anything from inside.

Lori swung her long legs elegantly over the side of the table and rose. She put her arms around Krysty, hugging her tightly and feeling how the red-haired girl was trembling.

"Be fine," she said. "Them fuckers dead. Got what wanted. Don't cry, Krysty. Be fine. I won't talk. Nor you. Even if that giant mutie mongrel kills us. One day Doc and Ryan and J.B. an' Finn'll do for him. Beg pardon, but it's fucking true."

KRYSTY WROTH WAS STILL ANGRY with herself. If she'd waited, then a better chance might have come. A chance to chill the baron himself and go out on that. Or even a glimmer of a break. Now she'd have to invent a story that the men had freed her and that she'd been lucky enough to take them by surprise. It would be some hours before her strength would return.

Her acute hearing caught the noise of Tourment's clumsy braces creaking outside; then the bolt grated back. She held tightly on to Lori's hand to keep herself from trembling.

Chapter Nineteen

THE LIGHT FROM THE MOVIE PROJECTOR lanced through the humid darkness of the Adelphi Cinema, West Lowellton, centering on the glittering screen. Jak Lauren sat in the middle of a row of plush seats, with his top fighters in the rows around him. Ryan sat next to the lad, with Doc on one side, and J.B. and Finn a few seats down on the other side.

The albino had insisted they watch this, telling them it would last only about ten minutes. "It's all we got left. We watch special times. Like now. Kind of gives heart. How it was 'fore the winters came."

Though he was desperate to get on with the task of saving the women, Ryan knew that there was little point in rushing in like headless muties. The baron wouldn't have risen to his pomp and power if he were a stupe. That meant caution. He'd also captured Jak's father, so it would take a good plan to beat him.

Doc was astounded to find that some of the vid-house's equipment was still in working order. Jak showed them a booklet, dated January 2001, listing the attractions on at the Adelphi. They'd been in the middle of a retrospective season, with movies from the 1970s and 1980s. And even earlier. Names that meant nothing to Ryan or the others, but that brought a sparkle of enthusiasm to the rheumy eyes of Doc Tanner.

"John Ford and Sam Peckinpah," he exclaimed. "They were showing *The Wild Bunch* and *Ride the High Country*. With *She Wore a Yellow Ribbon* and *The Last Hurrah* the same day. That was Clint's final movie, 'fore he took up with all that politicking."

"We got bit of one left. *Culpepper Cattle Company*. Heard of it, wrinkly?"

Doc ignored the insulting nickname from the snow-haired lad. "Heard of it, sonny! By the three Kennedys! You'll ask me whether I've heard of…of, what's his name? Damn, it's left me."

"All else was gone. But in top shelf of closet was single round tin, and in it was piece of vid. Means a lot, Ryan."

So they sat and watched it. Doc was the only one there who knew what it was about, but his memory was sadly selective and imperfect. All he could recall, to the dumb fascination of Lauren and his gang, was that it was about a lad leaving home on a cattle drive and how he grew up and became a man. That a local land baron—the word aroused a mutter of hushed whispering—was going to drive some settlers off. There were some gunmen in it, and they finally came to the aid of the boy and the settlers.

It began with a scratching sound and much jerkiness, but it gradually improved. The volume was weak, coming through a single speaker, wired to the side of the screen. But it was enough. Ryan watched the flickering images with a naive wonderment. He was in a movie house, watching a film!

There were some wagons being dragged into a line by the gunmen. The settlers, kneeling in prayer, were singing "Amazing Grace." In the distance was the unmistakable outline of the local baron and his own team of blasters.

"Comes back to me," whispered Doc, along the row. "Names and the faces. Gary Grimes is the kid. That's

Geoffrey Lewis with the kind of squint. Bo Hopkins, giggling there, with the smooth face. Man with long hair...
don't know. Could have maybe been Wayne Sutherlin. He
was in it. The other man's an actor called Luke Askew.
One of my favorites. What happened to..."

"Shut up, Doc," hissed J.B.

"Hell of a firefight," sighed Finn. "Way to fucking go."

At first, the defenders gunned down several of the hired
pistoleers. But there were too many of them, and one by
one the defenders were picked off. Crimson sprayed as
they died in slow-motion. Finally it was the kid and the old
man who led the attack. The boy had a blaster nearly as big
as he was, but he froze and was about to get himself
chilled. Then the one whom Doc had said was called Luke
Askew rose—from the dead, it seemed—and stabbed the
attacker, the two men falling together, locked in each other's arms.

Ryan felt the short hairs rising on the back of his neck
as the single, pure voice of a woman came swelling with the
old hymn again. The skinny preacher with crazed cowardly eyes told the boy they wouldn't stay.

Told him that the land they'd wanted—which the men
had died for—was not meant for them. It was tainted with
blood, and they were moving on. In the end the kid drew
on the man in black, insisting that they bury his friends
before they moved on, and grudgingly the settlers agreed.
At the last, with the lines of "Amazing Grace" still ringing out, the boy dropped his blaster beside the graves and
rode away.

"Though we are dead, ten thousand years," sang the
woman; and all around the vid-house, Lauren's gang sang.
Several people were weeping at the beauty and power of
the film, well over a century from the past.

Ryan felt a prickling behind his own eyes.

"Son of a fucking bitch, ain't it," said a grizzled man behind him. "Always kind of lifts me. Makes me want to get out and ice the baron on my fucking ownsome."

The lights returned, making everyone blink. Ryan glanced around him, seeing the ragged army he was about to help. And he saw why the short piece of film was so important to Jak Lauren's people.

The battle appeared hopeless, against overwhelming odds. Yet the faded images, with the crackling sound track, typified the desperate lonely, struggles that were taking place all over Deathlands. Ryan was understanding it more and more. It was a natural process. Groups arose, some promoting only themselves, others trying to clean up the world. As he saw it, it wasn't enough just to worry about your own survival. Sometimes you had to stand up and fight for things you believed in.

It was that courage that Ryan saw in the ratlike teenager and his raggled army.

"Time we talked."

"Sure. You four, and me and my five top chillers. That set with you?"

"Yeah. Want to know all 'bout the Baron Tourment. His ville. Where he lives. Where he'll keep prisoners. Sec men. Blasters. All that."

"And more," said J.B. "We know all that, we can get the plans made."

Ryan stood up, stretching. "Some food and drink. Need to be ready by dark."

Jak Lauren peeled back his lips in an icy grin. "Be dark in around five hours. Time for real good plan. We were lost, now we're found."

"Mebbe," said Ryan.

Chapter Twenty

THE CELLAR DOOR OF the Best Western Snowy Egret inched open, then stopped. It opened a finger's-breadth more, then stopped again. The two women heard the deep resonant voice of Baron Tourment laughing quietly.

"Very good. Oh, very good."

Krysty wondered for an insane moment whether she could possibly take out the chieftain of Lafayette, realizing immediately that the butchering of the two guards had left her too drained even to wrestle a kitten.

"I am impressed, ladies. Fucking impressed. Oh, yes, I am."

Inside the room, it was almost silent. Just the hypnotic buzzing of a blowfly, conjured from nowhere to feast on the banquet of blood that poured from the mouth of the one sec man, the groin of the other. The baron's voice resonated from outside the room.

"Alain and Neal. Two of the best, if that roguish Mephisto is to be believed. Are you to be believed, Mephisto? Eh?"

"They were good. You sure they're chilled?"

"Can't you taste their souls fleeing from their useless carcasses? Such a sour, yet sweet flavor. No, they are dead, are they not, sluts?"

"Come an' find out, cripple," taunted Krysty.

"Good." Baron Tourment sounded as if he were genuinely amused. "Two more on the account."

At last he appeared, his head bent to avoid the low ceiling, the white-suited sec boss at his elbow. Both men were holding M-16s. The baron's weapon was plated with gold, its stock studded with semiprecious stones. Mephisto's rifle was comparatively plain and uncluttered, except for the head of a red-eyed cockerel, done in opals and rubies.

Krysty and Lori, licking their dry lips, stood beside the tables.

"How did they chill 'em?" asked Mephisto.

Tourment shook his head. "Don't matter. It's the redhead. She's got some real power. They got careless. They got dead. End of that story."

He lifted the barrel of his blaster, covering both women. His eyes searched Krysty's, until she felt he was somehow trying to suck her soul from her body.

"Go fuck a dead shark," she said, trying to provoke him again.

"Perhaps I shall allow you that pleasure, girl," he replied. "Or, perhaps a live gator. See how your power works on that. But I feel your power is exhausted."

Krysty knew she was right: the massive baron was a doomie. But he wasn't able to see what she was thinking. Her mind was locked too tight for him to penetrate. She said nothing, staring him out.

"We should find out where they are," interrupted Mephisto. "Get after 'em 'fore dark. If'n we wait, they could be anywhere."

Tourment sighed. "Such haste, my dear sec boss. If they are in league with the snow wolf, they will have gone to his skulking place in the vid-palace."

"Said we should have blown that apart."

"Only last week one of our swampwags was taken by the little bastard. The time is not ready yet." There was a snap in his voice that made Mephisto hastily step back.

Krysty could feel herself strengthening. She'd expended much more energy in destroying enemies far more powerful than the two sec men in the past, and hence her recovery would be quicker. Lori, at her side, stood straight and tall. Only the faintest trembling told Krysty how tense the young girl was.

"Enough of this. Come with us, and I'll show you what happens to anyone standing against the anger of Baron Tourment, high priest of Lafayette, lord of Mardy, nightstalker and spirit-raiser."

"And all round shit," completed Krysty, relishing his hesitant stumbling toward her on the creaking frames. She saw the finger whiten on the trigger of the pretty M-16.

"Come," he said, gesturing with the gun. "See how the kin of the snow wolf, your friend, is treated."

Outside, there were a dozen armed sec men waiting to escort them through the echoing basement corridors of the large motel.

His head bent to avoid some of the painted metal pipes that festooned the ceilings, the baron led the way toward steep iron stairs. He negotiated them slowly and with obvious difficulty, leaning on Mephisto to steady himself. Krysty whistled tunelessly between her teeth at the delay.

JAK LAUREN STALKED around the auditorium, the tiny pieces of metal sewn into his clothes glinting in the overhead lamp so that at times he seemed to be wearing a suit of dancing lights. They'd been talking for an hour, not even stopping when bowls of hot stew were brought in from the kitchen of a nearby house.

The meat was a light pinkish-gray, tough and salty, in a broth with fresh vegetables. Finn devoured his and asked for more. Only when he'd nearly finished the second helping did he ask what it was.

The woman with the scar across her neck grinned, but no smile could ever light up her stony eyes. "What's your guess, Finnegan?"

"Some kind of bird. Or mebbe horse."

"Nope. It's gator meat. Killed this morning, so it's real fresh."

If she'd expected disgust from the fat gunman, she was disappointed. Finn laughed and held out the chipped dish for a third helping. "Day or so back one of them fuckers tried to fucking eat me, lady. Nice to know I'm getting my own back."

The albino joined in the laughter, clapping his approval of Finn's response. "Same way chill baron and all," he said.

"Not unless we get the details of this plan worked out," called Ryan. "We got a lot of pieces, and none of them stick together. You showed us the plan of the Best Western and told us how many men and what kind of weapons they got."

"And you showed us what you got," added J.B. "You sure you told us all?"

Jak stopped pacing and turned toward the slight figure of the Armorer. "Sure. Blasters. Ammo. Grens. Some high-ex but not much. Two flamers we captured when we got the swampwag last week."

"There's that gas-jelly, Jak," called a balding man with a drooping mustache.

"What?" snapped J.B. "How's that?"

"Yeah. Year or more back, three of us, one was Pa, near got jumped by sec men up near old highway. Hid in brush and found a war wag from before the winters. Army. Two smaller wags with it. Few blasters, fucked by water and mud. But in back was drums this gas-jelly.''

"How many? How big?" asked J.B., glancing across at Ryan, who was searching his memory for a long-forgotten piece of information.

"Twenty. All 'bout this high," he said, holding his hand about four feet from the floor. "Opened one. Sticky. Fuck, was it sticky! Tried dipping a hunk of wood in it, and it burned like gas. But we couldn't see no use for it.''

"Jelly that burns like gas," said J.B., turning to Ryan with a blissful smile. It was the happiest that Ryan had seen him in months. "Know what it is, Ryan?"

But it was Doc who replied. "I know, Mr. Dix."

"What?"

"It's napalm."

BARON TOURMENT led them onto a low concrete dock that jutted into an expanse of murky water. It faced west, toward a red sun that was sliding nearer the horizon, sinking behind bayous lined with stunted trees, their roots tangling above the brown slime.

The stone dock was mud-smeared, chipped and broken where it came in contact with the water. It stood about three feet above the swamp, on pilings of rusted iron. Several wide-bottomed metal canoes were tied to the pier. Across the water Krysty could make out the silhouette of a building, open on two sides, a stone table at its center. Her sight was exceedingly sharp, and she could see metal rings at each corner of the table and the thick stains that ran down from the top.

Sec guards ranged around them as they stood there in the cooling late afternoon, with the baron and Mephisto at their head.

"Now for you to meet an old friend, ladies. The father of your leader."

Krysty felt Lori stiffen, the word "Ryan" on her lips, and nudged her into silence.

"Our leader?" she said.

"Jak Lauren, slut. The white wolf himself. We hold the coward's own father." Raising his voice and clapping his hands together, he ordered, "Bring him here. And the pitch."

The air filled with the tang of hot tar as four sec men struggled with an iron caldron that bubbled and smoked. Two others brought out a prisoner cuffed between them. He was short and frail, wearing only rags of cotton, with a pair of rubber sandals flapping on his feet.

"Father Lauren," said the baron. "Have you three met before?"

The man, who looked to be close to Doc's age, ignored the baron, staring stubbornly at his own feet. Lori shook her head and looked away. Krysty was puzzled. It seemed as though Tourment genuinely thought they knew each other. If it wasn't a trick, then what did he think was going on? She knew the leader of the other gang in West Lowellton, the snow wolf, was the bitter enemy of the baron. If he was called Jak Lauren, then this old man was his father. Why had the baron brought him out? What was he trying to prove?

There wasn't long to wait. Tourment gestured for Mephisto to approach. The sec boss sidled to the front of the group and drew a long, slim-bladed stiletto from a sheath at the back of his belt. He grinned as he showed it to the women.

"His son will be angry. I don't care," said Tourment. "I don't fear him. Or any of you. Even the man with one eye."

At a sign from his chief, one of the sec men stooped and picked up a paddle from the nearest canoe. He slapped it a few times on the water, the noise echoing across the lagoon until it faded. Tourment waved his hand again, and the man stopped.

"I decided this would be best. It will show you and the others what happens to those who stand against me, show the pack in Lowellton what awaits them. And I shall take some fucking delight in it. Start, dear Mephisto."

The sec boss moved in front of the old man, weaving the knife in his fingers. He glanced around to make sure the pitcher of hot tar was ready and then bowed to the two women.

"Watch," he whispered to them.

J.B. REMOVED HIS FEDORA and banged it against the back of one of the seats, raising a cloud of dust. "We're wasting fucking time," he said, his voice grim. "You're more like damned kids than men who want to fight." He looked around the old cinema at the faces of the gang, mocking them with obvious anger. "We got to go first. We got to have the best blasters. We got to drive the swampwag. We got to... mother-fucking stupes." He rubbed his eyes, showing his fatigue.

"He's right," said Ryan. "It's close to dark. We got us a good plan. One that might just work. And all we've done for the last hour is pick our asses and chew round and round and waste time."

Jak Lauren stood up and moved to join Ryan. "This is our ville, Ryan. Our enemy. Our battle."

"Then fucking fight it on your fucking own," spat Finnegan, shaking his head in disgust. "You're like fucking kids at a fucking game. It's my ball, so you can't fucking play."

There was a burst of chattering and shouting angrily directed at Finn. But Ryan shouted louder than anyone and even considered firing a triple burst into the star-embossed ceiling.

"This is it," he called, when the noise died a little. "Our way or not at all. It's what we do and we do well. It's not up for argument. Get it?"

Lauren nodded. "Sure. Guess it's the only way. Your way."

"Sure. Now we can talk details. Just you and us and six of your best."

The kid sucked on his teeth. In that unguarded moment Ryan glimpsed the child of fourteen living inside the body of the trained killer. "Yeah. Not all of us are good with blasters. You see, Ryan, we all read an' write. Pa made sure of that. Years ago. And his Pa. There's men and women here with all the skills. They know 'lectrics, power, water, farming, crops, land . . . how to do all that. They all got a real skill."

"What's your skill, young fellow?" asked Doc Tanner.

The snow wolf didn't hesitate. "I'm the best at butchering men," he said.

LORI WAS DOUBLED OVER on her knees, her skirt riding up to reveal her buttocks and attracting lustful glances from many of the sec men. She was vomiting copiously, threads of yellowish vomit dangling from her mouth, splattering on the concrete. Krysty stood close to her, watching what Mephisto was doing, determined not to give way and show any weakness.

First he had sliced off all the old man's fingers, one by one, first holding the wrist on one hand, then the other, to gain enough purchase to force the blade through the knuckle joints. Blood spurted, and the old man struggled and cried out, but the sec men were too strong for him. That was when Krysty saw the reason for the caldron of smoking pitch.

At a nod from Mephisto, the guards thrust their prisoner's hands into the scalding, sticky liquid. Instantly there came the hiss of steam and the smell of scorched flesh. Lauren's body stiffened, then went limp. Tar coated his wrists, sealing off the leaking stumps of his fingers so he didn't bleed to death.

"Bring him round. I want him conscious for all of this," said Baron Tourment quietly.

The nearest sec man slapped the old man hard across the face. A ringing round-arm blow that jerked the skull on the thin neck. His cheeks swollen and bruised, Lauren jerked back to awareness. He started to moan; Tourment gripped him by the jaw.

"Listen to me. This is for your son and all his stupe killing. He'll hear of this and know what awaits him." He let go and looked at Krysty Wroth. "And this waits for you after our talk."

She ignored him.

Tourment extended a hand to Mephisto, who dropped the severed fingers of their captive into the huge pale palm. Ten pieces of bloodless meat, jointed, with chipped nails tipping them. The baron smiled and walked to the edge of the dock, scattering the fingers on the surface of the water with a joyous gesture of release.

"First course, my pets," he called.

Krysty noticed that the front of the man's elegant breeches was swollen with a truly frightening erection; she looked away. Mephisto, at a signal from the baron, picked up a large cleaver and ran a thumb along the edge, like a lover caressing his mistress's body.

Fifty yards out into the Atchafalaya Swamp, there was a rippling of water. Then a long spade-shaped head protruded, eyes glittering under ridges of bone, the ferocious snout raised to the evening air.

"DO WE ALL AGREE?" asked Ryan Cawdor, facing the entire West Lowellton street gang.

Nobody spoke: they all watched him with a sullen, grudging respect. "Well," said Doc Tanner. "They don't disagree, Ryan."

"We go midnight," said Jak Lauren. "Plan sounds good to me."

"Best we got," Ryan said. "It works, and you get to drain the swamps and build your windmills around dawn tomorrow."

"It don't work, and we get to dig us some graves," replied the boy, his wolfish eyes glittering.

LORI SHOOK as though she was suffering from some dreadful ague. She held her head in her hands, her palms pressed hard against her ears to try to shut out the hideous mewing cries of the tortured old man. Krysty, her face set like marble, determined not to show the gloating baron and his sniggering sec boss any weakness, watched without flinching. She spoke only once.

"I'll never forget this. And I'll be there when the score is settled with you and your sick, stinking filth. I swear it by Gaia."

They laughed.

By then Father Lauren was close to death. Mephisto had hacked away at both feet, sawing them off at the ankles, again using the hot tar to curtail the bleeding and cauterize the wounds

Out in the lagoon, the massive cayman waited patiently for each severed limb and bit of flesh. Its jaws, gaping wide enough to swallow a swampwag wheel, snapped at each white foot, gulped it down with no discernible effort or pleasure. Then the creature disappeared into the murk until only its eyes broke the scummy surface.

"Hands next, baron?" asked the sec boss, looking down in irritation at some specks of blood that dirtied his nice clean suit.

"Maybe his cock, Mephisto. Or his ears. Maybe his lips or nose. So many choices. Yes. Ears and then nose. No, wait. Be difficult to use the pitch on his face. That can come later. Hands next and then cock."

Krysty judged that merciful Death finally spread its mantle over the old man at about the moment when the kneeling sec boss began to hew clumsily at his remaining wrist with the cleaver. The blood, no longer spurting vigorously from the stumps, simply oozed sluggishly across the stained concrete.

"He's gone," said Mephisto, disappointed.

"Throw his hands to our pet?"

"What about the rest of the fucker?"

"Carry on with cock and then do his face. There's the big flagpole in front of the motel. Haul what's left up there with a notice about what happens to enemies of Baron Tourment. Leave it to the crows."

The warm humid Louisiana evening was closing in around them as the girls were driven back to the cellar at gunpoint. Once more, the baron bound them to the tables. Leaving them, he said, "Later, sluts. We can talk later."

RYAN CAWDOR WAS RESTLESSLY pacing around the lobby of the Adelphi Cinema, watching darkness descend on the neighborhood. At Jak Lauren's orders, most of his small army was resting or asleep, with a skeleton crew on sentry patrol. Doc had also fallen asleep, after having entreated Ryan to wake him should there be any news or action. Finnegan had found his way into the kitchen and was stoking up his boilers, ready for the firefight to come.

J.B. joined Ryan, and the two old friends walked together. "Not long," he said.

"No. I wish we could recce some around the baron's ville."

"Why not?" asked the Armorer.

"Yeah," said Ryan. "Why not? I'll check with the kid and get us a map of the region. They've got good ones. Seen 'em. Just you and me, J.B., like old times. What d'you say?"

J.B. rubbed his fingers contemplatively over the darkening stubble on his chin. Then he grinned. "Yeah," he said.

Chapter Twenty-One

JAK LAUREN WASN'T keen on their going out so soon before the attack. His hair flowed about his shoulders as he gesticulated, waving his hands.

"What the fuck you want to do this? We got maps. You know where the ville is. We'll be with you. Fucking stay here."

Ryan shook his head. "No. If'n you fear us going to 'tray you to Tourment, we're leaving Finn and Doc here with you. If we go to fight with you, we want to see what we can first. Be back in good time. It's only seven now. Our plans are to leave here at eleven, so we'll be back by then, three hours from now. I want to go and look at what we're tackling."

"Too late to change plans," said the boy, almost reproachfully.

"Why change 'em?" asked J.B. "Fine as they are. Just fine."

RYAN AND J.B. each carried one of the hand-torches from the Holiday Inn on their belts, as well as their usual armaments. The weather was calm, the air still. Jak opened the maps one more time, showing them where and where not to walk. He pointed out swamps that had risen over old highways or trails that were patrolled by the Baron's sec men. Both men listened carefully, committing the information to memory.

"Come back safe," said the boy, patting them both on the shoulder as they left the lobby of the old vid-house. Ryan half grinned, still finding it hard to believe that this war-leader was a lad of just fourteen.

IN SOME WAYS the recce was abortive. They found their way along the abandoned suburban streets, past the entrance to a massive shopping mall, taking the route that the albino kid had shown them. A couple of times they were startled by animals—once by a massive armadillo, with its family in tow, crossing the blacktop in front of them. Another time they never saw the creature, but they heard it moving through high brush at the back of some houses. They stopped where they were and waited for it to pass.

Eventually they managed to get within sight of the Best Western Snowy Egret, but the area was crawling with sec patrols, moving in groups of five or six, using generator-powered searchlights that cut through the night, making it impossible to approach within a hundred yards.

"Have to take them out first thing," said J.B. as they crouched in a grove of whitebeams on the edges of a large derelict mansion.

"Easy with this." Ryan patted the butt of the G-12 with its bulky night sight. "Soon as we open up, they'll know what's going down."

"If the plan works, they won't have time to do nothing 'bout it."

Ryan peered at the front of the big building. "No gates." He was about to crawl back when his eye was caught by something. "Fireblast!"

"What?"

"There. That pole."

J.B. followed his pointing finger, finally making out the tall metal bar rising vertically in front of the motel. The lights were dazzling, and it was some seconds before his eyes adjusted to take in what it was that dangled from a rope some thirty feet in the air.

"Man or woman?" he whispered.

Ryan had brought a small, powerful pair of night glasses with him, and he reached from them, his heart sinking. It was undeniably a naked corpse. The rope was knotted around its neck, but the lamps threw it into a sharp contrast of brightness and shadow, making it hard to see it clearly.

He focused the glasses, taking a deep breath to hold them steady. "Bastard," he breathed.

"Not one of the women?"

"No, J.B., it's not Krysty or Lori. It's a man up there."

"But it looks like there's no—"

"Yeah. That's right, friend. It's been castrated. And there's no hands neither. And no feet."

"The bastards! Like some dirt-crazies that shrink heads or take hair."

"The eyes, nose and ears are gone, as well."

"Who do...?"

"Looks like an old man. Could be past fifty. I reckon it's the lad's father."

"Whitey's old man?" This was the nickname that Ryan had given him. "Yeah. That would figure what we know of this baron."

Ryan pocketed the binoculars. "Let's go. Tell the kid what we've seen."

He wriggled away, with J.B. at his heels, ready to return to the old cinema.

THEY WERE ABOUT HALFWAY BACK when they heard boot-heels ringing on the overgrown, gravel road. Ryan hesitated only a second before pointing to the left, then dived over a rotting picket fence and moved quickly along the side of a trim little house. He felt J.B. at his back and stopped once they were both safely around the corner.

"Wait," he whispered, peering toward the street. Six men, making up the sec patrol, were marching toward their base. Most of them were smoking and carried M-16s slung across their chests. Ryan's keen nostrils caught the unmistakable aroma of maryjane drifting over the weed-infested garden. The sound of their footsteps vanished away down the road, and Ryan and J.B. were able to relax again.

"Could have took them," said the Armorer, easing his finger off the trigger of his Mini-Uzi. "Hit 'em all in one burst."

"They'd have heard it and figured it was the start of the attack. This Tourment may be the meanest fucker in the land, but he can't be a total stupe. He'll know we might come after the women. No point giving him any warning."

J.B. nodded. "Guess so. Let's move."

"Wait."

"What now, Ryan? You don't want to take a leak, do you? Trader always said when you first joined you was always sneaking off to take a piss before the shooting started. That it?"

"No. What the fuck's that there? In the middle of the garden, by that dead rosebush?"

It was a metallic dome that rose about three feet above the matted surface of what had once been a neatly trimmed lawn, now overrun with crabgrass. Ryan picked his way through the knee-high weeds, then bent over the strange protuberance.

"What's your guess? We could do with Doc here. That old bastard knows more about the times before the long winters than any man does. Or should."

"Small redoubt?" guessed J.B., tapping on the top with the butt of his blaster.

"Private one. Wait. Didn't you once tell me 'bout the last years, when folks installed their own nuke shelters. This could be one, still here."

The Armorer set his weight against a large wheel set in the top, but it didn't budge. "Bolted."

"Yeah. But look at the rust round it. Might go if'n we both give it a try together. Come on. Heave on three. One, two *three*!"

There was a brittle snap as corroded metal gave up its resistance. The wheel then turned fairly easily, with a thin grating sound that made Ryan look behind him. "Check the road. I'll come get you when it's open."

It took thirty or more turns before Ryan heard a latch disengage, and he was able to lift the trap. It was enormously thick, obviously counterbalanced by weights; it opened with a clunk. There was a faint hissing, and a waft of overpoweringly stale air, so dry and sour that it almost seemed to Ryan to clutch at his throat, like a hundred-year-old wraith.

J.B. joined him as he flashed his torch into the entrance. They saw a tunnel that dropped vertically about thirty feet, with a white-painted set of ladders, its rungs throwing sharp shadows.

"Going in, Ryan?"

"We got time. I'd kind of like to see inside one of these places."

He went first, slinging his H&K caseless over his shoulder. It was obvious that the shelter hadn't been opened for a century. It was probably one of the few totally safe places in all of Deathlands.

THERE WAS A DOOR at the bottom, with a simple catch on it. Stuck to it with contact adhesive was a flowery notice. It said: "Don 'n' Peggy's place. If you got no beer, you can't come in."

A smaller card said: "This is the golden door that has a silver lining."

The shelter was small and cramped, with a living space opening to a couple of bunks. There was a kitchen area and toilet and washbasin. Beyond that was another door that hid the controls, generator, air purifier, water recycler and stores.

Ryan saw the two corpses immediately.

Unlike those above ground, these hadn't deteriorated into skeletons. They were mummified bodies, leathery lips peeled back off yellowed teeth. The skin had shrunk and tightened across the faces, showing the skulls that lay beneath.

The woman, with long black hair, lay on one of the bunks, looking as though she'd been laid out in a funeral home. The skeletal hands were folded neatly on her shrunken breasts. She wore pale blue dungarees, stained and filthy, with a black and white badge pinned to the shoulder strap. Both J.B. and Ryan recognized it from old books as the emblem of a society that opposed all forms of nuke growth.

"Didn't do her no good," said J.B., his voice flat and muffled in the cramped metal tomb.

The man's body was in the john, huddled over the chemical toilet-bowl, almost as if he was at prayer.

"Looks like he died puking," commented Ryan.

There was plenty of food in tins. J.B. switched on the water purifier and found it still functioned. Ryan sat down on a canvas chair, looked around the shelter and saw a primitive vid-machine, with a camera wired to it. He pressed the button marked Battery, and a faint red light glowed on the display, as if some tiny hibernating creature had just been awakened.

"It works, J.B.—it works."

He wasn't totally surprised. In some of the better-protected redoubts that they'd found during the years with the Trader, they'd quite often come across battery-operated machinery that still functioned. But generally the charge was only held for a few minutes, and then the equipment would grind to a halt forever.

"Press the On button on the telly there."

J.B. hit the starter, and the screen lightened, revealing a jagged pattern of gray and white. Ryan had already noticed that there was a reel sitting in the vid-machine. He leaned forward and pressed the control to set it in motion.

"You don't think there's..." The voice of the Armorer faded away into a stillness that verged on awe.

The jagged dashes and dots changed to colored splashes and streaks. The speaker crackled, and then they heard the sound of music.

"Testing, five and four and three. Coming through real good. Just turn off my new Pogues compact. There." The music ceased.

Suddenly something appeared on the screen, a great blurred outline, like a football. It vanished, and then they saw the head and shoulders of a man who sat in the same chair where Ryan now sat. He looked to be around fifty years of age, with thinning black hair and a small neat mustache. He had plump, well-shaved cheeks and immaculate teeth. Teeth so good they couldn't possibly have been genuine. He wore a bright shirt, decorated with garish bananas and pineapples. On his right hand was a ruby fraternity ring and on his wrist a platinum Rolex watch.

"Hi there to the future." There was a sheepish grin on his face, and he seemed a little embarrassed at his own presentation. "My name's Donald Haggard, and I'm an optometrist here in West Lowellton, part of the great city of Lafayette in the great state of Louisiana. Don't know rightly why I'm telling you this, because I guess you'll know all that. I've just broken off from Christmas brunch to tell you a little 'bout . . . Guess I damned near forgot to tell you the date. It's December 25, in the year 2000. Wanted to make this here vid as a kinda record, I guess, of what's going on here right now."

While Ryan and J.B. sat there, spellbound by this message from a dead man, Don Haggard went on to outline the political situation. The tensions between East and West, the problems in Libya, in South Africa, in the Philippines, in Cuba. In the northern cities of Great Britain and in Israel.

"Seems like the whole world is just waiting for someone to push the first button."

He talked a little about his wife, Peggy, who worked locally in telephone sales, and their three sons, Johnny, Dwight and Merle.

"Guess you know from that what kind of music I'm into," he guffawed. J.B. and Ryan looked at each other, blankly.

The picture wobbled, and the gears of the vid-machine grated and whined as if they were about to give up. Ryan leaned in the chair and pressed the Fast Forward button, letting it go ahead for several seconds.

"Don't have time to watch all this, J.B.," he said. "Mebbe take it with us."

"Stop it here."

Don was back, looking rather less cool and in control than he had on Christmas Day. "Things don't," he began. "Sorry. Start with date. It's January 15, 2001. Yeah. Government tells us not to worry. Motherfuckers. Not to worry. They don't live out in the open. They've got their bunkers and hideouts. Me an' Peggy'll be fine. What about them good old boys of ours? Where do they go? Can't come in here. Built for two. Jesus on the fucking cross, what a mess!"

"Can't have been a big magnetic pulse in the skies round here," commented J.B. "Would have cut off all the electrics."

Haggard rambled on a while longer, cursing the politicians, both Russian and American, for letting things slide to the brink of war.

Ryan ran the tape farther forward, watching the dancing picture and halting it when there was an obvious change of time.

"January 24." Looking at his watch, Don went on. "Late morning, I think. Watch stopped. Guess it's around ten-thirty. Peggy's worse, crying and throwing up and taking on so."

Don looked terrible. His shirt was stained and dirty, and he was pale and unshaven. His eyes were sunken, and he had obviously been weeping. "I'm real fine, folks. Whoever you are. Felt the bangs again a day back. Last night, maybe. Not sure. But I'm real fine and so's Peggy. Just a mite sickly. See my hand shaking some. Should have stocked up on liquor. Never thought 'bout that when I built this place. Saved our lives, I guess. Can't tell for sure. Haven't been up top. Won't yet."

J.B. walked across the room and removed a knife from a neat mounting on the wall. "Tekna." He held it up, showing Ryan the five holes in the hilt and the distinctive double sawing edge. "Surgical steel with a high chrome content. Haven't seen one in years. I'll take it." Sheathing it, he hooked it on his belt.

Ryan pushed the Fast Forward control, stopping it when the man's head vanished in a blur of visual static. He glanced at his chron again, seeing they still had a little time. To watch this film was even more amazing than being in a vid-house or a Holiday Inn. Seeing this vid was to witness the beginning of the long winters, as it was happening. The neutron bombs had fallen, infecting everyone with a lethal burst of nuke energy.

"Twenty-fifth January. Air filter doesn't fucking work properly 'gainst what the Reds dosed us with. I can feel it rotting my fucking bones. Peggy's worse. I'm going up top to see one time. If anyone ever sees this, you'll know what it's like."

The camera showed the walls of the tunnel and angled shots of the ladder as Haggard carried it up. He panted and sighed, stopping a couple of times to gather breath. Then there was a break, presumably while he cautiously opened the hatch and peered out. The next shot was in his garden, the man providing his own commentary on what they were seeing.

"Lotsa smoke all round. Looks like there's houses fired toward 'fayette. Our house is standing good."

Wobbling and jerking as Haggard carried the camera with him, shooting as he went, the film showed a murky scene, poorly lit on account of the smoke drifting by. At first it didn't seem the holocaust that Ryan and J.B. knew it to have been.

Then it began.

The commentary began to stammer and fade, sinking to a spasmodic muttering that identified people here and there. It finally faded to silence, and the sound track only picked up a low keening, with a piercing scream intermittently shattering the quiet.

The land was a massive charnel house. A land that was filled only with the dead and the dying. A high wind whipped clouds across the sky, which seemed to be a dark purple, like bruised flesh. Wherever the lens probed, there was death. Young and old, frail and hale, all felled by the same single swipe of the nuclear scythe. The nuking had been cunning and selective, hitting only creatures that breathed, sparing all the buildings.

"Tom Adey and his young kid...Beulah and her gran...little Melanie and her folks...Pop Maczyzk... new married couple moved into the Wainwright place last week."

Dead and dying.

On porches and in the road. One body hung out of a burned car, the head, arms and upper torso untouched by the flames; the lower torso and the legs were charred and blackened; the mouth was open in a soundless scream of ultimate agony.

Dogs crawled along the sidewalk, snapping at their own hind paws, eyes rolling, tongues hanging from their jaws. A wheelchair was caught by the vid camera, tipped on one side, wheels slowly rotating in the wind, its occupant vanished.

The camera swung wildly through 180 degrees, pointing at the ground, its shots very jerky and fast.

"He's heading back here," said Ryan. "Had enough. Poor fucker can't take any more of what happened to his neighborhood."

The picture went blank, and J.B. moved toward the television, thinking it was over. But it wasn't.

Not quite.

A face swam into approximate focus. The face of a mortally ill, dying man, still recognizable as Don Haggard, but drawn and yellow and thin. Dark seams furrowed his face from his nose to the corners of his mouth, and the eyes were veiled with a dreadful fatigue. He wore a plaid shirt that was moist with vomit and what looked like drying blood.

The voice was hoarse and labored. The tape ran on with long pauses as the man seemed to fight to remember how to speak.

"Donald Haggard here of West Lowellton. Don't know the date no more. Been six days since Peg passed away. Poor old dear been sleeping more and finally slipped from me while I slept. I got the sickness like everyone. Been shitting so much I can't keep me clean no more. Lost all my dignity. Puked blood today. Can't be soon 'fore I join my darling. Guess our boys are long dead. Hope they died quicker and easier than folks round here. Conceived in fucking liberty... We can't hallow or consecrate this ground...." He was overtaken by a coughing fit, his body shaking. "Last full measure of devotion... It shall not perish from the earth. No, no, no."

"Turn it off, J.B.," said Ryan.

Don Haggard's voice was weakening. "Heard knocking a whiles back, but I couldn't ... wouldn't have ... not going out again." The man staggered to his feet, swaying to and fro, pointing a finger at the camera. "Do you feel fucking lucky, punk?" he said, to the bewilderment of two people a century later.

That was the last he said.

Then there was the noise of someone being violently sick—a choking, tearing sound that went on and on until J.B. pushed the Fast Forward button again. Don Haggard never reappeared, though the tape ran right on through to its end and automatically rewound itself.

"Going to take it?" asked the Armorer.

"No. Like robbing a grave. Not right. Leave it here."

They switched off everything, gently pulling the door shut and climbing out into the cool of the late evening. Ryan lowered the exit hatch, swinging the wheel-lock on it, making sure that no casual predator would disturb the last resting place of Don and Peggy Haggard of West Lowellton, Louisiana.

They returned to the Adelphi Cinema without incident and rejoined Jak Lauren in good time for the last firefight.

Chapter Twenty-Two

RYAN WAS IMPRESSED WITH the regimented hold that the fourteen-year-old boy had over his small army. Jak had ordered silence, and that was what he got. Each man and woman understood his or her role in the assault; they oiled and greased their weapons, and carefully wrapped rags around them to prevent noise. A few of the men checked the captured swampwag to make sure the steering was smooth.

The heavy casks of napalm were loaded into the rear of the buggy, the tops having been painstakingly cut off by hand. Old blankets were wadded between them to stop them from rolling and clattering.

Under the direction of J. B. Dix, grens were wired to various points around the swampwag, their pins secured with loops of fishing line, cut to an agreed length of 120 yards.

Just after midnight, they were ready to go.

BARON TOURMENT hadn't yet returned to the cellar. Bound and helpless, the girls lay in total darkness with only the rhythmic clunking of the nearby ice machine and the distant chattering of one of the elevators to break the stillness.

They talked for a while. Krysty tried to keep the younger girl's spirits up, telling her that Ryan and Doc and the others would surely come for them.

Eventually, around midnight, both of them managed to fall asleep.

THE GEARS SET IN NEUTRAL, the buggy, pushed by teams of fighters, rolled on its massive tires. The tall woman with the jagged scar across her neck sat at the controls. She was reputedly the best driver in the small army, and the success or failure of the first part of the plan depended upon her skill and nerve and timing.

Finn walked with two of the older men, all three of them carrying flamers. Tanks of propellant, with a nozzle like a garden hose, were supported across their shoulders by a web of faded canvas strapping.

"You sure that slope's steep enough at the front?" asked J. B. Dix.

"Yeah. There's a hill out of sight of the motel. We get it there and then let her go. By the time they see it coming, speed'll be well up. Too fucking late to do much. Leah jumps, and Finn and his men get to work."

It took them close on two hours, with stops for frequent pauses for everyone to gather breath. Even Doc insisted on taking his share of heaving at the lumbering vehicle, though it nearly exhausted him. His ebony sword stick was in his belt, the massive Le Mat pistol, over two hundred years old, in its holster.

KRYSTY DREAMED that she lay in an archaic wooden wagon, with a fluttering top of white material. It was set amongst a grove of green-leaved sycamores, with sun-baked fields all around it. There were men, women and children, hunkered down in the grass behind the wagon, in old-fashioned clothes. The women in long cotton dresses and poke bonnets. Dark suits for the men. By another wagon she saw four men and a boy, loading antique blasters, laughing as they did so. Somehow, though there was no enemy in sight, Krysty knew that a battle was about to go down. A bloody firefight against a superior force.

"TWO-SEVENTEEN," said Ryan Cawdor, angling his chron to catch the stray moonbeams that filtered through the trees. From far below they heard noise around the Best Western Snowy Egret: men calling out orders; laughter; a shrill scream, followed by more laughter.

Leah stood quietly by the swampwag, dwarfed by the wheels, her scarred face in shadow. She pulled on leather gauntlets, brushing her hair back from her eyes. Nearly a foot shorter, Jak Lauren stood beside her, his own hair tied into a silvery ponytail.

"Jump and roll once you're sure it's on course. And get the fuck out. Finn and flamers are going to be right behind. Is that okay, Leah?"

"Sure. I won't let you down, Jak." Leah looked across at Ryan. "Won't let anyone down."

She swung up, seating herself, waving a gloved hand to show her readiness. There was the faint sound of metal on metal as she released the brake. Some of the men set their shoulders to the back of the swampwag, and it began to move forward, gaining speed on the slope.

"Go, Finn," called Ryan, urging them on. The buggy was going faster than they'd guessed, and he saw suddenly that the three men with the flamers were going to have a serious problem getting close enough if the grens didn't do their stuff. The thin lines paid out behind the swampwag, each held by one of Jak's people.

Lauren led them down the hill after the swampwag, slowing as he reached the edge of the covering trees. Ryan patted him on the shoulder, turning to J.B. and Doc and six men he'd picked earlier.

"Going round the back, Whitey. See you inside. Good luck."

And they were gone. They cut to the left along a side road that would wind about and bring them to the rear entrance of the motel, through its abandoned parking lot, by the shell of the swimming pool.

It was surprisingly late before any of the baron's sec men saw the swampwag noiselessly hurtling toward them. Ryan heard the first shouts and a crackle of spasmodic fire. He watched the big buggy move within a hundred yards of the main entrance, driven straight as an arrow by Leah.

"Now. Jump, girl," he said, knowing there was no way she could hear.

Bullets sparked off the front of the vehicle, whining into the night. The searchlights jerked and danced as they sought the rushing attackers. Finn and his two comrades were caught and held by the beams, frozen in the stark light.

"Now, J.B.," said Ryan, carefully aiming the Heckler & Koch. The Armorer stood in the center of the blacktop, his legs spread, the Uzi braced against his hip. Both men opened fire simultaneously, their guns on continuous burst. Their aim was good enough, even at that range, to smash both searchlights instantly. There was a tinkling of glass, and wounded men cried out as they fell. The front of the motel was immediately plunged into darkness.

Then everything started to happen more or less as they'd planned it.

But Leah's death hadn't been part of the plan. She was supposed to jump. Instead, she stayed at the steering controls, making sure that the swampwag hit smack in the center of the main entrance. It crashed with an enormous metallic crumpling noise, half overturning, spilling its load of napalm. The impact was so tremendous that some of the grens were jerked free of their mountings, with only two remaining in place.

Ryan saw the crash, watching as Leah's body was thrown high in the air, arms and legs like a disjointed doll's. She hit the motel with crushing force, sliding down the wall and lying still.

"Fireblast!" he swore. "She didn't . . ."

The grens went off, almost together, splattering the napalm over a wide area but failing to ignite it. J.B. had warned that the sticky gas might have lost some of its combustibility; that was why Finn was there as back-up. Now he was needed.

Although Ryan and the others should have been moving to the rear of the Best Western, they waited to see what would happen. If the flamers didn't work, then the whole attack was going to fail.

"Come on, Finn, you old bastard," Ryan muttered.

The firefight was gaining momentum. Bullets hissed and snapped all around the front of the building as the Baron's sec army came tumbling out to repel the attack. Jak Lauren was leading a group of fighters down the hill, darting from side to side to use what little cover there was. All along the front of the fortress, picking their way through the sticky, stinking mess of napalm, the sec men were gathering their strength.

One of the men beside Finnegan fell soundlessly, shot through the head, his blood and brains splashing over the road. They were a scant sixty yards or so from the wrecked swampwag, and bullets started to bracket them. J.B. had wanted to get closer.

"Fuck that!" shouted Finn, dropping to his knees, opening the valve and pressing the ignite button. He pressed it a second time when nothing happened. At his side, one of Jak's men also knelt, fumbling with the controls. A spray of lead centered on his chest, and he went toppling on his back, the flamer falling limply from his dying grasp.

Finn pressed the button a third time.

Ryan held his breath.

KRYSTY AWOKE, tugged from her dream. Straining her exceptional hearing, she caught the muffled roar of an explosion. And shouting. A lot of shouting.

"Lori," she called. "Wake up, Lori. They're here. Wake up!"

THE JET OF FLAME, dripping beads of golden fire all along its magical length, struck the center of the ruined swamp-wag, playing over it, instantly igniting the hundreds of gallons of napalm.

Finn jumped to one side, releasing the main control of the flamer, burying his face in his hands at the cataclysmic explosion. Jak Lauren and his group stopped in their tracks, shrinking back from the inferno that raged outside the motel. The sec guards were destroyed in the blink of an eye, converted from fighting men to dancing puppets, tugged by strings of fire. Their thin, helpless screams were drowned by the ferocious roar of the flames. The entire front of the building caught fire, and lakes of smoking crimson spread inside through shattered windows and doors. In less than one minute, the whole place was ablaze.

The men with Ryan and J.B. stood and gaped. Night became dazzling day. The shooting stopped for a few moments, replaced by the noise of the fire and the screeching of hundreds of wild birds, erupting from the trees all around. Ryan saw a great slim-necked white bird with an enormous wingspan flying majestically away over the burning motel.

"Now," he said, breaking the others from their shocked contemplation. "Come on. To the back."

BARON TOURMENT HAD been sleeping, his arm resting across the hips of a slim Cajun girl. Her tanned body was covered with bites and scratches, and she had slithered into a merciful, drugged sleep.

Mephisto burst into the room, his clothes crumpled, a blaster in his hand.

"They're here! For fuck's sake, Baron, get up and fight or run!"

"Who? The one-eyed man?"

"Don't know. Move this slut outta the way." He pulled the girl to the floor; moaning, she resumed her slumber. "Bombs. Fire-sprays. Blasters. It's a fucking war out there."

Tourment reached for his braces and buckled them on while Mephisto outlined what had been happening.

"Whole place is burning. Must be twenty dead. Could be more. It's bad. Real bad, Baron."

Tourment hitched on his belt, with the twin pistols in it. Stub-gripped Ruger GP-110s, a matched pair of silver-plated revolvers that had been taken from one of the gun stores in downtown Lafayette years back.

"How many out there?"

Mephisto shook his head. His own customized M-16, with its ornate cockerel's head, dangled from his right hand, almost as if he'd forgotten he was still holding it. "Don't know. Plenty. Thought I saw the snow wolf."

"And the man with one eye?"

"Who?"

Tourment reached for his trembling sec boss and grabbed him by the front of his jacket. "You heard me, offal! Was there a man there with only one eye? He's the one to be feared. I know it. I've seen it."

"Didn't . . . didn't see him. Time's racing, Baron. The place is lost. Got to get out."

"Side way, canoes," said the giant black, striding to the door of his suite. "Get the two women and bring 'em."

"Too late for that," said Mephisto, his voice rising until it was almost a hysterical scream. "Don't you . . . it's fucking over. We lost. One fucking bang and a damburst of fire, and we're done."

KRYSTY LAY STILL, resting, harvesting the layers of calmness. Knowing that if the motel was under attack by Ryan, then it would not be long before Baron Tourment, or one of his sec men, remembered them and came looking for them. That could be the moment when her special powers might be most needed. Lori, at her side, lay still, whistling to herself to keep her spirits up.

HALF A DOZEN SWAMPWAGS were already rolling around the back of the blazing building, with sec men still clambering into them, ready to run. Exchanging fire with Ryan's party, all of them fell dead, with only a single casualty in the attackers' group.

"Blow the buggies?" asked one of Jak's men.

"No. You'll need 'em after this is done."

"You figure we're winning?" asked another of them as they neared a large rear entrance.

"Yeah. Leah gave us better than we'd hoped for. When this is finished, you ought to build her a bitching great statue and bring your children to look at it every fucking anniversary."

There was a foot of stagnant slimy green water at the bottom of the pool. It reflected the flames that were already beginning to break through the roof of the Best Western. One of the sec men came sprinting around the corner of the motel, heading toward them, clutching a suitcase. He saw them but didn't check his stride, figuring them for his own comrades.

"Mine," said Ryan, putting a single round from the H&K through the man's neck. It kicked him back, his feet flying up in front of him as though a wire had been pulled around his neck.

"Rat abandoning the sinking ship," commented Doc Tanner.

The door was unguarded and unbolted. To their left they heard shooting. Their nostrils filled with the acrid stink of poisonous smoke. The speed with which the fire spread was startling. Ryan realized that he hadn't really taken into account the way a dried-out hundred-year-old husk of a building would blaze. The plan had been even better than he could have dreamed. A single crushing blow.

"All we gotta do is find the girls and get clear," he said. "Whitey figured the basement. Best get to it 'fore we all go up."

OUT FRONT, Jak Lauren had managed to stop crying. Seeing his father's hideously mutilated corpse dangling from the flagpole, like some obscene trophy of battle, had created an ocean of grief and anger within him. In his fourteen years, the boy had seen enough killing to last most people a full lifetime. But for his father to die now, with victory suddenly and magically within their grasp—that was bitter.

The tears lasted only a minute or two before his iron self-control returned and he led his people in a screaming charge. Taking the firefight into the burning building, they massacred anyone around. He used a .357 Magnum with a satin nickel finish, spare ammunition rattling in the pockets of his torn jacket. So far only a half dozen of his group had gone down, compared to more than two-thirds of the Baron's defending sec men.

One of the gaudy sluts came running toward the boy, her mouth open in a scream of horror and agony, burning na-palm dappling her naked shoulders and back. Jak stead-ied his right wrist with his left hand and shot her carefully between the eyes.

He was greatly tempted to stop and lower his father's body from the pole. But that would take time and men, and both were vital to maintain the momentum of the at-tack. What had been his father was no longer around. It didn't seem to matter what happened to his dismembered corpse.

KRYSTY MANAGED A SMILE as Ryan came kicking in through the cellar door, the G-12 raking the room, ready to butcher anyone there.

"Hi, lover," she said.

"Hi. How's it gone?"

"Could have gone a whole lot worse if'n you'd left it till tomorrow. That Tourment is one evil fucker. And his sec boss isn't any better."

Doc had rushed straight to Lori, and laying down his sword stick, embraced her while she wept. J.B. pushed past him, the Tekna knife in his hand. The keen edge parted the cords that bound the girl to the table; he turned and re-leased Krysty the same way.

Smoke was billowing in from the corridor, making them cough. Someone ran past outside, loudly yelling for help.

"We winning?" asked Krysty.

"Yeah," replied the Armorer.

"Looks that way," said Ryan, steadying the girl as she stood up. She brushed the fiery hair off her face, smiling at him.

"The Baron been chilled yet? Or Mephisto?"

"No. Unless Whitey's got 'em."

"I'd like 'em," she said. "Half hour in here with them tied like we were."

There was a look of venomous hatred in her eyes that Ryan had never seen before.

Some of Lauren's men were getting anxious. "Fire's getting close," said one. "Best go help Jak."

"Sure. We'll go out the same way and round the far side. By the lagoon."

He couldn't understand why Krysty shuddered at the word.

Doc was still comforting Lori; the tall blonde hung on to him, her face buried in his chest. J.B. was fumbling with the knife, resheathing it. Ryan's arm was around Krysty.

Then Mephisto appeared silently in the doorway, with two sec men at his elbow. All three of them had M-16s.

"You're all fucking dead," he said, favoring them with a graveyard smile.

Chapter Twenty-Three

"ONE MOVE, AND YOU'RE all swamp-fodder." The sec boss looked mad, his eyes bulging, white froth hanging from the corners of his lips. His suit was stained with soot and mud and was torn across one shoulder. But the muzzle of his carbine was rock-steady.

The men on either side of him were typical stony-eyed sec men, their uniforms also smoke-stained and scruffy; their guns covered the five people in the cellar.

It was desperate ill-luck that none of the three men in Ryan's party were able to get immediately at a blaster.

"Baron's making ready to leave the ville. Set up house somewheres else. I'm going with him with a few good men like Rafe and Pierre here. You bastards have done in one night what the dirt-poor under the snow wolf haven't done in years." He stared at Ryan Cawdor with an intense curiosity. "Baron been doomseeing you, mister. Man with only one eye. Figured it would be his ending."

Ryan said nothing, easing away from Krysty, freezing as one of the sec men shifted his aim to cover him more closely. J.B. hadn't moved an inch since Mephisto appeared. Doc had let go of Lori, standing with his hands on his hips, looking contemptuously at the three gunmen.

"Don't look like his ending, mister. Looks more like your ending."

"Why don't you take us to see the Baron?" asked Krysty. "You know he likes me and the straw hair. Might be angered if you don't."

The sec boss shook his head. "Sorry, slut. It's going to be here. And it's going to be now."

Ryan's reflexes were stretched adrenaline-tight, ready for a last desperate, hopeless try, before they were all ripped apart.

It was Lori who checked the executions. She took a step away from Doc, teetering as she often did on her ridiculously high heels, drawing eyes as she wobbled. "I'm sick," she said. "Got to take clothes off." Her speech was slurred as if she were drugged.

"Get the..." began Mephisto, his voice drifting away as the beautiful blond girl hoisted up her scanty red skirt and began to peel off her panties.

Directly in front of the sec men, Ryan and J.B. were unable to risk any sudden moves. Doc Tanner stood a little more to one side, his shoulders stooped—a defeated old man, waiting for death.

Suddenly the defeated old man had a cannon in his right hand.

It was his thirty-six caliber percussion Le Mat revolver, nine-chambered. But the unique quality of the pistol was that it had a second smooth-bore barrel, chambered to take an eighteen bore single scattergun round.

There was a smile on the wrinkled cheeks and a merry twinkle in the old man's eyes as he squeezed the narrow trigger.

The boom of the explosion drowned out the crackling of the flames from the corridor. A great burst of black powder smoke filled the cellar, blinding everyone. Ryan heard screaming as he pushed Krysty to one side, the G-12 falling ready to his hands and snapping off a double burst toward the doorway.

The Armorer's Uzi barked a quarter-second later. Some bullets whipcracked off the stone walls, pinging and ricocheting off the metal pipes. Some tore into soft flesh.

As the smoke cleared, it was almost as though a master magician had performed a skillful illusion. Mephisto and the two sec men had disappeared. Then Ryan made out a pair of boots, sprawled in a corner of the corridor, moving spasmodically.

He edged sideways, seeing that all three of the baron's men were down and done. The single round from Doc's blaster, at point-blank range, had been perfectly aimed. The shot spread just enough to hit all three men at face level. Both guards lay kicking, one mumbling for aid through a mouth filled with blood. The lead had ripped into their eyes and cheeks, tearing flesh from bone. The impact had been sufficient to send them all staggering backward, easy prey to the torrent of lead that followed from J.B. and Ryan.

Doc joined them, beaming at his success, manipulating the action on the smoking Le Mat, ejecting the spent cartridge and reloading from one of the capacious pockets in his old frock coat. He shifted the hammer so that it rested over one of the thirty-six caliber rounds.

"Upon my soul, Mr. Cawdor, but that was vastly enjoyable. To see the wicked so smitten and righteousness triumphant."

"Early days, Doc," grinned Ryan, watching the wounded sec men. "But you done real good. And you, Lori," he called. "Fucking great."

"Thank you," said the girl, breathing hard with excitement. "Wanted to see the motherfuckers drown in their own shit and blood."

"You done that," J.B. commented dryly.

"The matter is not quite concluded," Doc said, looking down at the three men. One of the guards was already still, his chest and stomach ripped apart by the G-12 or the Uzi, his blood and bone and intestines mingling on the floor. The second sec man was dying, his face shredded from taking the worst of the Le Mat's shot. He was moaning, rolling from side to side, his hands holding his ribs from where blood oozed.

"The quality of mercy is not strained," said Doc. Still smiling broadly, he knelt and placed the muzzle of his pistol into the raw hole where the sec man's mouth would have been. He squeezed the trigger. The bullet bounced the man's head off the stone, killing him instantly. Doc thumbed back the hammer once more, turning to look at Mephisto.

The sec boss was dying. Several pieces of shot had pocked his face, one bursting his left eye. And more bullets had stitched across his chest from Ryan's and J.B.'s shooting. But he still breathed, flat on his back, his carbine thrown several feet away. Smoke drifted down from the main part of the burning building, and the heat was growing appreciably.

The firing from the front entrance had slackened. Ryan guessed that Jak Lauren's army had vanquished most of the baron's shattered forces.

Mephisto blinked up through the blood that ran down over his one good eye. "Still won't catch Baron. Too clever for you."

Krysty looked coldly down at him. A sudden anger washed over her, and she spat in the dying man's face, wanting to tear and hurt him. Lori was at her side, also looking down at the sec boss with bitter hatred on her lovely features.

"Bastard killer," Lori said, lifting her foot and stamping down with all her weight. The heel of the red leather boot struck Mephisto in the center of his one good eye, splattering it to a bloody liquid. The tinkling silver spur hooked in the corner of the socket, and the girl jerked at it. Mephisto shrieked in stunning pain as his head was rolled backward and forward. Finally the spur was wrenched clear, tearing the flesh away like raw meat.

Doc straightened, leveling the antebellum pistol, squeezing the trigger once more. The ball splintered the blood-slick forehead of the sec boss, killing him.

"Should have left him gut-shot," said J.B.

"Better dead," Doc said, holstering the heavy gun.

Ryan looked along the corridor. The billowing smoke was tearing at his lungs. "Gonna be roasted if'n we don't move fast."

"That mother said the baron was making a run. Which way?" asked Krysty.

"Got to be across the far side. By the lagoon."

"There is boats there," said Lori.

"Boats?"

"Canoes. Small ones," amplified Krysty. "And the biggest mother of a gator I ever seen in my life. Makes the one that tried for Finn look like a baby."

Ryan hesitated, then turned to the Armorer. "J.B.? We gotta go help Whitey and his group? Sounds like it's going well."

"Want me to go check? And you go after the baron?"

"Yeah. Take Doc and the women."

"Sure."

"I'll come," said Krysty.

Ryan shook his head. "Way I look at this, it's kind of personal. It's like a debt."

"You don't owe anything to anybody, Ryan," said Doc Tanner.

"Except myself. Now let's move."

THE BLAZE HAD BECOME a full-fledged firestorm. A gusting wind tugged and howled about the inferno that had once been the Best Western Snowy Egret. Jak's men were already mopping up, trailing and killing any of the bewildered and demoralized sec men they could find.

Some had managed to escape the withering fire of the assault party and headed blindly toward the depths of the swamps. As Ryan and his group emerged from the smoke at the rear of the motel, Jak saw them and came dancing over. Hearing their news, he told them of his own total success.

"Not total if some of the sec guards have 'scaped free," said J.B.

"The Cajuns don't love 'em. With Tourment gone, they'll kill 'em all. Cajuns or the swampies."

"I'm going after the baron. Seems he's gone 'cross the lagoon in a canoe." Ryan pointed to the left of the raging fire.

"I'm coming," said Jak.

"No. He's mine."

The boy pointed behind them, to the mutilated corpse of his father, still hanging from the flagpole. "Not after that. Mine."

"Time's wasting," J.B. said.

Ryan looked into the boy's crimson eyes, seeing the flames reflected in them; the mane of white hair, torn free from its binding, swayed in the strong wind. Ryan was a good judge of men, and he saw that he would have to kill the fourteen-year-old if he wanted to stop him from going after Tourment.

"First one there chills him, Whitey," he said, turning and leading the lad toward the lagoon and the mysterious island.

Chapter Twenty-Four

So FEROCIOUS WAS the blaze, so all-consuming, that within twenty minutes of the swampwag crashing into the front of the motel, virtually the entire building had been devoured, leaving only columns of twisted metal and stone and a windblown mound of glowing ashes.

Jak Lauren overtook the older man, leaping easily over the corpses of the sec men strewn along their way, turning and grinning at Ryan, his teeth bared in animal pleasure. The big .357 was in his right hand. Through the parking lot they ran, blinking as the wind blew a golden cascade of sparks all around them.

"There," shouted Whitey. "No sign."

The concrete dock, scattered with cinders, was deserted. Near the metal boats they saw the body of a sec man sprawled near the edge of the water, his neck snapped with a single crushing blow. Jak Lauren gestured at it. "Baron's work. Least we know we're on the trail of giant bastard."

The moon still sailed above the light clouds, its silvery glow strong enough to cast blurred shadows all around. The surface of the muddy lagoon glittered and danced with a million points of white, like a watery galaxy of stars. On the far side, Ryan could make out land, and a peculiar building standing on it.

"What's that?"

"Tourment's voodoo temple. Sacrifices of hornless goats. Girls slaughtered. Children defiled. The dead made to live."

"And the living made to die," completed Ryan.

There was no sign of life on the island opposite. Ryan squatted down, shading his eye against the moonlight, trying to make out what was happening. He saw some low shrubs and stunted live oak trees: enough cover to hide a platoon.

"What's on the other side?" he asked.

"Swamp comes on far edge. Way through in good light. Trails like gut-slit moccasin snake. Baron never find in this dark. Wait up, then try. Don't forget his legs real fucking weak. Like crutches. Die in thick mud. We take care, and we get him."

The lad slipped to the edge of the dock, looked searchingly over the water, then untied one of the boats and climbed in. Ryan went to join him, but Jak was too quick.

"Take your turn, Ryan. He's mine. See you later." And he was gone, the paddle slicing in and out of the ooze, the canoe darting, arrow-straight, toward the far bank.

"Fireblast!" hissed Ryan, taking the next boat along, easing himself into it cautiously. He was aware of how low in the water he was now set and recalled that there were giant mutie alligators infesting the swamp.

By the time he mastered the flimsy craft, rotating it twice before attaining the right direction, Jak Lauren has already grounded his canoe and hopped out on the slippery shore. He waved triumphantly at Ryan before disappearing into the brush, his white hair blazing like a beacon.

Halfway across the lagoon, Ryan's paddle grated against something hard and serrated. Something that moved away with a sullen reluctance. It felt a little like a massive submerged log, but every nerve in Ryan's body told him that it wasn't.

He worked harder, bending all his muscles into each thrusting stroke, feeling the boat shoot forward faster, a gurgling wave breaking under the bow. His ears caught a strange sound behind him: a thin, hissing noise, like escaping steam. Out of the corner of his eye he saw the water parting and something chasing after him.

The instant the bow of the canoe slid into the pebbles and mud, he leaped from it. His blaster ready, he spun around to face what had been pursuing him. But the water was calm and still, with only the faintest suggestion of a ripple toward the deeper part of the swamp.

He was motionless for a moment, gathering his self-control about him like a protective cloak, checking his bearings. In the moonlight, he could barely make out the tracks of the albino through the mud. But he saw a rowboat a few yards farther along, toward the building. Examining it, he discovered some extraordinary marks in the mud. Someone had fallen, and fallen again, and dragged himself along by hand. There was one clear print, and Ryan stooped and placed his own hand in the seeping mark. The fingers were nearly four inches longer than his.

"Fuck it," he sighed. Tourment was going to be a difficult man to take if it came to close combat between them. The mud also showed the truth of the leg-supports. Great furrows vanished into the bushes where the land was less wet. Despite, or perhaps because of his enormous size, the baron wasn't going to find it easy to move.

The fire was dying behind him as he set out to move inland. The temple was open, and it was obvious that nobody was hiding there. The island was apparently no more than a half mile in length, but he had no idea how wide it was. The undergrowth closed in around him.

He never heard the swampies.

One moment he was up and walking; the next he was rolling over on his hands and knees, the G-12 pulled from his grip, someone's arm around his throat, another attacker hanging on his waist, kicking at his legs. There was the stench of gasoline and sweat as he grappled with the oily bodies.

Despite the shock of the sudden attack, Ryan was able to immediately retaliate. Heaving up, feeling the hold loosen on his waist, he snapped an elbow back as hard as he could, hearing a rib break, and a strangled gasp of pain. The arm was off his throat, and he was able to wriggle to his feet, drawing the panga, the best weapon for hand-to-hand combat.

There were three of them.

Two men and a woman. Muties, like the ones they'd seen on the day they arrived in Louisiana. All of them were around five feet tall, stumpy, squat and muscular. Dressed in torn pants and shirts, they had flapping sandals of hacked rubber on their feet. They stared at him blankly, the sockets of their eyes surrounded by odd scars. The woman held a small crossbow, and the men were armed with machetes shorter and narrower than Ryan's own weapon.

They breathed noisily through open mouths, their arms hanging by their sides. Standing gazing at Ryan, they seemed to be waiting for him to make the first move. Suddenly the woman raised the bow, aiming it jerkily at Ryan's belly.

The thought darted through his mind that this was a squalid and foolish way to die. Alone in the muddy darks, gut-shot with a wooden arrow. He tensed, ready for a desperate dive at her, his senses telling him it would be too late and too slow.

The bow twanged, and the shaft hissed through the air several yards over his head. Ryan stared as the woman staggered sideways, her nail-less fingers plucking at the hilt of the slim dagger that sprouted from her neck like a bizarre pendant.

"Take the others, stupe!" hissed Jak Lauren, darting from the undergrowth, a knife in each hand.

The fountain of blood from the woman's severed neck pattered around them; she fell to her knees, then rolled heavily on her back. Her legs spread, and Ryan noticed with revulsion that a small residual penis dangled from her naked belly.

An instant later one of the swampies was on top of him, its dank, noxious breath hot in his face. The machete hissed toward him, and he wriggled around, blocking the blow with his forearm. He stamped on the creature's foot, making it mew like a kitten, breaking away from him.

"Cut its throat!" called Jak Lauren, who was fencing around the other mutie, his knife glinting in the moonlight.

The noise might warn Baron Tourment that they were close. So it was important that they dispose of this threat swiftly.

The swampie came shuffling in, waving its steel blade, grunting with the effort of each feinting blow. Ryan backed off, considering drawing the SIG-Sauer P-226 9 mm blaster. But the ground underfoot was slippery. One mistake, and he would be down and done for.

He darted in and back, stooping as though he'd slipped, one hand going down into the slimy mud. As he straightened, he saw the mutie looming over him, blank eyes like a shark's. Ryan threw a handful of dirt straight into those eyes. The swampie staggered away, grunting in anger.

The eighteen-inch blade of Ryan's panga flitted out and back and out again. Slick with blood. He cut the swampie across the lower forearm, and again across the top of the right thigh. Both had been deep, slashing blows that opened up the flesh into scarlet lips. The creature's machete dropped, and it hopped back, squeaking feebly.

Ryan waited, remembering how hard it had been to kill the living-dead muties before. Dodging around his opponent, Jak Lauren had been grabbed around the chest. But the mutie howled in pain, releasing him, looking in bewilderment at its stubby fingers, which streamed with blood from a dozen cuts; the tiny slivers of razor-steel sewn into the albino's clothing again proved their worth.

The other swampie was moving in on Ryan again, stooping to reach for the fallen blade, fumbling in the dark mud. It was an opportunity that couldn't be missed. Ryan stepped once forward and once to the side, blade up, muscles poised for the downward hack. Steel whispered in the moonlight, then came a solid thunk and grating sound. The panga eventually sliced clean through the mutie's scrawny neck, decapitating it, the head rolling into the mud, the body slithering at Ryan's feet, jerking and twitching.

Wiping blood from his face, Ryan turned to see if the boy needed aid. But there was no need for worry.

Jak Lauren was amazingly, dazzlingly fast in hand-to-hand combat. Maybe the best Ryan Cawdor had ever seen. He switched the knife from side to side quicker than the eye could follow. The mutie lumbered after him, making great ineffectual swings with its machete that would have sliced the lad in half if they'd landed. Jak pulled away, then sprinting in toward the swampie, took off with a great spring and actually leaped clear over the man. Turning a somersault in the air, he still had the control to slash at the creature's face. The thin knife cut across the eyes, blinding the mutie with streaking blood.

"Off with head, Ryan," called Jak, landing in an easy forward roll, coming up in a fighter's crouch.

Dodging the mutie's helpless lunge at him, Ryan took a half step to one side and hacked with the panga at the neck. The living-dead mutie had a heavy build, and the blow failed to totally behead it. But the steel severed the spinal column and most of the flesh and muscle. The body fell, spouting blood that seemed black by the light of the moon. The round brutish head remained attached to the shoulders by a stringy thread of gristle and sinew, rolling behind it like an afterthought as the body pitched and jerked.

Ryan stooped to cleanse the blade of his panga in the stubby grass. At his shoulder, Jak Lauren was grinning. "Easy as shooting sec men," he said.

"Tourment'll have heard the fight."

"Let him. Can't get off here. With his crooked legs, he can't run or swim. I'll take him."

"Or me," said Ryan, sheathing the panga, then he picked up his G-12, wiping it clean of mud.

"Yeah. You or me, Ryan." Like a swamp wraith, the boy was off and running, visible mainly by the glimmer of his stark white hair.

THE BARON nearly managed to fool them. Despite his bulk and his clumsiness, he succeeded in lying quiet in the undergrowth until they passed. Then he made a lumbering charge for the boats before they could turn and follow. But Ryan heard him and yelled out a warning to Jak Lauren.

"Boats, Whitey!"

As Ryan sprinted back along the twisting trail, his boots kicking up spray around him, he glimpsed a monstrously

tall man, striding as if he wore stilts, near the narrow strip
of beach where the canoes waited. A triple burst from the
G-12, fired on the run, didn't come within ten paces of
Tourment, but it was enough to make him stumble and
dive sideways for cover behind a low mud bank. Ryan, in
turn, leaped off the path, finishing up flat against the
trunk of a fallen tree, slippery with moss and cold to the
touch.

A couple of shots smashed into the wood, only inches
from his head, and he flattened down. He tried to identify
the flat barking of the blaster. If J.B. had been there he
probably would have guessed not only the model of the
gun, but even figured out the year of manufacture; all
Ryan could tell was that it was a big handgun. He strained
his ears and caught the giveaway triple click of a hammer
being cocked. That meant a revolver, which probably
meant six rounds, but Ryan wasn't about to stake his life
on that.

There was a blur of movement, topped with a streak of
white, and Jak Lauren dived to the ground behind another toppled tree a few yards away.

"Yonder," called Ryan, waving the barrel of his handgun.

Two more shots were snapped off, both coming close.
Jak fired once with his Magnum, its six-inch barrel
gleaming in the moonlight.

"We got him," he yelled. "Got him cold as dead gator
meat."

"Want to talk, snow wolf?" came the voice, calm and
measured. Utterly unhurried.

"Want to kill, bastard," replied Jak Lauren.

"Want to talk, one-eye?"

"Want to kill you, Baron," replied Ryan Cawdor. His
words were rewarded with three spaced bullets, the last

shot showering him with splinters of chipped wood. Glancing around the side, he was able to see the gun being withdrawn, and recognized it as a Ruger GP-110. Six shot.

"Fired seven. Means two guns. Would have heard him reload," he called to Jak Lauren. "Five rounds left," he said, raising his voice so it would carry to their adversary. "Five left, Baron. Another few minutes there'll be men coming over. It's done."

"I can find plenty of jack. More cards than either of you would see in a lifetime."

"Rather piss in your face," shouted Jak, snapping off a couple of rounds from the Magnum, the bullets kicking up a spray of earth near the top of the rise.

"One-eye?"

"Yeah, Baron?"

"I'll give you everything."

Ryan sniffed audibly. "Been offered a lot of things in my life, Baron. Never everything. What would I do with everything?"

"That's our last word? What's your name?"

"Ryan Cawdor. Yeah, it's my last word. Come out or stay there. It's all one. Quick or slow, Baron. Easy or hard."

The reply was two bullets in his direction, and two at the tree that sheltered Jak Lauren. That left him only one round, unless he had another hidden blaster or was going to reload.

"That's it. One left for myself. Would have liked to take you scum with me. *Au revoir, mes amis.*" This was followed by a single muffled shot.

"Goodbye, Baron," said Ryan, motioning for Jak to remain where he was. "Could be a trick. Likely is."

But it wasn't.

They were both startled by an animal howl of searing agony. The huge figure of the Baron appeared, crashing over the top of the rise, both hands clutching his face, stumbling on the creaking metal and leather frames, falling to his hands and knees, rolling and rising again. He howled in dreadful pain.

"Watch him, Ryan," warned Jak Lauren.

Through the dim light, Ryan could see that this wasn't a ruse. Tourment must have put the muzzle of the Ruger into his mouth, intending to pull the trigger and blow away his brains. Removing the possibility of an execution at the hands of the snow wolf and his followers. But, as is surprisingly common, he'd screwed it up. The gun hadn't been angled correctly, and the abrupt kick as he pulled the trigger had thrown off the aim.

As he fell again, hard, one of the leg-supports snapped in half, making it impossible for him to rise. Ryan could see the damage more clearly. It looked like the heavy caliber bullet had angled up and sideways, smashing the upper jaw, boring through the top of his mouth, exiting through the cheekbone, just below the right eye.

It had torn the eye itself from the socket, leaving it hanging on his cheek, like a pendulous ornament.

Ryan stood up, leveling the G-12, ready to chill the wounded man.

"Pull that trigger, and I'll ice you, Ryan," came the cold voice of Jak Lauren, also standing, his big Magnum looking absurdly large in his small fist. But it was very steady.

"What do you want, Whitey?"

"Couple things." He walked to stand by the thrashing man, and leveling the pistol, carefully shot Tourment four times. Once through each elbow and the center of each knee. The giant black man rolled helplessly, moaning in pain, unable to move.

His face like stone, Jak unbuttoned the front of his trousers. Keeping his threat, he urinated in the baron's upturned face, the yellow liquid splashing in the man's eyes and mouth, making him gag and choke.

"That's for my father. The bullets are for all my friends. But this last is for me," said the boy, holstering the pistol and unwinding a length of thin cord from around his waist and beckoning for Ryan to help him.

Ryan Cawdor had always seen the justice of making the punishment fit the crime. For a man as blackly evil as Baron Tourment, that wasn't a simple matter. But Jak's plan was simple and would fit the bill.

IT WASN'T EASY to manhandle the flopping, screaming giant down to the water, and roll him into the soft warm mud of the shallows while he tried to scream through his broken jaw and smashed mouth. Blood kept choking him, and he coughed and moaned.

The rope was tied around his waist, the other end knotted to the stern of one of the canoes. Both Jak and Ryan got into it, pushing off and paddling as hard as they could. The cord tightened, and for a few moments they were paddling and getting nowhere. Then the Baron was sucked free of the slime, rolling and flailing in their wake.

Jak looked back, nodding in satisfaction. Stopping for a moment, he slapped at the brown water with the flat of the wooden paddle.

"What's that for?" asked Ryan.

"You see," replied the boy.

Glancing over his shoulder, Ryan saw a huge log, motionless on the far shore, suddenly jerk into clumsy, waddling life and slither into the water and disappear. A V-shaped ripple on the surface of the swamp, arrowing toward them, indicated that the beast was approaching.

Ryan bent to his paddling, but Jak Lauren had stopped once more, gazing back at the floundering figure of the baron with an expression of gentle content on his narrow, scarred features.

In turn, Ryan stopped. Ahead of them the last portion of the roof of the Best Western Snowy Egret collapsed in a great shower of sparks, soaring skyward. For a moment, smoke billowed across the lagoon, making it difficult to make out what was happening. Then it cleared.

The cayman was swimming alongside the towed body. It reared out of the water for a moment, its eyes gazing into the ruined face of its master as though it couldn't believe what it saw. Then the jaws opened, gaping, row on row of teeth.

And closed.

RYAN WOULD NEVER FORGET that sickening crunch of bone and meat being devoured, stripped from a living body.

By the time they had paddled back to the dock where the others waited for them, the end of the rope was just a bloodied knot.

Nothing else remained.

Chapter Twenty-Five

"NO, WHITEY."

"Come on, Ryan."

"No. Your fucking place is here. They're your people. We helped you beat the baron. Now it's up to you."

"I'm coming."

"No, you're not. What about the windmills? The clearing and draining of the land? The planting of crops and the founding of a settled ville for you and your folks?"

Jak Lauren was still immovable. Three days had passed since the battle at the motel. The dead were buried, the last of the sec men hunted down and slaughtered. The Cajuns had been to West Lowellton, learned that the rumors were true. That the bad days were truly over and peace had come to the Atchafalaya Swamp.

Now, with Ryan and his party all fed and their various minor cuts and wounds tended, it was time for them to be moving on. But Jak Lauren had insisted on talking privately with them on an overgrown patch behind the Adelphi Cinema.

Mainly, he and Ryan did the talking.

The boy's hair, recently washed, had dried into a great torrent of purest white that foamed about his narrow shoulders. His red eyes were blazing with the intensity of his feelings.

"Pa set this up so's if we ever won fighting, then there's all skills here. I told you that. My only skill's killing. No need for that here. Not now. Come with you."

The others sat in a circle in the grass, looking at the skinny young boy. Doc's arm was around Lori; her head was on his shoulder. J.B. was playing with his fedora, turning it around and around in his lap, avoiding Ryan's eye. Finn was picking his teeth after three helpings of gator stew. Krysty sat quietly beside Ryan.

"But they need you, Whitey."

"No. I . . . I need you, Ryan."

There was no doubt that the kid was a great fighter. Rough around the edges, but he would be a useful addition to them. Seven had been a good number. After Henn's death, there was a sort of vacancy.

"I don't know."

Jak shook his head, his face vanishing beneath the white froth of his hair. "My work's done, Ryan. My people will stay here forever now. Now the shadow's been lifted. Like a strong wind, you helped rid the land of vermin."

"Yeah," said Ryan, still doubtful of taking a child of fourteen into their select group.

"If'n you don't, then you might see it hard to find that gateway you spoke of."

"That a threat, Whitey?" asked J.B.

"More promise," replied the kid.

Doc Tanner began to laugh at Jak's nerve. Lori joined him, then Krysty and Finn. Finally J.B. glanced at Ryan, and the two old friends also began to laugh.

So it was decided.

THE FAREWELLS WERE BRIEF.

Jak led them away, through the suburbs of West Lowellton, toward the edges of the swamps. The sun was shining and the neat rows of white houses looked as though their inhabitants had just slipped down to the shopping mall and would be back at any minute.

Guided by the albino, they reached the low redoubt before the sun was setting, finding it as they had left it.

The walls of seamless pale stone were tinted a gentle pink by the sun's lowering rays. Inside, it was clean and trim, and Ryan took over, leading them along the corridors. The air inside was hot and humid, and he could feel himself sweating.

"Easy as this to get in," said Jak, his voice more subdued than usual. "Never guessed. Folks scared of it."

They walked through the anteroom with its serried rows of flickering lights and chattering tapes. The door of the gateway stood open, as they had left it. On the way they collected the clothes and provisions that they had earlier abandoned, and Ryan again possessed his beloved long coat with the white fur trim.

The walls of the trans-mat chamber were dark blue smoked glass, armored and thick, with the now-familiar pattern of raised metal disks on both the floor and ceiling.

"Going to be like being knocked out, Whitey," said Ryan. "Sit down and close your eyes. When you wake, we'll be somewhere else. Don't know where. It'll be fine."

"Sure," said the kid.

All of them sat down, their backs against the walls. Ryan waited a moment, his hand on the door. "Here we go," he said, shutting it firmly.

He sat down and closed his eye, hearing the quiet voice of Jak Lauren, singing to himself.

Once I was lost, but now I'm found.
Was blind, but now I see.

Ryan's head began to swim as the trans-mat jump began, and the words of the old, old hymn faded from him.

His last conscious thought before the dark pool engulfed him was a hope that this time they'd find someplace that wasn't so damned hot.

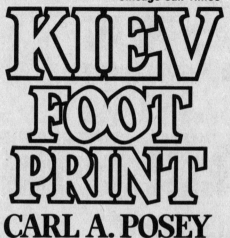

"An exciting, well-paced tale
of complex deception, fast action."
—*Chicago Sun-Times*

KIEV FOOT PRINT

CARL A. POSEY
Author of *Prospero Drill* and *Red Danube*

Miles above Earth, the space shuttle *Excalibur* floats lifelessly, its brave crew destroyed in a bizarre, unexplained accident. But as gravity slowly begins to reclaim the deadly debris, an on-board nuclear reactor transforms the crippled spacecraft into a lethal time bomb—a thermonuclear bullet locked on an unalterable course, aiming strait for the heart of Soviet Russia.

CATASTROPHE OR CONSPIRACY?

K-1